Without WAX

a documentary novel

William Walsh

CASPERIAN BOOKS

This is a work of fiction. All the characters and events portrayed in this book are either fictitious or are used fictitiously.

Portions of this novel have appeared in *New York Tyrant*, *Juked*, *Keyhole*, and *Old Crow*

www.casperianbooks.com

Cover by Kim Edge Ambler

ISBN-10: 1-934081-01-9
ISBN-13: 978-1-934081-01-3

Table of Contents

Prologue

Shaving

Wax Williams didn't get any hair between his legs until the summer before ninth grade. His first instinct was to shave it off. He knew that his father shaved his face every day and that his mother shaved her legs and under her arms. He figured they both also shaved between their legs. He didn't know for sure if they did, but he knew that he shouldn't ask.

The first time he shaved himself, he used his father's menthol shaving cream, which stung him in a cold way. His testicles tightened up and ached. He shaved quickly—eyes tearing, hands shaking. He nicked himself twice.

One week later, when his hair had come back in and an itchy rash had appeared, he shaved again, this time using the beauty soap his mother kept in a little plastic box in the bathroom vanity. It was easier going the second time, but he stopped shaving and wiped the soap off without rinsing when his penis became hard as he pinched the head lightly to reach a spot he was trying to shave underneath.

He knew what was happening. Erection. He knew that it was also called a hard-on. He had them when he woke up in the morning. He'd read that this was normal in the second to last chapter of his eighth grade health book, even though his class never officially got that far in the book and had been instructed not to read past the chapters that had been assigned. Originally, Wax's class was supposed to cover the whole book, but after the textbook had been reviewed by the school board, there was a vote against including sex education in the eighth grade curriculum. Ms. Boynkin, Wax's health teacher, would pass the books out at the beginning of each class and collect them before the bell rang to end class. These books could not be taken home. She would circle the classroom as the students read, making sure that nobody looked beyond the day's lesson. The trick was to read forward during one of the open book tests. You could flip through the pages quickly then, undetected, and get an eyeful of the nude anatomy drawings in the final chapters. But you couldn't look for too long. You had to flip back to where you were supposed to be.

Wax shaved about once a week for the rest of the summer. One night he said to his father, "I shave now."

His father looked closely at Wax's chin and rubbed the back of his hand on his cheek. "Sandpaper," he said, before turning back to his newspaper.

Wax had expected his father to understand the larger implication of his shaving, but he had seemed oblivious. It was possible that his father was avoiding the subject.

***

Wax knew that beginning in high school you had to start showering after gym. It was school policy. A letter of notification came from the high school in the middle of the summer. Mrs. Williams read part of the letter aloud at the supper table in an angry voice: "As proper hygiene is imperative to the overall health of every student at Ampersand High School, students will be required to shower following physical education. Each boy/girl is to bring his/her own soap and a clean, dry towel. They will be afforded ample time to properly shower before the start of their next class. Thank you for your cooperation with this policy."

She handed the letter to Mr. Williams who quickly reread the letter, then looked at the list of things each student had to have for physical education.

"I don't like it," Mrs. Williams said. "I think boys just misbehave in situations like this. It's unnecessary."

Mrs. Williams said Wax should cover himself in front of the other boys and make sure that he didn't look at the other boys and that if there was any horseplay in the shower he was to step out of the shower and dress for class. If this got him into trouble, she would go straight down to the school and stand up for him.

A week before classes started, Wax decided that he would begin shaving every day so he wouldn't be stubbly. He was thinking about having to shower with all the other boys after gym class. He figured that if he had stubble, someone would say something about it. He didn't want any stubble.

He was scheduled to take physical education fourth period every Wednesday and Friday. His mother packed his gym bag for him with a new bar of soap in a plastic sandwich bag and a new white towel that she had bought when they had gone shopping for school clothes. She also packed his gym uniform, white shorts, and a reversible shirt in the Ampersand colors—green and gold. The idea was that you could turn the shirt inside out when teams were divided up, though in basketball, which was all they would ever play in gym, Coach Dunkin always made the teams Shirts vs. Skins.

Wax was also supposed to have an athletic supporter (it was on the boys' list), but Mrs. Williams had crossed it off in the store without buying one. When he asked her about it later on at home, she told him that she would not buy an athletic supporter for him. "You don't need one," she said. "They're disgusting and filthy, and I'll be the one who has to wash it."

Wax didn't ask her about it again because he knew she was still upset about the showering policy. She kept asking Wax if he was nervous about having to shower with the other boys. "Are you afraid?" she asked.

He told her, honestly, that he wasn't. He had seen a movie once about kids away at summer camp who all had to shower together at the same time. The movie made it look like fun, the way the stalls were low enough so you could see the head of the boy next door. He also thought of how the army doctors on M*A*S*H showered together but in separate stalls.

But then he found out that the showers at Ampersand High School weren't divided into stalls. There was just a wide-open corner of the locker room with eight columns that each had shower nozzles spraying in four different directions. Coach Dunkin turned them all on at once with a large knob that looked like a ship's wheel. You had to huddle around the columns with three other guys and duck your head under the nozzle. The water went down two large rusty drains embedded in the tiled floor.

Some of the boys from third period gym were still in the showers when Wax entered the locker room. They were all tenth graders. Wax could see them through the steam, laughing and pushing each other around. He was surprised that none of them covered themselves, like his mother had told him to.

Coach Dunkin was tall and overweight with a sweaty red face and a whistle on a shoestring around his neck. He was sitting on a small table by the showers handing out combination locks from an old laundry basket to Wax's fourth period class. There must have been a hundred locks in the basket, all with a three-number combination taped across the dial.

"What's your name?" Wax was startled by how loud Coach Dunkin's voice was.

"Wax Williams."

"Your real name, not your nickname."

"That's my real name," Wax said.

Coach Dunkin looked at his clipboard, then looked at Wax. "Wax Williams," he said, putting a heavy old lock in Wax's hand. "Make sure this combination works before you lock up your clothes."

Wax moved toward a row of lockers. One of the boys on the bench told him to pick an empty locker. Wax sat down next to the boy, but faced the row of lockers on the other side of the bench. The boy started undressing. He took off his shirt, pants, and underwear, and then stood naked for a moment looking through his gym bag. His back was turned to Wax, but there were other boys who, Wax thought, could probably see the boy from the front.

The idea of taking his clothes off in front of everybody now made Wax uncomfortable and anxious. He began thinking of ways to undress that would not leave him exposed to the other boys. He knew he wouldn't have to get out of his underwear because he didn't have a jockstrap to change into, but suddenly the idea of just being seen in his underwear made him feel self-conscious and scared. And then there was the shower after gym. Wax resolved that he wouldn't get caught fumbling through his gym bag with no clothes on. He would have his gym uniform ready to put on before he got out of his clothes, and he wouldn't get out of his shirt and pants at the same time. He would take off his shirt first, put on his gym shirt, then take off his pants and put on his gym shorts.

The boy standing next to him was still naked. He had his gym uniform, towel, soap, and jockstrap out of his bag, but he wasn't changing. It seemed to Wax that the boy was purposely showing himself to the two boys on the other side of the bench. They both looked away, but they kept taking quick looks at the naked boy every few seconds.

The naked boy turned to face Wax as he stepped into his jockstrap. Wax saw that the boy had hair. Wax stood quickly and took a step back and looked into the big shower area. He felt a panic in his throat and worried that he was going to trip on his own feet as he moved toward the shower. He could feel his face getting hot.

Coach Dunkin blew his whistle, told the boys in the shower to get the lead out. Then he turned the big knob to shut the water down in all the showers. Wax heard groans from the shower and one of the boys yelled, "But, Coach, my balls are still soapy."

Coach Dunkin laughed and said, "Girls love soapy balls."

The tenth graders emerged from the shower then. They were all a lot taller than Wax. He looked at the floor and also noticed that their feet were much bigger than his. He didn't look up; still, he could see that all the boys coming out of the shower had hair. They weren't shaved. Not one of them.

"Coach," Wax said. He tried to say it in the same tone as the boy from the shower who had said his balls were soapy, but his voice sounded much smaller and didn't seem to carry in the echoing locker room.

Coach Dunkin didn't take his eyes from his clipboard. Wax worried that the coach might not have heard him, or worse, that he had decided to ignore him.

"Coach," he said again, louder this time.

Coach Dunkin finally looked up. "I already gave you a lock, didn't I?"

"I don't have an athletic supporter," Wax said.

"Why not?"

"My mother said she wouldn't buy one for me."

"Don't bullshit me, son."

A few of the tenth graders started to gather behind and beside Wax, toweling off as they listened to Wax tell Coach Dunkin that his mother had refused to buy a jockstrap for him because she didn't want to have to wash it.

The tenth graders laughed when Wax said that.

"You don't have to wash them," one boy said.

Another boy said. "I didn't wash mine once my whole freshman year."

Coach Dunkin said, "You're excused from gym for today. But you make sure you have five dollars next class. I'll have a cup and a strap for you. You tell your mother the money's for Glee Club."

"Thank you," Wax said.

Then Coach Dunkin said, "But no singing in the showers."

All the tenth graders laughed and Wax did too, but he didn't know what was funny.

Chapter One

All Doll

JOEL HANDLE (DIRECTOR): Wax Williams wears two robes. The outer robe is white terry cloth, floor-length, stolen, I'm sure, from some hotel. The inner robe is red satin, strategically cut to mid-thigh. His penis—eighteen inches flaccid, twenty-plus at its fullest arousal—hangs below the hem of the inner robe, his only costume for *All Doll*, a short film we're shooting of Wax having sex with a transparent inflatable doll. I am directing and my wife, Eva, is producing.

EVA HANDLE (PRODUCER): The point of the short robe is that it is too short to cover all of his long cock. It's really quite a visual.

DEE-DEE SHARP (HAIR AND MAKEUP): I am responsible for grooming Wax below the waist. It's my job to make sure Wax looks his best—every inch of him. He keeps a simple trim of the pubes. Not too spare. I also apply a light foundation and powdered blush to his penis and sack for close-ups.

BEN BETTIS (CAMERAMAN): This is the second day of a two-day shoot. On day one I got all my shots of the quote-unquote lab—the clock on the wall set at various time intervals, some of the fake technical equipment, the blinking monitors, the test tubes and beakers and shit. I shot the doll alone from a slew of angles and a few of her POV shots of the ceiling. I rolled some tape of the Old Lab Lady: entering the lab, exiting the lab, that kind of thing. She did a few great peek takes over her clipboard.

Hilda Flüke (Non-performing Talent, cast as the Old Lab Lady): My only screen direction in the script was to pace around the perimeter of the lab and observe Wax Williams as he works away on the blow-up doll. Eva and Joel thought that I would be more comfortable if my part were filmed without Wax being present. They booked me for two days—the day before Wax did his scene and the day after. They promised to get my shots done with me alone on the set. They'd edit my performance with Wax's to give the appearance that I was present during his exhibition with the doll. They were trying to save me embarrassment, I suppose, because I am old. I have been a professional actress for forty years and no acting work can make me feel embarrassed. And I really wanted to meet the young man.

Dee-Dee Sharp: It's a scientific experiment to see how deeply a woman is penetrated by Wax. It's a high-concept piece, Ty Boyce says.

Hilda Flüke: I'm told that there may be a voice-over for my character that hasn't yet been written. I'll read it like it's a report, scientific findings of my study. I can't wait to voice that.

Eva Handle: The transparent inflatable doll is handmade. And we have a camera port in the back so you can see Wax's cock after he enters the doll. We call it cum-cam.

Joseph Wheeler (President and CEO of New Day Engineered Plastics): Joel and Eva explained what they wanted with this doll. A doll that you could see through. Transparent. Easy, I thought. Just remove the flesh pigment from the plastics material during our next manufacturing run of inflatable dolls. But not so easy after all: the plastic without the flesh pigment was clear, but it had a greenish cast to it, which did not photograph well. We played some with the mix and got the plastic pretty pure—very clear. But, in doing so, the material became brittle and it split easily. Days of testing ensued with lots of trial and error. This is chemistry—an art form, really. In the end, we got a few hundred yards of a transparent material that photographs very well and that has a pretty good feel to it, I'm told. But it is thicker than the plastic skin of our standard dolls and therefore could not be machine-stitched. We did that by hand, producing five transparent dolls. Three we're keeping for marketing purposes—conventions, plant tours, client parties. The Handles got the other two. If their little movie is a success, we'll have created a market for these things, I'm sure. So we'll have to keep working on the mix—get the clear plastic thin enough for mass production.

TY BOYCE (SCREENWRITER): Wax was once asked what he felt so deep inside of a woman. His answer was metaphysical. "Sometimes great warmth," he said. "And other times a sad coldness." That quote inspired me to write this movie.

EVA HANDLE: Wax had not done any video work in more than nine months when we approached him with *All Doll.* He fulfilled his contract with Lyle Mammon when they shot *SpanksGiving IV,* and he had quietly announced his retirement from adult film work at that time. He had gotten lots of offers from West Coast producers, but prior to speaking with Joel and me, he had declined all new proposals. We'd sent him a number of conventional scripts, all of which he turned down politely.

JOEL HANDLE: Wax told me that he decided to work with us for simple cash flow reasons. He didn't want to juggle his investments, nor did he want to raid his savings. He was only making $3,000 for his personal appearances, and in a lot of ways that's much harder work. He figured the twenty grand we are paying him for *All Doll* would last him a good six months.

TY BOYCE: We are working a small crew. Ben is shooting and doing all of his own lighting. Joel is directing and running sound. Eva dresses the set. Dee-Dee does hair and makeup. I am running lines to Wax and working through a few missing story points when Mammon arrives.

DEE-DEE SHARP: Lyle Mammon is a man you always smell before you see him. He's what you'd call many-scented. He always wears at least three competing fragrances. At first you whiff a floral scent, then something a little citrusy, then his base musk. He smells like the perfume counter at Macy's.

JOEL HANDLE: We'd hardly shot anything with Wax when Mammon shows up, the fucker. He's not supposed to show his face anywhere near the shoot. He isn't even supposed to know when we're shooting. But there he is, standing in the middle of my set with this six-foot four-inch Amazon.

BEN BETTIS: Mammon initially seems interested only in the breakfast buffet that is laid out. He helps himself to two danishes and some coffee. You could bake a cake with the amount of sugar he puts in his coffee.

EVA HANDLE: Mammon is wearing a very tight blue suit that might have fit him two years ago.

JOEL HANDLE: Mammon introduces his companion as Mancy, stressing the "M" in a ridiculous way. She quickly corrects him and tells everybody that her name is Nancy. She has a deep voice. Mammon corrects himself. "Excuse me," he says. "This is Nancy." Then he makes some joke about pre-ops being very sensitive about their new names. Everybody laughs because we always laugh at everything Mammon says when he's trying to be funny. It makes life easier.

DEE-DEE SHARP: Facially Mancy resembles Pat Riley, the basketball coach. Long, narrow face. Deep dimple on a wide chin. Small, close-set eyes. Prominent nose. High, narrow forehead. She has her short black hair wet-combed straight back over her ears, which aren't pierced. The wristwatch she has on is a large, men's digital with a thick, black band. She has on low-cut jeans and a white tank top. She is very tall and strong looking—the most muscular woman.

BEN BETTIS: We're all supposed to care that Mammon's companion for the day is of uncertain gender. Wax Williams, meanwhile, is looking real unhappy to see Lyle Mammon. He obviously thought he was working for the Handles, for their new production company. But Mammon showing up signals to Wax that Lyle Mammon is involved in the production. It's possible that Mammon is simply paying a courtesy call to the set, but something about his attitude and bearing tells me that this is not a social visit. No. Mammon is checking in on one of his productions. If I can figure that out, I'm sure Wax can.

LYLE MAMMON: We're not on speaking terms presently, Wax and I. But the business relationship will resume, that's understood—mutually.

JOEL HANDLE: Clearly Wax understands that Mammon's presence on the set means that the feature is being financed, circuitously, by Mammon. I feel strongly that this requires an honest conversation between me and Wax and Eva.

***

It would be sinister, Wax thinks, if it weren't so ridiculous. He was naive to think he could work in the adult entertainment business again without, in some way, working for Lyle Mammon. Mammon's reach is simply too far reaching. He has a hand in almost every production company on the East Coast, and an interest in most of the action in Vegas and LA.

Joel Handle says, "We thought you knew Lyle was our financier."

Eva Handle says, "We didn't know there were any lingering problems between you and Lyle."

Two lies, Wax knows. But he isn't upset. Being told lies doesn't bother him anymore. You have to care to get mad, to feel tricked. He decides to be just as honest with Eva and Joel as they have been with him.

"It's not a problem," Wax says. "It's nice to see Lyle again."

He can tell that the Handles believe every word he says.

***

EVA HANDLE: Nobody really cares or would be surprised to learn that Mammon has decided to cross-pollinate one of his nubile concubines with one of his musclebound sidekicks to produce the musclebound—but still somehow nubile—Mancy. Who cares? Only Mammon. He's trying to make some joke. Is she a he or a she? We all really want to know because the question is hanging in the air and it's only fair that we know. We're trying to get some work done, and why leave a question like that unanswered?

DEE-DEE SHARP: The question persists: Is she a trannie or what? Tell us already. The suspense is bothering me.

***

"Who's the hole?" Mammon says to Wax, pointing to the inflatable doll.

Wax doesn't answer, keeps his gaze in the opposite direction, still pretending that he doesn't know Mammon's on set. This greeting, he feels, is inappropriate. Wax hasn't seen Mammon in nine months. The man should have something nice to say. But that's Mammon.

Mammon tries to make another joke, "Don't fall in love, son," he says. "That doll might have taken your breath away at first sight, but some day she'll be gone like the wind."

Only Mancy laughs. Mammon turns to face her, says, "Shut up, numbnuts."

Nodding toward Mammon, Wax asks Ty Boyce, "What's *he* doing here?"

"That's a fine how do you do," says Mammon.

Wax puts the long robe back on.

"I'll be leaving soon," Mammon says. "I knew you'd be here. I wanted to see you. Say hello. See how you're doing. It's been a while."

"I'm fine," Wax says.

"Mancy here wanted to meet you."

"It's Nancy," Mammon's companion says. She holds her hand out, and Wax shakes it and gives her a polite smile.

Mammon places a hand on Wax's back, trying now to bring him into the Mancy subplot. "She-males can run hot or cold."

"I'm a girl," says Mancy. "Since birth."

***

JOEL HANDLE: She unbuttons her jeans and pulls them down to show all assembled her clean-shaven, female private parts. And, yes, she's definitely a woman. No doubt about it. But Mammon says, "Your doctor did a great job, Mancy. It looks like you could make a baby with that thing."

EVA HANDLE: We're all staring at her shaved cookie, and then off comes her tank top. Like it was necessary. Her fake breasts are absolutely square. Square. Two blocks resting on her hard pectorals. Little sharp-looking nipples, small areola. She does a few flexing poses at Mammon's urging.

Ben Bettis: Dee-Dee—trying to lighten the mood a bit—points to Lyle's hair and asks him if he's gotten himself a new wig. And Mammon says, "Hell, no. This is not a toupee. I still have all my feathers."

Dee-Dee Sharp: I'm the best straight man Lyle Mammon ever had. No matter what I say, he makes a joke. First day I worked with Wax, I asked Lyle if I should rouge Wax's foreskin. He looked at me and he said, "Honey, that ain't no foreskin. That's a fiveskin."

Eva Handle: Wax is such a sweet guy. Before he gets busy with the doll, he tells me he is worried that he might let us down. He hasn't had sex in a long while—months and months—and he wonders if his equipment will work. Will he be able to get hard enough to enter this doll? He has performance anxiety. Not unnatural; normal, given the situation. Healthy, even. Doubt motivates. A man like Wax needs a certain amount of insecurity, I think, if only to temper the potential for ego.

Dee-Dee Sharp: Someone makes a crack about the doll being the best actor that Wax has ever worked opposite. Wax says, "You know, people are always so critical of porno actors. We might not be good actors, but the truth is nobody knows how to act before they have sex—or after. We do real good at the sex, and that's what counts."

***

"What are you using for lube?" Mammon asks Wax.

Wax gives Mammon a look that says, "What's it to you?"

"Professional curiosity," Mammon says.

Wax hands Mammon a tube of a nationally advertised lubricant. Mammon throws it over his shoulder. "Stuff'll give you crotch-rot," he says, and he calls Mancy over, fishes around in her oversized shoulder bag. "New product," he says, showing Wax a tube of something called Human Touch. He reads aloud from its label. "Scientifically formulated for use with adult toys... dildos, buttplugs, dolls, pocket pussies, etc."

***

JOEL HANDLE: I don't think Wax is feeling anything while we are shooting *All Doll.* I bet he doesn't feel any of it, not even his orgasm. Wax has no difficulty attaining a good erection. He shows us a diamond cutter of a hard-on, but it's just an autonomic response, a reflex. He's already been paid.

TY BOYCE: Erection is a big part of Wax's job description—to become erect and to stay erect, no matter what. The fact that his arousal is spent (or misspent) on a blow-up doll—a transparent blow-up doll—does not make a difference. It is an exercise of this imagination, an arousal of the mind. Wax seems genuinely pleased that his head has not failed his body, regardless of how joyless the task.

DEE-DEE SHARP: I was surprised by how hot it was to see Wax work the doll. I thought it was going to look pervy. And Wax is so not a perv.

TY BOYCE: Wax was attuned to the inflated doll's every sigh and suspiration.

NANCY KEENING (MAMMON'S COMPANION): The blow-up doll keeps deflating. Every time Wax gets himself inside and starts pumping, the thing pops a seam. Whoosh!

EVA HANDLE: Wax looks pissed. But he keeps his cool. He waits patiently while Joel heat-seals the broken seams on the doll.

BEN BETTIS: Condensation has formed on Camera One during a particularly close close-up. That makes me think that the cum-cam is probably fogging up, too. We only need a few good minutes of footage from the cum-cam, but there is no way to tell if we'll even get a minute's worth.

***

"We have some doubts about the cum-cam, Wax," says Joel Handle.

Wax doesn't say anything.

"I was just told by Ben that the doll is steaming up inside. Condensation."

Wax says, "We can keep taking short breaks. Let her de-fog."

"But the money shot. We're not sure the cum-cam will get the money shot."

"I can pull out for the money," Wax says. "I thought I was going to anyway."

"We thought we'd have you shoot your load inside—cum-cam. No?"

"No."

***

DEE-DEE SHARP: The lipstick is all kissed off the blow-up doll. Kind of a sad sight.

TY BOYCE: The doll looks tired, unfulfilled, cranky.

EVA HANDLE: The doll deflates again. Wax cradles her in his arms. He considers the doll's impassive face. He's still in character—whatever that means. Then his hands find the part to inflate the doll—the little stem on the back of her neck. He feverishly begins to blow into the doll's stem. It verges on comical.

JOEL HANDLE: Wax withdraws from the doll only twice more. The first, unscripted time to apply some additional lube with a sure hand. The second withdrawal is for the money shot—the exterior ejaculation. The wet moment we've all been waiting for.

DEE-DEE SHARP: Wax calls to me for a towel. He cleans the doll up himself. He looks a bit flushed in the cheeks. He isn't sweating, but he is a little out of breath. He asks for a glass of ice water, and I get it for him. His hands are very cold. He looks a little shaky.

JOEL HANDLE: Usually there's an ovation after a scene is cut. Everybody claps for the performers and it's a release for those of us working behind the scenes because we have to be so very quiet while we're shooting. But when Wax is done with the doll, there is no applause.

LYLE MAMMON: The plan was this: After Wax blew his load, I was supposed to suggest that the doll should come to life. So I pick up the deflated bag of a doll, and I say, "She's alive!" And everybody on set laughs, and then I say, "I don't want to butt in, Eva, but I see a new direction to take this thing." Eva and Joel tell me to be quiet, that they got what they wanted and the shoot is over. But I say, "No, I see a better ending, and I can't let the day's shooting end without sharing the idea. Even if you don't want to shoot this new idea that I envision, I have to tell you what it is."

JOEL HANDLE: There was no plan set up with Lyle Mammon. Really. We did not talk before the shoot. He just shows up, and then he tells us he has a better way to end the movie.

LYLE MAMMON: Wax says, "Tell us your great idea, Lyle. Tell us the idea that you have to share." And I know that I have drawn Wax in and that he knows what I'm going to say and he knows that he's going to do what I suggest, and he knows that I know this. And I also know that this boy doesn't hate me. I shouldn't call him a boy anymore—he's almost twenty-four. But he doesn't hate me and he doesn't hate the work he does, at least no more than any man hates his job.

BEN BETTIS: I'm surprised that Wax gives Mammon entry into the conversation.

***

"Wax," Mammon says. "I looked at Ty Boyce's original treatment weeks ago, and I said at the time that the script needed a pretty girl, even if you're not gonna fuck her. Maybe that old lady in the lab coat lends some authenticity to the proceedings, but that's worth nothing in a film like this. It's not hot. Every element in an adult film has to add heat. That's axiomatic—ask anyone.

"The other thing is this: you in a movie alone is like a homo tape. Guys aren't gonna buy it. They want to see you put it to a hot girl. If they buy this tape and bring it home to watch and the only naked person in it is you, then to them it's a homo tape and they're gonna be fucking mad. There's certainly a market for you in a movie alone, but it's a homo market. Don't matter that the doll's a girl doll. There's guys—straight guys—who rent every movie you make, and they ain't gonna rent this one if it's just you and a rubber doll and some old fat lady watching."

"The script does need a little fleshing out," says Eva Handle. "No pun intended."

Mammon chuckles, rests a hand on Wax's shoulder, "We need more flesh—female flesh—and less inflated rubber."

"Think about it," says Ty Boyce. "We need a sexy female focus. Otherwise it's just some guy with a big dick and a rubber doll."

***

DEE-DEE SHARP: Wax says, "This was supposed to be me solo." He's talking in a much louder voice than I've ever heard him use before, but he still sounds reasonable. There's an edge in his voice that he meant to be heard. He says, "There wasn't supposed to be any cast besides me and the doll, and the old lady taking notes. The treatment said that the researcher would only be observing me. She was described as matronly. It said she might give me instructions in a Germanic accent."

EVA HANDLE: Wax has a briefcase with him that he goes to now. There isn't much in that briefcase of his—the treatment for *All Doll* that he's after, a calculator, a row of new pens, a mini-stapler, a pad of paper, some of his toiletries—toothbrush, travel-size tube of toothpaste, a razor.

BEN BETTS: The talk turns to the contract. Joel agrees with Wax when Wax says that a contract's a contract. But the point that Joel really wants to make is that Wax's contract does not give him final script approval or any say in casting decisions.

EVA HANDLE: Wax signed the contract when all we had was a three-paragraph treatment from Ty Boyce. And that's all we really had when we scheduled shooting.

JOEL HANDLE: I don't think that Lyle is helping our cause. A conversation with him can be like trying to catch your breath under water. Wax looks like a man ready to walk. He can. He's done what we paid him to do.

EVA HANDLE: Wax pulls Ty Boyce aside and I hear him say, "There's no way I'm screwing Mancy." And as if on cue, onto the set walks this beautiful young woman.

BEN BETTIS: Her name's Janna SayQua. I met her once before at one of Mammon's parties. I don't know if she's done any work for him yet.

DEE-DEE SHARP: Janna is a very cute girl: big brown eyes; tiny nose; pouty lips; very petite; good hair—chestnut with blond highlights that somebody did for her the right way.

JOEL HANDLE: She looks like a doll. She has a doll face. Mammon cast that right about her.

LYLE MAMMON: I say to Wax, "Let me make an introduction. Janna SayQua, this is Wax Williams. Wax, this is Janna."

DEE-DEE SHARP: Janna's hair and makeup are already done, which pisses me off. That's $75 out of my pocket. Her skin is tanned just a tad past perfect, but she isn't freckled. I would insist on giving her a manicure—since there's always a lot of close-up hand action in Wax's movies—but her nails look recently done. She is ready to work.

LYLE MAMMON: I invited Janna because I know she's the type of girl that Wax finds irresistible. I figured he hadn't had a real piece of ass since he'd stopped working for me. That's nine months; a long time for a guy who is used getting laid every day. Plus, she looks the part.

BEN BETTIS: Ideally, I like to meet the actors that I'll be shooting at least a day or two before we roll film. Even if I don't get an opportunity to get light levels on them or take some instant photos, I can get a pretty good idea about how to shoot them, how to light them. It can get tricky if you're shooting someone whose face you've never seen before. You need to see their angles and how their coloring represents on film. Do I want to pop on a lens filter for close-ups or use some lens gels? On *All Doll,* I was rolling four cameras with a mix of a few different film stocks, including black and white, and an ancient video camcorder. Not to mention the stupid fucking cum-cam.

JANNA SAYQUA: It isn't a very friendly set. Nobody seems happy to see me. Nobody even talks to me, except for Lyle.

DEE-DEE SHARP: She knows her way around the set like she's been here before. Her arrival isn't some coincidence, though Mammon expects us all to see it that way.

JANNA SAYQUA: I'm delighted to finally meet Wax. He is polite to me, professional, but not exactly warm. I mean, we are going to have sex in like twenty minutes. He could show me a smile, give me a hug. Something.

LYLE MAMMON: Janna is an exquisite implantee. Perhaps the best tit job I've seen in eighteen years. Saline implants wired to the ribcage. No visible scars. Nipples set high with aching, full-popped erections. She has a really sweet face, too. Big eyes. Beautiful hair down to her ass. She has this charming way of handling a soft cock. She works it lightly in her hands and lets it spill over her slender wrists on the way to her mouth.

EVA HANDLE: Janna's tits are tit-job big, but they're in proportion to her small frame. She has retained a natural silhouette. But she also seems the type who'll go up a cup size six months from now.

JOEL HANDLE: I tell Wax we can do a lot with Janna that we can't with Hilda Flüke. It doesn't have to be sex. It can be flirting. He can flirt with Janna and it's sexy fun. If he flirts with Hilda Flüke it's creepy. With Janna we can take things a step further. She can flash Wax to get him excited to do the experiment. She can sit on one of the high lab stools and accidentally on purpose show Wax a nice beaver shot. I'm trying to baby step her into the movie. She's in the same costume as Hilda Flüke, except eight times smaller and tight, tight, tight. Eva says, "Wax, we shoot Janna doing the same things as Hilda Flüke and we make it like you're imagining old Hilda Flüke is a hot young thing."

***

Janna's stealing shy looks at Wax, half listening to everything that Mammon says. Wax gets the idea that he'll be talked into fucking her on camera. Forget the contract, he's being duped. But he decides quickly that if that's the case, he'll let it happen. It makes sense. He wouldn't be hesitant at all if Mammon hadn't shown up. Had Handle and his wife been straight with him all along, he'd be happy to do a scene with Janna as the lab lady and allow for any form of spontaneous sexual interaction.

Then Mammon says, "How about Janna assists you getting into the doll? She grips your cock at the base and at the head and she guides you into the doll. She has such beautiful little hands and she has a charming way with a soft cock."

Wax listens to the idea with little interest.

"Before she puts you into the doll," Mammon continues, exerting more and more ownership of the movie, "maybe she measures you and traces an outline of your cock onto some graph paper. and then she applies the lube that I gave you...and she could improvise a little pep talk about how what you're about to do will advance the science of penetration."

"Maybe you don't even fuck her," says Joel Handle. "Janna could just stand there and watch you. The camera keeps cutting to close-ups of her face alternating with the doll's and we can see that she's getting hot just watching you. But she's fighting her urges to pull you off the doll and hop on your big bone because she's a scientist. But she's also a red-blooded girl and, hell, if you're screwing a blow-up doll she may as well open her lab coat and start touching herself all over. Maybe she could improvise a dildo with some oversized test tube or she could straddle the long lens of a microscope and bring herself off."

"A guy can rent a tape like that and feel good about himself," Mammon says. "He's not watching it to see what you do with your big dick. He's watching to see what Janna's gonna do next."

***

DEE-DEE SHARP: I remember a time when Wax made an effort to get to know all of his costars. He'd make arrangements to meet them a few weeks before shooting was scheduled to start, have dinner somewhere, talk. But he had to give that up fast. Getting to know the girls worked counter to his ability to get an erection on set. It's like the better he knew them the less they turned him on.

JANNA SAYQUA: The doll comes to life. That was Lyle's idea. And I'm the doll. Here I am, alive and fucking.

EVA HANDLE: I'm prepared to throw out everything we shot yesterday with Hilda Fluke. Who wants to see some fat-ass matronly scientist watch a young stud fuck an inflatable doll? It's a lot sexier for the viewer if a pretty, young scientist is running this experiment.

HILDA FLUKE: I come to the set on day two—even though I'm not scheduled—and there's some young little cunt in a white lab coat, tighter than any scientist would wear. Beneath her lab coat she's wearing lingerie. She's holding a clipboard—the same one that I used the day before. She has her hair piled up high on her head. She's wearing glasses at the tip of her nose to show that she's smart. I say to Eva Handle, "Looks like you recast the role of the matronly lab lady." She hands me four hundred-dollar bills and quietly points to the door.

***

"Think of it as a transubstantiation," says Ty Boyce. "Rubber and air become flesh and blood. You screw the doll to life. Or, less dramatic, Janna's the fantasy that you're having while you work away on your inflatable girlfriend. We intercut the footage to show your ongoing fantasy. Either way, the viewer gets to see you do a real girl. Not just the doll."

Janna approaches Wax slowly. Ben Bettis, who has been rolling tape throughout the discussion, follows her. Mammon and Mancy step out of the frame. Joel Handle calls for quiet on the set. He and his wife kneel on the floor just outside of the shot.

It has begun.

Janna puts a light hand on the belt of Wax's robe, grips it loosely, doesn't say anything. She removes her glasses, takes the pin from her hair and shakes it loose. She opens Wax's robe. Takes hold of his cock with her right hand, lets the length of it spill over the top of her left hand, gets to her knees, and opens her mouth to take the head of Wax's cock.

Wax hears Mammon say to Ty Boyce, "Janna has a real charming way with a soft cock."

***

Eva Handle: Janna does with her mouth things that the doll simply could not do.

Lyle Mammon: It's a pleasure to see Wax work again and to see a new young starlet begin a promising career. Oral still makes or breaks a girl in this business.

Ben Bettis: As she takes Wax into her mouth, Janna gets this cute grid of symmetrical dimples on her chin.

Janna SayQua: I can feel the head of his cock touching the back of my neck from inside my mouth.

Dee-Dee Sharp: We're watching Wax and Janna, and the set is very quiet, just the sound of them. Mammon whispers in my ear, "They've become the beast with two backs... that's from Shakespeare."

Eva Handle: They are very hot together. Maybe it all seems hotter because watching Wax with the deflating doll only makes you realize how hot real sex is.

Ben Bettis: About a minute before Wax is ready to blow, I feel a hand on my back. It's Mammon. He points to the doll, deflated in the corner. I back up a step or two and my shot now includes the doll in the background. I have to give Mammon a thumbs-up on that one. The guy has an eye.

Dee-Dee Sharp: Wax's money shot with Janna is surprisingly copious. I'm amazed he got wood so soon after finishing the doll, and then he blows a load on Janna's chest that looks like it was three days in the making. Lots of batter, as Mammon likes to say.

Ty Boyce: I clocked them at just over twenty-five minutes. A natural five minutes oral. Ten plus minutes missionary, then legs up. They kissed enough, hard and soft. Neither made any odd sounds. He paid good attention to her breasts. Eight minutes good doggie. Switched positions smoothly. She appeared to orgasm two times. Then a few final minutes more missionary. Wax blows a belly to chest load. Add to that the twelve minutes Wax did with the doll. Add to that (maybe) the footage of old Hilda Flüke farting around in the lab. We have a movie that could cut a few different ways.

JOEL HANDLE: And this time there is applause. It was quite a performance and all of us cheer and Janna has this thrilled-beyond-satisfaction look on her face and even Wax is smiling. We all are clapping like hell.

LYLE MAMMON: Wax stands and holds out a hand to help Janna up. But before she can take hold of his hand, Wax collapses.

Consumer Profile

Boothgirl

You don't like to rent tapes to play at home. There's no thrill in that. Every girl you know has done that at least once. You get off going to the video booths at Sunrise Arcade on Route 2A in Ampersand Falls. It seemed daring the first time you did it, and it has never stopped feeling that way.

In artsy R-rated movies with erotic content, they show the woman naked presenting herself to a seducer. They show foreplay that's either meant to be awkward or pass as adventurous. They may show tight close-ups of the woman's body and they might even show her seducer's ass. But there's a fadeout as the sex begins. You don't see the lovers again until morning. The woman's nudity then is never as flattering as it was during the seduction. She makes attempts to cover up with the sheets. She's disheveled, and he's a little distant. They're in an inexpensive hotel room. When she walks across the floor to the bathroom, she does so without grace. She takes heavy steps and appears a little wobbly on her feet. She's not a kitten anymore. She's a cow. She's heading for the pisser and the only question is will she close the door behind herself. (You hate these movies but you watch them on cable late at night, wishing you could go to the booths to watch something real.)

The video booths at Sunrise Arcade are on the second floor. The staircase up is narrow and littered, and it's not good to meet anyone coming down the stairs. The men coming down the stairs come down the stairs at a fast clip, almost running. At the top of the stairs is a large room with black walls and a row of black lights overhead on a low ceiling. Porn movie posters are on the walls. The booths sit in the center of the room like an island of doors, four doors on each side. One of the doors has a sign that says, "Personnel Only." This door has a different kind of knob on it—one that locks from the outside. Behind this door there isn't a television screen and a machine that takes five-dollar bills. Behind this door is a bank of VCRs connected in some smart way to the eleven televisions in the eleven peep booths.

You bring along a smart little flashlight the size of a pen; just one AAA battery inside. You always have a notebook. You are Boothgirl and you are a poet. MFA from Wadsworth University. A few dozen publications in small but respectable literary journals and a chapbook entitled *Crooked Cleavage Blues*. You're always able to get some writing done in the booths—mostly revision work. That's rare for a writer to find—a place to revise. You don't push it. You bring along one poem. Take it apart a few times in the booth, half watching the video that's playing.

The men standing outside the booths always seem surprised to see you there. A girl. Mostly they ignore you. Pretend they don't see you. Some of them will nod to you as they nod to one another, but that's it and you don't know what that nod means. Never any conversation. You want to tell them, confidentially, "I come here to write. And to play with myself—like you."

Boothgirl earns a living teaching freshman composition and, when you're lucky, an introductory course on literature—The Modern Novel, The American Short Story.

Inside the booth. Fasten the hook-and-eye latch. Insert a five-dollar bill in the machine, and in a few seconds a video will come on. You love most of all the movies of Wax Williams, and it's a special treat to find one showing in the booths. But that's rare. Usually they are playing unknown performers. Obscure titles. Lowdown productions. Amateurs—videos that nobody buys.

A pretty woman with bad skin is sitting alone on a hotel bed. Only the bottom of the seascape above the bed is visible. The fixed shot appears designed to capture the loneliness and horniness of the setting. You feel stupid for noticing such details, but you want to find some deliberate creative thought behind each video. After ten seconds pass, you conclude that the only reason this woman's legs fall below what can be seen by the camera is that she must have bad legs. You don't want to see this woman's heavy legs flailing in the air while some fatty humps away on top of her. You advance the channel to a gay video. Two slim men stand side by side, masturbating, kissing, giggling. You watch, wondering how long it will take them to start blowing each other. You won't be able to watch much of that, you think. At one time you wanted nothing more than to see that, but once you had, you were bothered. To your mind, men didn't do it right, which was a big surprise. You had expected to learn new technique and to witness a love for the act and a level of professionalism that you weren't always able to muster. What you saw in your first boy-boy video was disappointing. One guy closed his eyes too tight when he did it, and the other guy hardly ever took the guy in his mouth—it was more of a hand job with some weird licking. You had figured that gay guys were the only ones who gave earnest blowjobs. Wrong.

Boothgirl takes out a notebook and begins to write:
Girls like you aren't born until high school. Born at sixteen years old. You give birth to yourself, you glamorous creature, you beautiful girl. But you're so young. Baby woman. You just started menstruating. You like it. You like menstruating—you are that young. Last week your pee-pee was an inert slit. Now it's an open mouth, a gaping open wound—dripping. A weeping eye socket with no eyeball. And hairy. Always wet. Slick. Touch it.

You estimate the dimension of the booth to be four feet by six feet. The walls are painted flat black, and the only lighting in the booth is a forty-watt recessed bulb in the dropped ceiling. The television screen is twenty-seven inches wide. The television sits in the wall at about chest height. There's thick plexiglass protecting the television screen. Guys come on the plexiglass. Some of them wipe it off and toss the used tissue and napkins from fast food restaurants and donut shops on the floor. There are built-in seats in some of the booths. They're a bit low for sitting comfortably, but they're at the right height for you to get a leg up.

Boothgirl tells the class, "Question every word, every choice." You tell them, "Complete poems are sometimes not quite really done." You tell them, "You can love a word and find that you have to part with it in the end."

All through high school your panties were perpetually wet. Soaking wet. The only time your panties were dry was when you weren't wearing them. You thought about sex all day long and masturbated constantly. You looked at porn and read erotica. You liked porn better. You stole three triple X videos from the adult section of the video store, and hooked up the family VCR to the old black-and-white TV in your bedroom. You faked being sick for a week so you could stay home alone from school and watch those three tapes all day long, over and over.

You saw nobody upstairs at the booths your first time, but you knew that you weren't alone. The next time, there were three men standing outside the booths. They each stood alone, but your instinct told you that they had arrived together, all in suits and ties—working men from the offices downtown. Finally they entered separate booths. The doors from a few closed booths opened then, and the men in those booths stepped out and began jiggling the handles of the occupied booths. Some of those doors opened, and the men stepped in. Then you had a stupid realization—something you should have understood before you ever stepped into Sunrise Arcade. Men came to the booths to meet up with other men. It was a cruising spot. They blew each other in the booths.

You went to Tijuana once for spring break and saw a donkey show. Everyone was talking about the donkey show, "You gotta see the donkey show." And there were so many strip joints and hookers all over the streets. The donkey show was at a dirty club that was more like a barn. The show was a woman fucking a donkey. It was insane to see. So loud. Screaming loud. You felt sorry for the woman and sorry for the donkey. People watching, drunk, whooping so loudly, and the donkey was just crazy. Hay on the floor. The woman was pulling on the donkey's tail and his cock, and then she swung herself under the donkey and this old guy with her strapped her ankles across the donkey's back and then he guided the donkey's cock into her. Fucking crazy.

Not just damp or moist or humid, but slick. Slippery. Syrupy. So you touch it. You rub the middle finger of your left hand against your clit. Then you slide your hand under your panties. Put you pencil behind your ear. You think, *Rub my hole.* And you slip your middle finger inside. Rub. Finger. Finger in your hole. Christ. You feel your whole body heat up. Dark booth. The movie on shows two girls sharing a double-headed dong, their legs like mating scissors.

You like to compare yourself to the women in the videos. You can be truthful with yourself and very objective in seeing that most of these women are built in a way that you aren't. They are almost all very skinny and with big, fake tits. You don't hold that against them, don't look down on them for getting boob jobs. Augmentation. Forgetting the tits and the skinny waists and tiny asses, you think your face compares better to almost every woman that you've ever seen in an adult film. You have better hair, too—better styled, at least. Hop, skip, and jump. You could be one of these women. These women like sex and so do you. They have no inhibitions—look at what they do for a living—and you are as close to having no inhibitions as a woman can get and not be in porno.

Boothgirl writes in a little notebook:
The little girl in the picture stood a few feet from her mother with her hands on her hips, just like her mother. She had inherited her mother's facial features and many of her mannerisms. She always listened closely when grownups were talking—she liked hearing what they said, and she used her new words with her playmates.

It was like you had a fever. Your teenage pussy was on fire and you felt your face getting flushed and you sweated, too. You couldn't wear makeup most days because you sweat so much, and makeup seemed to make things worse and caused you to sweat more and break out. One day a pig of a boy called you a sweaty bitch. And another boy named Michael Glass stood up for you. He said, "Girls don't sweat; they glisten." Oh, you wanted to take Michael Glass home and watch dirty videos with him and fuck him. You wrote in your journal, "He has to get inside my wet hole. Michael Glass. My drenched twat. My hot cunt. Michael Glass."

Some days you feel silly being there. In a booth. A poet with a notebook and a pencil, come to revise a work in progress and look at a few dirty movies. Five dollars for every fifteen minutes.

One day in your junior year you wore no panties to school and a short skirt. You could feel how wet you were. Dripping. Dripping pussy. Slippery wet. You wanted to open your legs and let every boy in class fuck you. You took a desk in the back of the classroom and sat in such a way that your skirt was not under your ass. Your ass and wet pussy were right on the chair and the chair was still warm from whoever had sat there during the period before. You could squeeze the muscles in your thighs and ass and feel the lips of your vagina pucker against the warm chair.

And Boothgirl comes. Forget the prehistoric notion that promiscuous women—especially professional sex workers, strippers, hookers, porno queens—are not orgasmic. Boothgirl is orgasmic. Multiply so. You feel it in the soles of your feet if you're standing. You feel it deep in your still-virgin anus. Your forehead. Your ears. Across your chest. Your puffy nipples. Running up your throat.

You hadn't even menstruated once and you were in the tenth grade. Late bloomer. No tits either. Then, when you started getting your period, it didn't come every month. You got it like once every three months, and your friends told you that you were lucky. But your periods hit hard. Not cramps, more like a weight pulling on your pussy. Your legs went numb when you stood. But you liked it. You liked getting your period. Your mind was crazy with thoughts of fucking boys. You ate like a pig. Salty stuff. Sweet stuff. You just wanted a boy in your mouth.

You had a dream about being naked in a booth, so on your next visit you take your clothes off and stand naked in the tiny booth. It does not turn you on. You decide to stay undressed until you can understand why you aren't turned on. You light a cigarette—your first in the booths. Fifteen minutes pass. Your television screen goes blank. You are going to feed another five-dollar bill into the machine, when you realize that the absolute silence in your booth means that none of the other booths are occupied. You have a sudden urge to step out of your booth, naked. The thought seems to be an instruction—a dare—from your dream. You undo the latch on your door and open it. You step slowly out of the booth and walk quickly around the perimeter of the empty arcade.

You heard about Wax Williams from some boys in your algebra class. His cock was as long as his arm and he made porno movies. You stole a copy of *The Well-hung Jury* from the video store and watched it every day after school. You thought of nothing but Wax Williams all day long. He was from Ampersand, Massachusetts—a college town.

College was freedom and boys who kept their mouths shut and knew better than to talk about girls behind their backs. College boys, you found, would do what you told them. All the girls in your dorm were horny all the time, so you didn't feel like a freak anymore. Your first roommate wanted to kiss you, but you said, "No, thanks." You said, "I'm strictly dickly," and the girl laughed, so you kissed her anyway and then you let that girl eat you out all night long.

Boothgirl makes a list of other places she could go: apartment, a bar (any bar), cemetery (that's a place for poets to go and write), library, shopping, the park, gym, coffee shop. You have to be somewhere.

You wonder now if you'll ever get out of Ampersand. You'd come as a Wadsworth freshman. You stayed to get an MA in English, to work with Jeff Hector and edit his literary journal, *Folded, Stitched, Glued,* and become one of his lovers. Then you'd stayed on after finishing the writing program. You taught freshman composition at Wadsworth and at a community college a few towns away. Then Wadsworth expanded its graduate writing program and began offering an MFA in Creative Writing. So you enrolled in the program again and started fucking Jeff Hector again. He has a long and very thin penis—just like a pencil—because he's such a writer.

You give your class writing exercises, prompts to get them started. Nobody knows what to write about. "Write what you know," you'll say. "Or write about something you don't know." You have them stare at photos and write on a sheet of paper without looking at what they're writing. You tell them to begin their stories at the end of one day and end them at the beginning of the next day. You tell them to take a familiar, time-worn phrase and substitute a key word in that phrase to make a new epigram. There's no place like __________. __________ is where the heart is. The heart is a lonely __________. Your students look at you and then look at one another, suppressing their shrugs. You want to give up on them. Finally you say, "Just write something that I can grade."

You were good at figuring out which guys had big ones. You could just tell. A knack. You were hardly ever wrong. And you were lucky in your fucking. You never attracted any freaks, and you never got hooked up with boys who weren't strong enough to get dumped. You fucked whomever you wanted without regret or complications. You had a perfect knack for finding the ideal, well-hung, disease-free guy whenever you needed one. And it always went the same perfect way for you. Meet a guy. Catch his eye. Lure him from his friends (or girlfriend). Take him someplace and give him the fuck (or suck) of his life. Then part with a happy farewell. The guys always left when you wanted them to, and they always came back when you wanted them to. None of your girlfriends had this kind of luck. They all had bad dates with pricks who charmed the hell out of them, screwed them (usually badly), then lingered in their lives in complicated ways. Stood them up. Cheated on them. Or, the complete reverse, they dated guys who didn't know thing one about how to seduce a woman. Guys who dated them and dated them but never put the moves on them. Guys who then couldn't get the message that they didn't want to date a man ad nauseam, and that now their opportunity to get laid had passed. And these guys didn't go quietly. These were guys with heartaches that they couldn't heal and lusts that they couldn't implement. These guys wanted girls out of their league, and they thought the best way to win these girls was to ingratiate themselves with them. These guys went bald young and had little dicks.

Boothgirl writes:
She was good at judging knobs. She could predict what kind of knob a guy had before he whipped it out. She could look at guy and know in three seconds if he had a big knob or not.

You would say that yours was an imaginative and varied love life; rich with Richards, Bills, Tonys, and a few Bruces. You fucked half a hundred guys before you were eighteen, didn't get a single STD. No crabs. Not even a raw pussy. You had a cast-iron pussy. Built to withstand lots of activity. Resilient to disease and baby-making sperm. You're not afraid of big cocks. No. Listen: Put three fingers in my pussy, now. Sorry, my hand is already there. Yes, those are my fingers. You'll find a battery-operated phallus in a shoebox under my bed. Load it with fresh, long-life D-batteries, also in the shoebox. Ivory shaded dildo with imitation foreskin. A little cold on initial entry. But warms up quickly—physical principles of friction. That's what it's all about.

You hear a man enter the booth beside yours. You hear the machine accept his five-dollar bill. You hear his television come on to the same movie you're watching. You hear the man advance the channel past three other videos. He turns the volume up very loud. The bass soundtrack vibrates the plywood walls separating your booth from his, and above the volume of groan and the bass soundtrack you hear a hum and suddenly a large drill bit comes through the shaking wall followed by a penis. You look at this cock sticking into your booth. Then you look at the video on the screen. Girl-on-girl. Already you're writing about this cock. Purple. Bruised looking. Old. The oldest cock you've ever seen. Fifty, sixty years old. Big. Purple. Can't forget that it is purple. You remember reading once that steroid users have purple skin. This cock looks like it's been through a war. It's sticking through the wall half-hard. Alive. You'd have been less surprised if this thing had entered your booth through the television screen. That wouldn't have been scary. Through the wall the man says, "Come on, man. Come on." And you say, "What?" though you hadn't meant to speak at all. Then the cock disappears and you can see the man's eye through the hole and then his mouth. He says, "A girl." You say, "What the fuck?" And he says, "Get the fuck out of there." He's mad, and his anger makes you want to laugh. He pounds a fist against the thin wall. You unfasten the latch, open the door, and make your way to the stairs. On your way out of the store, you stop to look through the discount bin of previously viewed tapes. They're all marked down in price. Two for one; $9.99 and up. You buy *DormitOrgy, A Tale of Two Titties, Cuntraption,* and *Pornacopulia.*

Chapter Two

Roadwork

Mammon gave Mr. and Mrs. Williams payment of $10,000 in cash, all the money he had managed to accumulate in his forty-nine years on the planet. Mrs. Williams had typed up a document stating that, as Wax's legal guardians, Mr. and Mrs. Walter Williams authorized an apprenticeship with Lyle Mammon for a period of no more than five years, at which time, Mammon would grant Wax his leave. This was the second revision of the document that Mammon had seen. The first version referenced Wax as an "indentured worker" in Mammon's "kind charge."

Mammon balked at the language, and so did Mr. Williams. "You make it sound like we're selling our boy into slavery," he said.

Mrs. Williams told her husband to remain quiet, but she agreed to go over the contract one more time and make a few changes. She was, however, adamant about calling the $10,000 a cash loan, which Mammon felt she believed gave her and her husband the right to repay the amount (with an interest payment not specifically specified) and so void the nutty contract at some future date.

Mammon couldn't figure this lady out. She looked like standard issue mom, a nice lady from the office. But something else was going on with her. Mammon had no legal counsel, and he didn't see the need for such a document. He had some fears that Mrs. Williams would, one day, try to use this document as a means to get her boy back.

Mammon had insisted on looking Wax over before the contract was signed. Wax knew that Mammon had seen Dr. Johnson's unpublished paper on his treatment, a paper that contained nearly one hundred photographs of Wax at various stages of his development.

Mrs. Williams said, "Bathroom," and Mammon followed Wax to a narrow bathroom at the back of the ranch house.

Wax didn't have a problem stripping down for Mammon. He no longer had any self-conscious reflexes about standing naked before a clothed person for the purposes of an examination of his genitals. Three years of being expected to do so at the oddest times and places for Dr. Johnson or one of his colleagues had rid him of the adolescent shyness that many men carry with them into old age. So with his jeans and boxers down around his ankles in one crumpled roll, Wax stood before Mammon and placed his penis, long and thick, on a wicker clothes hamper. Mammon moved the unlit cigar stub from the left side of his mouth to the right. Didn't say a word. Half a minute later in the driveway, he amended the document with an alias, Lyle A. Mammonberg, which he explained was his honest-to-God real name.

"All right, then," Mrs. Williams said, though she seemed a bit suspicious. "I would like to see some identification."

"I have no ID whatsoever, Mrs. Williams. Never have."

"Not even a driver's license?"

"No," said Mammon, knowing that this lie would have to be convincing. "Mrs. Williams, I have never been gainfully employed—though I haven't been a criminal or involved in criminal activity. I have no social security number. No credit cards. No memberships. I've worked in show business. Nightclubs. Dinner theater. Standup comedy. MC'd at strip clubs. Managed a professional wrestler in the state of Washington. Work like that. Always paid cash under the table."

"No papers," Mrs. Williams said, accepting it as an impossible fact.

"My mother must have had a birth certificate for me at one time, but I have nothing now. Lyle Aaron Mammonberg. That's the name I started with. I've worked as Lyle Mammon for twenty-odd years. But I'll sign Mammonberg because, in all truth, Mrs. Williams, that is the only name that I can legally sign."

Without another word spoken, she opened the document again. Mammon signed a quick scribble, then watched Mrs. Williams countersign and instruct her husband to do the same. Wax stood inside the front doorway, leaning on the screen door. Mammon nodded at him. "Are you packed?"

The boy came out of the house then, two small suitcases and a book bag over his shoulders, and he headed straight for Mammon's white Continental. Didn't say goodbye. Didn't look back at the little house.

Mammon sprung the trunk on his Conti. "Toothbrush?" he asked. "Deodorant?"

Wax nodded.

"Tampons? Minipads?"

Wax laughed.

"Don't make your dirty jokes to my boy." Mrs. Williams last words to Mammon.

"Excuse me, Mrs. Williams," Mammon said.

Mr. Williams had followed his son to the car. He was a shrug of a man, sad-faced, standing with his hands behind his back—tall, but to no useful effect. "You look sad, Wax," he said. Getting no response, he spoke again. "You're leaving your home and family for God knows where. Of course you're sad."

Wax shook his father's hand and walked back to the front step to hug his mother. Mammon was glad to see this; it was a good way to depart.

And then they were in the car and off, Mammon and Wax. Up to full speed as soon as they turned onto Route 2A. Mammon wondered if the boy knew what was ahead of him. The kid wasn't dumb, but he was certainly naïve. Mammon had been clear at their first meeting that they'd be doing some business. "You're gonna put that great thing between your legs to work," he said. "But," he added quickly, "nothing queer. In case you're worried. And I'm not a pimp. You're gonna be screwing pretty girls. You'll be getting some good money, too. That money that I gave to your parents, that has nothing to do with you. Nothing to do with our business together. You don't owe me anything more than five years of work."

Mammon was surprised at how easy it was to talk to the boy. He listened good. Didn't have questions. Didn't interrupt. No wisecracks back. In fact, Wax seemed interested in everything that Mammon had to say. "You'll be working for me, Wax. I've never really been anybody's boss before. But I did manage a few comics after I got out of standup myself. I booked comics all up and down the coast. Maine to Florida. Clubs in Puerto Rico, too."

Wax perked up at the mention of Puerto Rico, so Mammon asked him if he'd ever been.

"No," he said. "What's it like there?"

"Beautiful beaches, very sunny. They have big casinos. Hot women with very round asses and little feet." Wax laughed. "We'll go soon. It'll be our first vacation, soon as we get some work done. Get some money in the bank. Fly down. Or maybe take a cruise ship."

Wax was smiling. Mammon liked that smile of his. This kid was gonna be a big star. The smile was capable of magic. A really sweet smile. Nothing dark behind that smile. No calculation. Charm, but not the effort to be charming. Just a nice smile. Clean face. Handsome face. The kid was much better looking than the photos that Doc Johnson had trotted out in that wacko paper of his. Good skin. Nice hair. Smart eyes. Male model material, really. A leading man in any era of cinema. He would be eighteen in six weeks.

***

WAX WILLIAMS: I didn't turn around to look back at my house, but I could picture my parents standing in the driveway, staring at Mammon's car as we drove away. Maybe they are standing there still, waving, just frozen in their shoes. I remember thinking that Mammon—this guy in a cheap suit with the silly big car—was just going to drive me around the block and drop me off again at the foot of my parent's driveway.

LYLE MAMMON: Wax's parents gave him their blessing, and then they basically disowned him. They took ten grand from me; then they took a powder themselves. Wax and I lit out on the road to make some bucks together. A simple plan. Wax would swing his thing at some of the finer strip clubs in the Northeast. We would use whatever we earned to bankroll our first adult feature.

WAX WILLIAMS: We weren't driving for very long when Lyle asked if I was hungry. I told him that I was, but my mother hadn't packed me any lunch. He laughed, and he said we would find a restaurant. He wanted to buy me lunch. He said he wanted to buy me lunch because lunch was a good way to start a business relationship.

TED ROMLING (BUSINESS CARD SAYS ROMLING VENTURES LLC, XXX DEVELOPMENT): This was the very first meal Wax had ever eaten that was not prepared by his mother. Lunch with Lyle Mammon. Hard to believe, but growing up, Wax had never even had a McDonald's hamburger—nothing but home-cooked meals. Brought his lunch to school every day in a brown paper bag.

LYLE MAMMON: I hired Ted Romling as a consultant well before the casting of *DormitOrgy.* He'd worked in the adult industry in one capacity or another for almost twenty years. He's very slick: sharp wardrobe, gold around his neck and on his wrists, shaved head that he kept very shiny. I didn't want for Wax to meet him too soon, so Ted shadowed us on the road, taking in some of Wax's early appearances. He videotaped Wax on stage and got some great stuff that we still haven't released.

TED ROMLING: Mammon told me in our first meeting that he wanted to make porn better. Quality. Good plots. Good sex. Realistic. Fun, but not laughable. He talked a good game. He talked like a guy looking for backing, and he could've gotten money from a dozen or more players in the industry. Any one of a dozen producers would've bankrolled a first feature with Wax Williams. But Mammon wanted to do it on his terms. He wanted to do it all. Develop a script, direct it, dupe ten thousand VHS tapes, design a box for it, and direct market it to adult retailers and through mail order. He didn't want to give up even a tenth of his stake in Wax. So step one was they hit the road.

***

They sat at the first available table in the restaurant. Mammon leaned his arms into the crumbs that had been left behind by the previous diner. Mammon was a man who took pains to be remembered by those in the service sector and, in turn, to remember those who had served him. He had a head full of waitress names and bartender nicknames that never failed him. He connected names to faces quickly and with lasting accuracy.

The fastest way to the bank, as Mammon saw it, would have been to serve simply as Wax's manager. It would have been an easier road, but not as rewarding financially. He could have rented Wax out to any production company that had ready capital and an experienced video production crew. Mammon could have taken his cut; recouped what he had given to the kid's cunt of a mother. But there was more to be made over the long haul, he was sure. Give the kid a few months' seasoning, do some roadwork, turn him into a performer. The strip circuit would help to establish him, generate a buzz.

***

LYLE MAMMON: I am an early riser. I wake up every morning at the first light of dawn. I had no need for an alarm clock or a motel wake-up call, especially when we had to get a move on to the next club. I do, however, like to take a quick power nap after each meal, breakfast included. Eating exhausts me. The dreams I have on a full stomach are quite different from the hunger dreams I used to suffer as a child, when I was routinely sent to bed without dinner. Hunger dreams, it is a scientific fact, can kill you.

***

"The water in the toilet bowl is blue," Wax reported from the bathroom.

"Then don't drink it," Mammon said.

"I don't have a straw," Wax said, quickly appropriating Mammon's sense of humor, which wasn't much different from that of Rollie Mignon, Wax's best friend since third grade.

Laughing, Mammon joined him in the little bathroom. He looked into the mirror, gave his hair a slicking with a wet comb, straightened his loud tie, and said, "I can't wait for tomorrow."

"Why?" Wax asked.

"Because I get better looking every day."

***

WAX WILLIAMS: Lyle was the first person that I had ever seen use two teabags to make one cup of tea. He also buttered both sides of his toast in the morning at breakfast.

***

During their first breakfast together, Mammon talked of nothing but the lunch they'd eaten at noon the day before. Lunch was Mammon's mistress, his only true love. The man lived for lunch. He loved what he called pub lunches: burgers and fries served in a basket with a cold beer.

***

LYLE MAMMON: There weren't all that many places for Wax to perform. There still aren't any strip clubs that I know of that feature only live nude men. It's a specialty showcase type thing, male strippers. Clubs'll do a ladies' night once a month, once a week if you're lucky. So we had to cover a lot of ground on those early trips. We'd go from Connecticut to New York to Pennsylvania to D.C. Maybe a dozen clubs. We'd wheel into the lot of the club a few hours before Wax was scheduled to perform on ladies' night—usually a Friday or Saturday night. So we arrive during the last hours of the dancing girls. Never a pretty scene. Lonely guys lingering over their beers, knowing they're going to get kicked out soon, sent on their way. Couple girls dancing on stage, watching the clock. It's a sad time at a strip club, the hour just prior to the start of a ladies' night. And always one guy who just isn't leaving. He wants one last eyeful before he goes on his way—maybe he's hoping that one of the dancers will sit with him at his table, run a finger under his chin, give him a little knee job under the table.

***

Wax came to know the Lyle Mammon story backwards and forwards on that first road trip. Mammon was very much a believer in recapitulation, especially in abbreviated forums, like short car rides, waiting rooms, and long-distance late-night phone calls. He liked to recollect his show biz failings. He saw himself as a victim of bad timing and undeserved screw-overs. His standup act was good—he had always known that it wasn't great—but his timing was bad and there were too many people in show biz who liked to screw people over. So years of jokes added up to nothing but a half-dozen unwinnable feuds and, to balance that out, a few friends who gave him a chance to reinvent himself—meaning, almost make a living—as a booking agent.

"Sold a few jokes to Buddy Hackett," was his most common refrain. "Sold a few jokes to Buddy Hackett," he said it often. "Mr. Buddy Hackett."

And then there were his unfunny monologues. His endless stream-of-consciousness riffing. "Fruit can be funny. Slip on a banana peel. Apple falls on your head and you discover gravity. A naked woman gives you an apple and when you eat it you're completely fucked out of God's paradise. William Tell takes a bow and arrow, shoots an apple off his son's head. Lucille Ball stomping grapes in a big wine vat with a bunch of chunky French peasants, and then she gets into a catfight with one of them. Blacks love watermelons. That's funny. Coconut-shell brassieres. The plum becomes a prune and it helps to keep you regular. A party girl eats a banana fellatio-style. She catches the attention of the intended man, and just as he begins to get aroused, she bites off the tip of the banana. His hands go to his crotch in reflex protection. Did you hear the one about the queer Irishman?"

"No," says Wax, too weary to deflect another punch line.

"He liked women better than beer."

"Good one."

"Did you hear the one about the queer burglar?"

"No."

"Couldn't blow the safe, so he went down on the elevator."

"I get it."

"You could laugh."

"I said I get it."

***

WAX WILLIAMS: One time Mammon pointed to a man on the street who had a full beard but no moustache. "See that guy," he said, "Abe Lincoln complex. You can't trust a man with an Abe Lincoln complex because he's probably a liar." He said, "Honest Abe, my ass." I don't know why, but Lyle had a thing against Abraham Lincoln. He hated him. He didn't like five-dollar bills or pennies because Lincoln's face was on them. If he was due back a five in change, he would ask the cashier for five ones instead. And pennies—he really hated pennies. He would pick the pennies out of his loose change and throw them away. Mammon said, "My father was the type of Jew who wore his yarmulke under his toupee. Didn't even bother to get me circumcised, the bastard. I'm the only uncut Jew in God's kingdom."

***

To minimize on expenses, Mammon and Wax doubled up on their road trips. Every dollar tucked in Wax's unaccommodating briefs went toward the production costs of his first full-length adult feature, which was still in the planning stages. Considering Wax's preternaturally large talent, funding could have been secured easily enough. However, Mammon did not want to do anything that might reduce his take. He didn't want to dilute his profit share or, worse, risk losing Wax to a producer with deeper pockets.

So they did without on the road. They skipped meals (just a few) and stayed in lousy motels. Mammon bought money orders with Wax's tip money, and sent the money orders to a post office box in Ampersand. He numbered each money order with the idea of showing Wax that all of the money would be accounted for upon their return to Ampersand. Of course, Wax showed little interest. He seemed to trust Mammon, having no reason not to.

"We have to live on nothing," Mammon said. "All we need on the road is gas, food, and lodging. No frills. No drinks, no smokes, no chicks." Wax nodded. "We're putting ourselves on a strict per diem. Do you know what that term means?"

"Yes."

"I haven't figured out what we'll need to cover everything, but it shouldn't take long to know." Mammon began keeping track of gas mileage and, without taking out a membership, he cadged a hotel/motel booklet from AAA. He made note of the cheapest beds on their route, and even managed to get the AAA discount at most stops. "Keep expenses down. We're not going to be staying at five-star hotels. We'll hit a town, find the cheapest flop, check in. A mattress is a mattress. Color TV. Shower. Shitter. That's it."

***

WAX WILLIAMS: I liked to watch Mammon break his aspirins in half and swallow them dry. This was the maximum amount of medication he allowed himself. Half an aspirin was all he ever needed. Aspirin worked on him in very small doses, which appealed to the cheapskate in him but worried the hypochondriac in him. He loved that a ten-pack tin of Bayer lasted him for months, but he worried about what this meant about his internal system. He said, "It doesn't say much for your bodily organs—and the blood in your veins—if you can only take a quarter of the recommended adult dosage." He was certain that it meant there were several defects with his heart, his liver, his you-name-it. His innards were all fouled up, he was sure of it.

TED ROMLING: Mammon liked to tease Wax about the little things he did—like the way Wax ate slowly and the way he was so neat about picking up after himself even in the fleabaggiest of hotels. They were together nearly every minute of the day, but Mammon never really gained much of an understanding about the way the boy's mind worked. I used to have the same problem with Wax. You just couldn't reach him. He wasn't very forthcoming. He kept his own counsel most of the time and didn't give much away with his facial expressions or through his body language.

***

"I know a diner not far from here makes a kick-ass chili," said ever-hungry Mammon.

"I don't think you're supposed to use the word ass to describe food."

"You can when you're talking chili. You can say kick-ass chili and there's no offense."

***

LYLE MAMMON: Wax's manners rivaled those of the clichéd Englishman in a stuffy movie. Like a cross between James Bond as played by Roger Moore and Mr. French—Sebastian Cabot—from *Family Affair.* Please and thank you. Please and thank you. It was like real etiquette, and you didn't notice it unless you were looking for it. We'd be on the set and the whole crew would break for lunch. I'd spring for some takeout. The rest of the slobs like me would just shovel it in. We'd clean our plates before Wax had even finished putting butter on his roll.

TED ROMLING: Wax'd give a subtle turn of his dinner plate to bring a baked potato from ten o'clock to three o'clock or to improve the cutting angle on his steak. Another kid his age would have just knuckled down on the fork to get the job done.

BERNIE LOUDE (CLUB OWNER): We've done a ladies' night here at Lucky Pete's once a month for the past six years. Wax was far and away the most popular of all the male dancers we ever featured. The ladies lined up to see him. And not many of the male performers make the successful crossover from clubs to video work. These dancing boys, they're hard to turn on, from what I've heard. They're in great shape and they can move on the dance floor, but no wood when it counts. They're showers, not growers, as the saying goes. Nothing gets them hard. Mostly because they're all half fags, but also because they're so used to being pawed and groped by women when they dance that they've trained themselves not to get turned on. They're always being cheered and ogled and they develop very big egos and that kills them sexually. My theory.

TED ROMLING: Bernie Loude let Wax and Mammon use his club as a rehearsal space for a few weeks before Wax's debut. They had to wait until Wax turned eighteen before he could start performing, and they had to teach him a few stage tricks.

LYLE MAMMON: We rehearsed a few hours every morning. Wax was not a natural on stage, but he wasn't bad. He took instruction well—his baseball coach would probably say the same thing. You only have to tell Wax something once and he knows it. I had a couple of the other dancing boys show Wax some moves. He was good with the pole. He liked to jump up and grab onto the pole and then hold his body in a straight, parallel pose. It was gymnastic.

BERNIE LOUDE: Wax's stage show? He refused to dance like the other guys in the revues. He has no natural rhythm and would not insult the women in his audience by pretending to entertain them through dance. He moved gracefully, though, like an athlete, and he eventually developed a sense of drama, of presentation on stage.

TED ROMLING: Mammon came up with the idea of a staged nude workout in the manner of the Greek athletes. And it was Mammon who researched and wrote and recorded a narration that played along as Wax did some calisthenics. First you heard "Theme from 2001: A Space Odyssey." Mammon recited some text ripped off from an encyclopedia about the Greek city-state and the origins of athletic competition. The lights came up. There was Wax sitting nude, center stage, in the pose of Rodin's "The Thinker." His penis was visible only to the women in the front rows, who would invariably gasp. As the music swelled, he stood. He stretched. He ran in place. He did a few minutes of jumping jacks. He performed a tribute to the great pugilists—hit a heavy bag for five minutes, and worked the speed bag, did some neat rope skipping. Some nights he wore a third boxing glove on the head of his penis. Always got a big laugh.

LYLE MAMMON: It's true. The first Olympic athletes in Greece competed in the nude and regularly exercised naked. The women were transfixed by Wax. I think that's the right word. They'd be very quiet at first. All eyes. Whispering. But not much tipping.

WAX WILLIAMS: Mammon wore rubber gloves when he counted our take in the motel later. He'd read something about a test that was done on a randomly selected dollar bill. Trace elements of fecal matter, semen, urine—among other things—on every bill. He liked me to watch him. Counting our money again, he'd say, "It is said to be a sign of insecurity."

LYLE MAMMON: The personal appearances were originally going to be a one-time thing, in and out, a summer of quick-hit, one-night stands on the beefcake circuit to infuse our still-forming production company with some much-needed capital to finance Wax Williams' debut adult feature. But it turned into a seasonal commitment. Wax didn't seem to mind. The performing rid him of any lingering, adolescent shyness—I sound like a shrink. It helped him forget about the string of bad, demeaning after-school jobs his mother forced on him, and the disappointment at the loss of his ability to play baseball. He enjoyed being on the road, I think. It was an education for him, and the money kept getting better. The first year we shared a motel room, divided the driving duties, and counted the money together.

BERNIE LOUDE: Mammon would schedule twelve minutes of standup from a local chick comic at every stop. He would help sweeten their material with some dick jokes that would tickle the women in the audience.

WAX WILLIAMS: I think that Mammon expected me to hate performing in clubs. He always stressed that it was a temporary job. But I didn't mind. I enjoyed it most of the time. I only had to do it twice a week at the most. The rest of the time we spent driving to the next club. The women were all older than me, since they had to be at least twenty-one to get in and I was only eighteen when I started. It was like a party. It's impossible to stand up on a stage in front of a hundred happy, cheering women—who are all throwing money at you—and not enjoy it.

LYLE MAMMON: Club owners would ask, "Does your boy have any videos?" I'd say, "He has yet to make his video debut." They'd say, "We can't promise you any stage time." I'd say to Wax, "Drop your pants for the man." And that was all it ever took. We'd get booked fast, and every booking made the next booking a little easier.

EILEEN T.: I'm a size queen, always have been. I remember when I ran girls' track my junior year in high school we would practice on rainy days inside the gym with the boys' basketball team. I noticed that I could see through the boys' gym shorts when they got sweaty. Our school colors were green and gold—tops green and shorts gold. The bright gold shorts that the boys' basketball team wore became almost transparent the wetter with sweat they got. The boys ran up and down the court and their shorts were see-through. And when they jumped for rebounds I saw everything in their shorts.

JANE M.: I had just gotten divorced. I was forty. I had no children and decided to move far away to live without family and friends. I just didn't want to be bothered by people who knew me.

TODD INSULIN (PHD CANDIDATE AT WADSWORTH UNIVERSITY, STUDYING GROUP BEHAVIOR IN EROTIC SITUATIONS): Men who frequent strip clubs do so mostly alone or, on occasion, in pairs. Often, the men who attend a strip club as a pair share a longstanding relationship—they're collegial pals or maintain some type of active, though not close or interdependent, business relationship. Also, a lot of these pairs are brothers. The only other set of male strip club clientele is the bachelor party group, which can range in size from six men to a dozen or more. The larger the bachelor party, the greater the potential for intergenerational familial males to be partaking together: brothers, sons, fathers, grandfathers, and uncles. Uncles and nephews are another common strip club pairing. Conversely, women visit strip clubs to see male performers almost exclusively in groups of four. I don't know why that is. Two women together might be scary for them because one could, theoretically, go off and do something crazy with one of the performers, leaving her friend alone to fend for herself. My best theory on the number four holds simply that four adult females can fit into a car better than five—nobody has to sit in the middle—and four women in a car is better than three, because three women in a car seems like an incomplete set—one woman would have to sit in the back seat all by herself and the decision surrounding which woman would sit alone in the back seat is the kind of decision that women, in general, like to avoid.

EILEEN T.: I started looking for books on ballet dancers and bullfighters and I'd just stare at their bulges. When I started college, I got photography books with male nude studies and books on figure drawing anatomy that had nude photos that you were supposed to draw. I made photocopies of the best pictures in the library. I was always occupied with the thought of penises. I wish there was a bona fide method to determine if a guy has a big one before it's too late. I mean, you have to be able to know. Guessing isn't good enough. You can choose a guy because he has a big bulge in his trousers, but then find out he's all balls—all potatoes and no meat.

TODD INSULIN: A strip club filled with female customers experiencing a performance by a male dancer is quite different from a strip club filled with male customers watching female dancers.

LYLE MAMMON: I remember the first club show Wax did. Crotch steam and nothing else was affecting the relative humidity of the club. The air conditioners were on full blast, but those horny ladies got a load of Wax Williams and they all got very damp and hot between the knees. Wax made them wilt. I heard one woman say to another, "Are you as wet as I am?"

EILEEN T.: I went to my first ladies' night alone while I was on a business trip to New Jersey. I was thirty-five years old and so very, very horny. The boys dancing were all so young and hot, but they wouldn't get fully naked. They kept themselves locked in tight with their little satin thongs. They'd give you a little peek when you tipped and a longer peek if you kept tipping. They'd stretch a leg over your shoulder and lean their package into your face and shake their hips and swing their package from side to side. I spent three hundred dollars that first night, and now I consider that the minimum amount for a good time.

JANE M.: Eileen made me come that first night. I had no interest, I thought, because I was in a no-sex, man-hating mindset after my divorce. I didn't want to go to a place and behave all gaga over some pretty boys who were probably gay anyway. But I went because Eileen said I had to see this boy Wax, who was so sweet and handsome and so different from the other boy dancers.

LYLE MAMMON: The women who came to see Wax were a nice bunch of girls: housewives and young unmarried women. They were a respectful bunch. They sat quietly when Wax was on stage. Didn't drink too much. Never got grabby with him. So we revved it up a bit.

JANE M.: Wax took the stage and did a few quick steps—almost a run and jump. He didn't move like the other dancers who had gone before him. He moved like a jock, not a dancer, but he wasn't clumsy. He was so young. His face was beautiful. He looked smart, shy. He looked friendly. You couldn't use those words to describe the other dancers. You could tell those boys all thought they were God's gift to women. Wax didn't parade himself around on stage. He responded to the audience, which was so loud. He was there to dance for us, to put on a show, to please us. He was honest about that in his performance. There was a give and take between us and him. He was treating us like we all were his teammates. He gave us all high-fives and had us doing the wave.

EILEEN T.: I got a kick out of Wax's manager, Lyle Mammon. Lyle was the only other man in the club, aside from the DJ and the dancers. He watched Wax closely as he moved on stage, and I could tell that all of Wax's moves had originated with his short, roly-poly manager. Seeing him mirror Wax's dance almost ruined the show for me. But all I had to do was focus back on that cock of Wax's.

JANE M.: Eileen pointed out how Wax's manager was mimicking his stage routine. It reminded me of girls I knew in high school who knew all the cheerleader routines but couldn't make the squad. They'd go to the pep rallies and to the games and sit in the stands and do the cheers in little movements along with the real cheerleaders. Sweet but pathetic.

EILEEN T.: I asked Mammon if I could meet his boy. He said no. He said the boy was shy, young. He said the kid wasn't the kind of performer who came offstage expecting a blowjob from a local skank.

TED ROMLING: I think that it is important to remember that Wax was very young when he started performing. He turned eighteen something like a month after he left his home with Mammon.

***

Another hot motel room. Neither Wax nor Mammon could sleep in the heat. The air conditioner was working, but it didn't quite do the job. Wax watched Mammon hold his pillow in front of the noisy air conditioner to cool it before he put his head back down.

***

WAX WILLAMS: The roadwork finally started to pay off. The money was adding up, and by the end of the second summer we had enough money to shoot the first feature. I just wanted to do it and get it over with. Lyle had been showing me some porno videos to get me ready for the job. It seemed easy enough. But I didn't tell him that I was still a virgin.

TED ROMLING: Florida during the rainy season, New England and a little bit of Canada in the winter. Ass-backward planning, as Mammon said. Wax made almost two hundred personal appearances that first year on the road, and they put more than eighty grand in the bank.

LYLE MAMMON: The money added up quickly, even though we barely broke even our very first road trip. We did Massachusetts, Rhode Island, Connecticut, and Jersey in six weeks. We made enough to cover gas, rooms, burgers. Almost nothing went in the bank. But we were laying the foundation for the next time we visited and the time after that. And each time we played return gigs, the crowds would double. We had to do separate admissions—two, three shows—some nights.

TED ROMLING: Wax must have seen plainly that a career in pornography was the best possible option for him. He might be a sideshow attraction all his life, but that would have to do. He accepted it. A high school guidance counselor might have read Wax as a bright kid with below-average social skills. But I feel that this was a position that Wax adopted rather than a skill deficit. Wax played shy, reserved, constantly half-embarrassed, while at the same time above-it-all. He played it that way because he thought it was the best way to play it—or maybe it was the only way he could play it. Anyway, to Mammon, the boy was an enigma.

LYLE MAMMON: We had trouble finding a suitable introductory movie role for Wax. All of the story ideas that Ted was floating to us were slanted toward an explanation of Wax's size. Wax is a space alien from a large-cocked planet. Or Wax is the happy victim of a radiation overdose. He's a hospital janitor who fell asleep on the X-ray table and somehow the X-ray machine switched on while he was sleeping and it focused on his crotch and he wakes up three times his previous size. Another one along the same lines involved Wax surviving a toxic spill at an atomic energy plant. He wades through some radioactive heavy water and instantly grows.

TED ROMLING: One story that I liked early on was a simple dream explanation of Wax's size. He's an average Joe taking a nap in front of the TV, and he dreams big. He dreams of himself as an exceptionally endowed porno stud.

LYLE MAMMON: The trouble with all the treatments we got was they all sought to explain Wax. I didn't want that. That would have left us with the task of always explaining his size in every movie. With every fucking movie we would have to invent some new reason for his bigness.

***

Mammon had a series of flat-out gynecological photos of Renee Salmon's vagina. She'd submitted the photos with the letter she'd written in answer to the very first ad Mammon took out looking for actresses to costar in *DormitOrgy*. Mammon was very pleased with the photos, Wax could tell. "This girl's got a vagina that is prettier than most faces." He handed the photos to Wax. Formal introduction.

"I don't know if she's simple or just naïve," Mammon continued. "But she's game and so far very amenable to everything detailed in the script."

The last photo was a simple headshot that looked a lot more professional than the others. Large brown eyes; olive skin; black hair, long and straight. She was smiling in a neutral way—just to show her teeth.

***

TED ROMLING: She was waif-waisted but with a new set of power tits and really good teeth and hair. Renee Salmon was the hottest girl I ever saw at a casting call, and her showing up like that—out of the blue in answer to an ad that Mammon had placed in the wrong newspaper—that's happenstance, or something. And that said to me that our production was charmed in some way. And that was true throughout the casting. I thought that Mammon was a fool to insist on a cast of first-timers, but turns out he was right and that's what still makes *DormitOrgy* so special.

WAX WILLIAMS: I remember the last night I performed at Lucky Pete's, which is just outside of Philadelphia. We were in the dressing room backstage and Mammon took out a fat-tipped felt marker and drew a Kilroy on the wall. The nose was extra long—extra phallic looking. Below the long nose he wrote, "Wax was here..."

DormitOrgy[1]

by Ty Boyce

Cast

Brandon Bailey: ....Wax Williams
Wendy:...............................Renee Salmon
Kelly: ....Kristine Pristine (née Christine Chirsky)
Lin Tsu:..............................Anna Eng
Drew Witherspoon: ....Wayne Notches
Security Guard:..................Paul Uncola
Second Security Guard:.....Lyle Mammon

[1]Titles are always hit and miss, according to Mammon. Sometimes they are clever, though usually they are groanable puns. Recently, porn titles have become merely functional—descriptive only of the sex acts featured.

FADE IN: EXT. BUILDING

Sign reads:

Wadsworth University
Becker Hall
A Co-Educational Dormitory

A graffiti wit has penned in a proofreader's caret to insert a 'g' between the letters 'r' and 'y' to spell: "DormitOrgy."[2]

INT. BRANDON'S ROOM

Usual fixtures: A single bed; bulging bureau; closet door open exposing disarray; dirty laundry on the floor; stereo components (music playing at low study volume); bookshelf made out of unfinished planks and stolen cinder blocks. Computer is on.

Sitting at the computer is BRANDON BAILEY[3]: a handsome prototypical college nerd-jock/jock-nerd. He's wearing a baseball cap, T-shirt, boxers, sports sandals. As he turns to look into computer screen, he puts on a pair of glasses, writes something in his notebook, keys some numbers into a spreadsheet. He looks[4] at a framed photo on the desk. Pictured in the photo are Brandon and KELLY in formal wear, toasting with champagne glasses raised. Also seen in the photo is a dark-haired, very attractive girl[5].

[2]The opening shot holds on the sign for a full ten seconds: long enough for a person to cough twice.
[3]The name Brandon Bailey is a composite born of two well-known TV characters: Brandon Walsh, from "Beverly Hills 90210" (Fox 1990–2000), and Bailey Salinger, from "Party of Five" (Fox 1994–2000).
[4]Wax's first moment on screen is a quiet one. It's a profile shot (stronger left side). He looks very young, collegiate, bright. His movements at the computer are a bit stiff, but his turn to look closer at the photo of himself, Kristine Pristine, and Renee Salmon—a Polaroid snapped an hour before the shoot—is assured, sexy.
[5]Renee Salmon has a longing look in the photo. Her eyes are on Wax.

INT. DORM HALLWAY

The two girls from the photo are walking along the hall. Blond Kelly[6] is wearing an oversized campus sweatshirt that hangs just low enough to cover her ass. She is barelegged. Her hair is up casually. She's got little white sockies on[7], but no shoes. Her dark-haired companion, WENDY[8], appears distressed. She's a little tipsy, having been drinking alone. She's wearing a short satin robe. Her hair is drawn back tightly. She's tiny, waifish. No shoes on. She seems happy to have Kelly's arm around her shoulder as the two make their way down the empty dorm hallway. They stop outside the door to Brandon's room.

WENDY:

(Points to the sign on the door, begins reading) Brandon Bailey is studying. (Turning to Kelly) See, Kelly. Do not disturb. I'll just call my gynecologist in the morning.

KELLY:

No way. This is an emergency. You can't leave it in there overnight. You'll get an infection.

Wendy tries to walk away, but Kelly reels her in, knocks on Brandon's door.

[6]Kristine Pristine. Most women sell a man with a smile. Kristine closed each sale with a frown. Something she picked up dancing in clubs. A pouty, wet-lipped, sexy frown that Mammon loved. It was powerful. It brought money out of wallets and flushed credit cards out of hiding.

[7]Mammon kept giving Kristine fresh socks between shots. It played heck with continuity, as shots later in the film show the soles of her socks to be bleachy clean, which was not the case in a few early shots.

[8]Renee Salmon was Mammon's second greatest discovery, after Wax Williams. Even though he had hired Ted Romling to consult on casting and to sift through the dozens of audition tapes and 8 x 10 headshots, Mammon found this gold on his own. Renee was just a wisp of a girl, nineteen years old. A willowy presence with deep brown, impenetrable eyes. She was a mile ahead of the other girls in the brains department. Much has been written about Wax's on- and off-screen romance with Renee Salmon. The relationship was not always genial, even during the making of their first feature together. At one point during the first day of shooting, Renee held up the ashtray she'd been using, offering it Wax. "Cigarette salad," she said. "Not hungry," said Wax.

BRANDON:
(His voice from the other side of door) Brandon Bailey is studying. Do not disturb.

KELLY:
Open up, Brandon. It's me.

INT. BRANDON'S ROOM

Brandon's eyebrows go up and down a la Groucho Marx. He waggles his yellow highlighting marker like it's a fat cigar. He picks up the photo. Kisses it. Holds the photo at arm's length to see that half his kiss landed on Wendy's face. He stands to answer the door.

Close-up registering Brandon's surprise to see both Kelly and Wendy before him. His first expression is delight to see Kelly, then disappointment to see that she's not alone.

BRANDON:
To what do I owe the pleasure?

KELLY:
(Leading Wendy into the room) Brandon, we have a situation.

WENDY:
An embarrassing situation.

KELLY:
Wendy here...

WENDY:
(Interrupting) A shameful situation. (Her inebriation[9] is more apparent.)

---

[9]Renee was drinking throughout the morning to gear up for this scene. She maintained a charming and professional tipsiness throughout the session.

KELLY:
Wendy, please.

BRANDON:
What's going on?

KELLY:
I'll just say it once, straight out. It's not embarrassing. It's nothing shameful. An accident has happened and we need your help.

The three exchange looks. Close-ups of expressions:

Brandon—Quizzical…

Kelly—Concerned, worried, anxious, but showing that she can keep a calm head in an emergency…

Wendy—Guilty, sultry. She bites her lower lip, levels her gaze at Brandon.

KELLY:
(To Brandon) Wendy was using a cucumber to masturbate with. Part of it broke off and she can't get it out of her… vagina.

WENDY:
(Laughs loudly) I'm glad you could say that. I couldn't have.

BRANDON:
Do you want me to drive you to the hospital?

KELLY & WENDY:
(Simultaneously) No!

KELLY:
(Sitting Wendy down at the foot of Brandon's unmade bed,

turning to face Brandon) Brandon. You need to retrieve that piece of cucumber.

WENDY:
Your mission, should you choose to accept it.

KELLY:
(Ignoring Wendy's comments) She can't do it alone.

WENDY:
You must enter the walled city. Locate and retrieve the thing that she said you have to get. Then return, leaving no trace of your visit. No fingerprints.

BRANDON:
This is weird. (But his expression shows that he is slowly warming to his mission.)

KELLY:
Just look at it this way. Your girlfriend is asking you to put your finger inside another woman. And you're helping a friend out of a predicament.

WENDY:
This twat will self-destruct in five seconds.

Kelly walks to the door, nodding for Brandon to come to her for a kiss before she leaves.

WENDY:
(Observes kiss closely) She's never kissed me that way before.

Brandon and Kelly continue kissing, oblivious to Wendy's comments from the bed.

KELLY:

(Exits looking over her shoulder) I'll be right outside. (To Brandon) Be careful in there.

Door closes. Brandon and Wendy look about the room uncomfortably, alternately staring at the ceiling and then at the floor. They finally exchange a direct look[10] of curiosity. Brandon approaches bed; sits beside Wendy.

WENDY:

(Solemn tone) Brandon, I'll understand if you don't want to go through with this.

BRANDON:

(After a thoughtful pause) A cucumber?

Wendy produces a large cucumber[11] from the pocket of her robe.

BRANDON:

It's huge. (Takes large cucumber from Wendy's tiny hand, considers it) You peeled it?

WENDY:

I was trying to sculpt[12] it in the proper shape of a penis. It was too bumpy.

BRANDON:

(Considers cucumber again) Three words for you, Wendy: high impact plastic. Battery operated, molded from the phallus of your favorite adult film star. There are a number of manufacturers marketing to the needs of lonely college

---

[10]Renee is a natural actress. She can portray emotion, unlike most of the other women who have acted opposite Wax who could only approximate lust and/or erotic vapidity. Still, Mammon was able to coach a bad performance out of Renee in her debut.

[11]Three extremely large cucumbers were purchased.

[12]Renee did the cucumber sculpting herself. She expertly peeled and carved the three cukes used during the shoot. She also insisted on putting each into service to make sure they had that used-as-a-dildo look to them.

coeds. You didn't have to cross over to the vegetable kingdom.

WENDY:
But how will my garden grow?

INT. DORM HALLWAY

Close-up of Kelly standing in the hallway outside Brandon's door. She's impatiently looking up and down the hallway. She puts an ear to the door, gets down on her knees to hear better.

CUT TO: Lingering shot from rear showing Kelly's shapely ass in a thong.

CUT TO: Shot of an attractive Asian coed (LIN[13]) approaching from rear, appreciatively clocking Kelly's exposed ass.

LIN:
Kelly? Is that you?

KELLY:
(Standing quickly, adjusting sweatshirt to cover herself better, stretching it nearly to her knees) Lin. I didn't hear you coming.

LIN:
Brandon not in? (Fishes a hand into her book bag.)

KELLY:
(Pointing to sign) Studying. I'm just waiting for him to finish up... studying so I can... surprise him. But I don't

[13]The role of Lin Tsu was cast before Renee and Kristine were discovered. Anna Eng was a very bright girl. Needed tuition money, figured nobody she knew would ever see the video. She had beautiful gold-tone skin. Very smooth face, no creases, small pores. She had good breasts. A few dark freckles across the top part of her cleavage.

want to...surprise him until I know he's done... studying.

LIN:
(Pulls key chain from book bag, inserts key in door, which is directly across from Brandon's door, opens door) Just interrupt him. He'll be glad to see you, I'm sure.

KELLY:
No! (Then toning down her response) He's studying.

LIN:
Whatever. (Enters her room, closes door.)

INT. BRANDON'S ROOM

Brandon kneels on the floor beside the bed, smiling nicely at Wendy. He rests a hand on her knee reassuringly.

WENDY:
(Digs heels into the mattress) Into the stirrups I go. Ready for the exploratory, Captain?

Brandon cracks his knuckles.

Wendy opens her robe to reveal that she is entirely nude, though her breasts remain partially concealed by her sheer robe.

Brandon swallows audibly.

Wendy opens her legs, reaches to her sex[14]—a shaved pubis—and spreads her labia neatly.

---

[14]This is kind of a quaint way to say vagina. Mammon had insisted on using the term in this first script and in all others thereafter because he had noticed that this was the preferred usage in "respectable erotica."

Brandon places his left hand on Wendy's right thigh, begins reaching upturned middle finger of right hand toward her sex.

Wendy takes Brandon's right hand, brings middle finger to her open mouth. Tongue visible. Eyes closed. She inserts Brandon's finger slowly into her mouth, sucks on it, pulls it out slowly. Her lips cling to Brandon's fingertip in a wet kiss.

WENDY:
Lubrication, Brandon.

Brandon inserts finger in Wendy's sex, moving in and about slowly, searchingly. Wendy responds with a sharp intake of breath, a pleased look on her face.

WENDY:
Yeah.

BRANDON:
(Not impolitely) Stay focused, Wendy.

Wendy opens her robe wider, touches her bare breasts, pinches the erect nipple of her left breast.

BRANDON:
Am I close? I don't feel anything.

WENDY:
Deeper, Brandon. Deeper.

Brandon fingers deeper, moving in and out. Tip of Wendy's long tongue touches tip of her nose. Legs spread wider.

Three-minute close-up of Brandon's hand—wet, moving fast. A spray of thick ejaculate appears across his knuckles. He ceases momentarily.

WENDY:
I'm the kind of girl who can squirt across the room[15].

BRANDON:
(Resumes fingering) I'm going to use two fingers, try to tweeze it.

WENDY:
Oh, Brandon. You're such a big tweeze.

Adjusting boxer shorts to cover obvious erection[16], Brandon enters Wendy with two fingers.

Wendy makes more pleased sounds.

INT. DORM HALLWAY

Kelly still has an ear to the door, which perks up at the sounds emanating from Brandon's room. She has the front of her sweatshirt bunched up in her hands and is stretching it out, obviously curious and beginning to get horny from what she's hearing. She looks up and notices the transom above Brandon's door. She rises up on her tiptoes, grips the doorjamb, and makes a futile attempt to do a chin-up in order to spy through the transom. Her sweatshirt rides up, leaving her ass fully exposed.

INT. LIN'S ROOM

Lin's looking through the peephole admiring Kelly's ass. Lin is wearing a white teddy, no panties, and she's eating ice cream from a pint container with an oversized spoon. One eye closed, she peers through the peephole, licks the back of the spoon, and begins touching herself.

---

[15]Renee brought this to the performance. It was a character trait that only she could have contributed to the role.

[16]Wax had great trouble staying inside his shorts. The crew shot around his early arousal, so as not to detract from the upcoming reveal.

POV camera shot through peephole of what Lin sees: Kelly's ass suspended in midair as she attempts one chin-up after another.

INT. DORM HALLWAY

Kelly finally falls to the floor, landing in a pretty heap. She sits cross-legged on the bare floor, runs a hand through her blond hair. Huffs. Puffs. Looks straight at Lin's door, then hears the sound of a spoon dropping on a tile floor.

INT. LIN'S ROOM

Lin, also on floor, reaches to retrieve spoon; her hand is between her legs.

INT. DORM HALLWAY

Kelly spots furniture arrangement in the hallway: two chairs, a love seat, and a small coffee table. Close-up of her face indicates that an idea has come to her.

INT. BRANDON'S ROOM

Wendy's legs are spread wider still. One foot rests on Brandon's right shoulder, the other is dug deep into the bed. Her right hand is working her clitoris furiously as Brandon reaches deeper.

Moaning louder, Wendy reaches with her free hand to turn up volume of Brandon's stereo.

BRANDON:

(Stops suddenly. Looks at right hand, flexes grip.) Cramping, Wendy.

WENDY:
(Without compassion) Back to work.

BRANDON:
I'm thinking maybe I could use my mouth to create a vacuum inside your...

WENDY:
(finishing his sentence)... Pussy!

BRANDON:
I could suck the cuke right out.

WENDY:
Yes. That just might work.

Brandon puts his nose to the grindstone, plants a deep sucking kiss on Wendy's sex. He flicks his tongue at her clit, licks at her fingers as they spread her labia.

INT. DORM HALLWAY

The camera begins slowly panning from the floor to the love seat with the coffee table lying across the arms, and two chairs on top of the coffee table, side by side. Kelly has a foot on each chair. The camera travels up the length of her legs: slender ankles, shapely calves, muscled thighs, tight ass.

CUT TO: Shot of Kelly's transom vantage POV shot of Brandon, face down between Wendy's legs.

CUT TO: Reaction shot of Kelly's face. It's obvious the sight of her boyfriend and best friend engaged in oral sex is a turn-on.

CUT TO: Lin's peephole POV of Kelly's ass.

Still licking the large spoon of ice cream, Lin opens the door to her room, entirely naked now, a pint container of ice cream and a second spoon in hand.

Kelly turns to see Lin as described. Brings a finger to her lips to shush Lin before she can speak, then motions for Lin to join her atop the stack of furniture.

Taking Kelly's offered hand, Lin steps up to look through transom.

INT. BRANDON'S ROOM

Camera angle shows transom POV of Brandon and Wendy, then pans down for a close-up of Wendy's face. After a moment, camera cuts to Wendy's POV of the two faces in the transom.

Wendy smiles, gives a small wave to Kelly and Lin.

Kelly and Lin simultaneously raise their ice cream spoons in salute.

INT. DORM HALLWAY

View from behind of Kelly and Lin as they continue to peep through the transom. Double ass shot. They're both eating from Lin's ice cream container, feeding large spoonfuls to one another while they enjoy the view. Their asses bump to the rhythm of the music from Brandon's stereo.

INT. BRANDON'S ROOM

Brandon and Wendy in position previously described.

Seeing Wendy gaze over his shoulder, Brandon turns face to look back at the transom.

CUT TO: POV camera showing Kelly and Lin duck out of view quickly.

BRANDON:
(Turning quickly to Wendy) You see that?

WENDY:
(Playing dumb) See what, Brandon?

BRANDON:
(Shakes head) I guess I'm just a little paranoid. Kelly's waiting on the other side of that door.

WENDY:
Kelly brought me here to you so you could help me. She's cool with this.

BRANDON:
(Resumes oral attempts to liberate the cucumber) All of this?

WENDY:
She knew what this mission would entail.

INT. DORM HALLWAY

A quietly giggling Kelly and Lin step down from their perches and begin to partially dismantle furniture stack, then assume positions side by side on the love seat.

LIN:
(Offering spoonful of ice cream to Kelly) What's going on, Kelly?

KELLY:
(Licks spoon clean, then licks at Lin's hand where some melted ice cream has dripped) I'm in the hallway of my

dormitory watching my boyfriend fuck my best friend. *And,* while doing so, I'm enjoying a snack with a beautiful, exotic young woman[17].

Lin pulls Kelly's sweatshirt off and kisses her deeply.

Camera remains in the hallway with Kelly and Lin as they make out and begin touching one another. Eventually Kelly stands on the love seat, positioning one foot on the armrest and the other on the back of the love seat. Lin begins oral sex on Kelly from behind as Kelly watches goings-on inside Brandon's room.

Camera begins alternating shots of Brandon and Wendy with shots of Kelly and Lin.

INT. BRANDON'S ROOM

Wendy sees Kelly's face in the transom, winks. Shot of Kelly returning wink, holding up her hands. Making a circle with the thumb and index finger of the left hand, she inserts the index finger of the right hand repeatedly. Wendy nods.

WENDY:
Fuck me, Brandon.

BRANDON:
No, I can't. I love Kelly.

WENDY:
It's okay with Kelly. She brought me here to you. Look. (Points to transom.)

Brandon turns, sees Kelly's smiling face in transom.

---

[17]Quote Mammon, "Definition of a good porno script: at least one lesbo scene and the pages aren't stuck together."

KELLY:

Go for it, Brandon.

Wendy frees Brandon's cock[18] from his boxer shorts, takes him into her mouth.

Brandon enjoys Wendy's oral for several minutes, then turns again to the transom: Two faces now, Kelly and Lin. Brandon grips Wendy by the hips, turns her, and mounts her in doggie position[19].

INT. DORM HALLWAY

Kelly and Lin resume their session. After several minutes pass, the loud sound of a basketball being dribbled can be heard in the hallway. Kelly and Lin hold their positions still, look into the dark shadows at the far end of the hallway.

KELLY:

(Above the sound of a dribbling basketball) Who's there?

Emerging from the shadows, a young black student-athlete, DREW WITHERSPOON, is seen doing some fancy dribbling of his basketball[20]. Dressed only in white briefs, the young man stops dribbling to say hello to Kelly and Lin by name.

---

[18] The reveal, as Mammon had been calling this moment, was almost lost... Ben Bettis's camera was not rolling. Mammon gave Wax a pep talk before this part of the scene began. He said, "It's like my old friend Harry Belafonte says, 'Just jump into the saddle and hold on to the bridle.'" Wax made no response to this advice.

[19] "It's just sex," Mammon said to Wax. "It's not an exact science. Forget the cameras. Concentrate on the girl. You've had sex before, right?" "Yeah," Wax lied, as any other nineteen-year-old male virgin would. We didn't know it at the time, but this would be Wax's first go at sexual intercourse. Mammon had assumed that Wax had already lost his virginity. But in truth, Wax hadn't yet. Mammon decided to make a fuckumentary of the making of Wax's debut, kill two birds with one stone. For release two years down the line, maybe later. Recycle footage with some extra shit that didn't make the cut, a new girl that Mammon would be sure to make a star of before releasing. Record a voice-over. Shoot some medical staff on call during the sex scene—young doctors, horny looking nurses, tight uniforms.

[20] Wayne Notches showed up on set with his own basketball because he thought we might forget his one and only prop.

KELLY:
Is that you, Drew?

LIN:
Drew Witherspoon?

KELLY & LIN:
(Chanting) Drew-ew, Drew-ew.

DREW:
(High-fives to Kelly and Lin, he plops down on the love seat between them) I won't even ask what y'all are doing.

KELLY:
It's not what we're doing, Drew. It's you. You're about to have a wet dream.

LIN:
Just don't do anything to wake yourself up.

Kelly and Lin peel off Drew's briefs. His penis bobs and waggles. Lin's on it first, Kelly gripping its thick base. After several minutes of Lin doing oral on Drew and Kelly kissing Drew, the threesome eventually configure into an oral triangle of Lin sucking Drew and Kelly licking Lin. Drew is standing on the love seat, looking through the transom, straddling Lin who sits on the love seat. Kelly is on her knees on the floor with her face on Lin's sex. This action is intercut with Brandon and Wendy still fucking hard doggie-style in Brandon's room.

INT. SECURITY ROOM

Black-and-white surveillance TV monitors showing empty hallways. A young SECURITY GUARD[21] is sipping coffee as he flips through screens.

[21]Paul Uncola was a funny-looking, large-cocked Italian oaf. He had one dramatic quality: stupidity. He projected dumb. He was an inept, big-peckered, lantern-jawed, clumsy motherfucker.

Screens of different hallways continue to flash on each of the three monitors until finally the cameras in the hallway outside of Brandon's room are called up.

Security Guard spit-takes coffee at the sight of Kelly, Lin, and Drew on the screens. He drops the coffee cup into his lap, spins in his chair, and reaches for a roll of paper towels. He inserts videotapes into three VCRs, presses the RECORD button on each machine, and picks up his walkie-talkie.

SECURITY GUARD:

Unit two to base.

RADIO:

Copy, unit two. Base over.

SECURITY GUARD:

I'm heading over to sector three to check out a small disturbance. Three students clowning around in the hallway. Nothing serious, two females and a male. Possibly inebriated. No backup required. I'll buzz you back if anything comes up. (Looks once more at three-way sex action on the surveillance screens.)

INT. BRANDON'S ROOM

Brandon and Wendy are still fucking hard doggie-style. They are both near climax.

WENDY:

(Reaching orgasm) Yes. Yes! (etc.)

Brandon pulls out.

Wendy turns quickly out of doggie position to take Brandon into her mouth. She grips his testicles, and rubs his penis on her face for a messy ejaculation[22].

INT. DORM HALLWAY

Kelly, Lin, and Drew are still actively engaged in their three-way on the small love seat. Lin is blowing Drew and Kelly is eating out Lin. Action is shown up close, then from a slight remove. The remove denotes the Security Guard's POV, as he observes the activities from the shadows. The action continues for several minutes, until Drew ejaculates on Lin's upturned face.

SECURITY GUARD:
(Approaches shining a flashlight on threesome) Don't move.

Naked threesome attempt to cover up their private parts.

SECURITY GUARD:
(Sternly) Put your hands up where I can see them.

Naked threesome comply.

SECURITY GUARD:
Names. (Flashes light on Kelly's face, then lets flashlight roam down to her breasts and crotch.)

KELLY:
Kelly Tanner.

---

[22]Wax's first money shot... exterior ejaculation. The money shot. The proof. Dick Johnson's Dirty Video Guide says, "Slow to arousal, but showing notable endurance and blasting not one but three spectacular money shots, newcummer Wax Williams spurts onto the scene with a tour de force performance in 'DormitOrgy.'"

LIN:

Lin Tsu.

Security Guard's flashlight jumps to Lin's face, breasts, and crotch.

DREW:

Drew Witherspoon, sir.

Security Guard's flashlight shows Drew's embarrassed face, then his penis.

INT. BRANDON'S ROOM

Brandon and Wendy listen at the door to the Security Guard questioning Kelly, Lin, and Drew. They hear:

SECURITY GUARD:

You three students here?

ALL:

Yes, sir.

INT. DORM HALLWAY

Kelly, Lin, and Drew stand naked before the Security Guard with their hands up high.

SECURITY GUARD:

(Pacing in front of threesome) You live in this dormitory?

ALL:

Yes, sir.

SECURITY GUARD:

Is this why your parents sent you away to this expensive institution of higher learning…to have sex in the hallway?

ALL:
No, sir.

SECURITY GUARD:
Can one of you explain what's going on here?

KELLY:
(Stepping forward, hands still up) It all started when my roommate had an accident with a cucumber.

SECURITY GUARD:
Don't fool with me, Miss.

LIN:
It's the truth, sir.

Door to Brandon's room opens. Wendy emerges, naked, ahead of Brandon, also naked. Their hands are up.

SECURITY GUARD:
The plot thickens.

WENDY:
It's all my fault, Mr. Security Guard.

BRANDON:
(Pointing to Kelly) That's my girlfriend, sir. She brought Wendy to my room so I could remove a piece of cucumber that Wendy got stuck in her . . .

WENDY:
. . . Pussy.

SECURITY GUARD:
(Steps up to Wendy) Was the cucumber liberated, Miss?

WENDY:

No.

SECURITY GUARD:

Allow me. (He brings Wendy's arms down. Gently spreads her feet further apart, then makes a playful adjustment to her breasts.) Close your eyes. Hold your breath now, and on the count of three, exhale. One. Two. Three. (He gives Wendy a light bonk on the top of her head.)

CUT TO: Shot of floor space between Wendy's bare feet.

The cucumber tip falls to the floor[23]. A cheer goes up.

Security Guard retrieves tip. Holds it up to the flashlight for closer inspection.

WENDY:

(Throws her arms around the Security Guard) My hero!

Wendy plants a long, deep kiss on the unsuspecting but not averse Security Guard. They continue to kiss, oblivious to the others.

Kelly and Brandon embrace and kiss deeply. Drew and Lin kiss. Before long, Wendy unzips the pants of the Security Guard. She takes his cock into her mouth[24].

Brandon and Kelly begin fucking[25] in a standing position. Kelly has her legs wrapped tightly around Brandon, who supports her weight easily. He presses her back against the wall, grips her shoulders.

---

[23]Only took one take. Perfect drop. Renee's a real professional. Released the cuke tip on cue.

[24]Mammon noted a look of jealousy on Wax's face as he watched Renee blow Paul Uncola.

[25]Kristine could not accommodate Wax. Several attempts were made. Lubes were applied. Toys, larger and larger, were employed to help pave the way. But no go. Mammon called it "cunt clench." In the end, the crew shot around it. Their sex was faked. Really faked. Thigh sex—completely intercrural.

Drew and Lin follow suit, with Lin facing the wall and Drew banging her hard from behind.

Camera cuts to and from each couple.

The Security Guard[26] is sitting naked on the love seat with Wendy astride him. She's wearing his hat.

Brandon and Kelly are fucking the hardest. They're whispering to each other.

BRANDON:
Did you see me fucking Wendy?

KELLY:
(Through clenched teeth) Yes.

BRANDON:
Did it turn you on?

KELLY:
Yes.

Drew and Lin are now stretched out on the bare floor. Drew's on his back. Lin's on top, facing away from Drew, stretched flat. She's rubbing her clit as she rides him.

The three couples continue the orgy to climaxes featuring exterior ejaculations by—in this order—Drew, the Security Guard, and Brandon.

---

[26]Mammon's direction was always minimalist, to the point. He'd indicate the girl Wax was to fuck and then recline on the nearest couch to watch. Like the age-old fashion tip that women should remove one article of clothing or accessory just before they step out on the town, Mammon always had his actresses take off one last stitch before he began rolling tape. Didn't matter if the girl was in just bra and panties, something had to come off. "Say the dialogue that's yours as if you're talking down to someone who is unimaginably dumb," he'd say. To Paul Uncola, he said, "Make sure when you're fucking her that you turn her ass into the camera as much as you can. Fart if you feel one coming on. Be natural. Swear if you can't remember the lines."

INT. SECURITY ROOM

On the black-and-white surveillance screens, the couples change partners. Kelly to the Security Guard. Wendy to Drew. Lin to Brandon. New partners start having sex.

Camera slowly draws back from black-and-white surveillance screens. The shoulders and head of a SECOND SECURITY GUARD[27] watching the monitors dominate the shot. His face and hands are off-screen, but it is obvious that he is masturbating to the action on his surveillance monitors.

INT. DORM HALLWAY

New couplings continue to orgasmic conclusion. Series of exterior ejaculations, popping in order: Security Guard, Drew, and Brandon.

INT. SECURITY ROOM

Black-and-white surveillance view of orgy shown over the shoulder of the masturbating Second Security Guard.

FADE TO BLACK

---

[27] Mammon insisted on playing the part of the second security guard. His face is not seen and he has only a few bits of dialogue spoken over the walkie-talkie, but he had to be in "DormitOrgy." The only other feature that Mammon appeared in was a how-to video called "So You Want to be a Pornstar?" He improvised a brief instructional scene on fellatio, telling a red-haired girl how to properly make use of her hands when giving a blowjob on camera: "Don't hold it like a steak knife, baby. Vary your grip. Squeeze it. Slap it. Rub it. Spit on it. But love it."

Consumer Profile

Tugger

Sunrise Arcade opens at 6:00 a.m. every day, and you always try to be the first customer through their doors. You don't have to be to work until 8:15, so you have plenty of time to look around to see what new stuff has come in. New titles have a way of sneaking up on the shelf. Most people don't realize that these magazines don't come out with month-to-month regularity. It's catch as catch can with many of the titles that you buy. Sometimes it's hard to keep up; you have to keep your eyes open. And then there's the way the owners of Sunrise Arcade always move the sections around—especially the video sections. That's maddening. But sometimes that sales tactic of theirs helps you to see a title that you haven't seen before. You know how to read point of purchase labels—the codes that show delivery dates—so you know a new video title when you see it.

Your name is Todd Tugman. Everyone has always called you Tugger. You haven't looked at yourself in the mirror since you were thirteen years old. You know what you look like. Your ears are lower than they should be, more a part of your neck than your head. Your eyes are too big. Your nose is too big. Your teeth are too small. Your chin is too small. Your hair used to be blond; now it's white and yellow. You wear glasses. Your glasses don't sit right on your face because your ears are too low.

You buy XXX magazines and videos. You are loyal to certain performers. Particularly Renee Salmon and Wax Williams. But you also like Cheryl Noble, Scott Kevlar, Muni Jacobs. Since your mom died two years ago, you've been saving most of what you buy. Before that, you threw your magazines and videos away so she wouldn't catch you with them. But now that she's dead, you don't have anyone that you have to hide it from. You bought new large shelves for all your videos and set them up in your mother's old bedroom. The videos are arranged alphabetically by title, except for two sections: one section contains all of your Renee Salmon videos, and the other section contains all of your Wax Williams videos. These two special sections meet on the shelf with the movies that they have made together—*DormitOrgy, Honey in the Mouth, Naked Guardian Angel, Vadge of Honor, Cuntraption.* Their movies are the only ones that you can watch again and again. Most of the other movies you watch only once or twice before putting them in their place on the shelves. You can't say what it is about those two—Wax and Renee—that makes them so special. They're just the best. Don't need the rest. You make a wish and you say a prayer that Wax and Renee will make more movies together.

Some mornings Sunrise Arcade is late to open. The owners oversleep. They own a place of business with the word "sunrise" in its name, but they have not made a commitment to get up early and to open on time. You *used* to call to check to see if they were open. The big owner would always answer with an unfriendly voice, "Sunrise Arcade." The little guy owner would answer all helpful, "Sunrise Arcade, how may I help you?" No matter who answered, you would hang up. But the big owner guessed that it was you always calling, so he told you to stop calling and hanging up. You said, "I just want to know if you're open." The big owner said, "If we're open we're open and you can come and see." You said, "I'm a good customer."

***

Last week you found advertisements in the phone book for paid escorts. You overheard a woman in the lunchroom say to another that there were hookers listed in the phone book. You had to see this for yourself. Sure enough, there are three escort services in the Ampersand/Ampersand Falls area. In addition to their alphabetical listing in the phone book, each escort service has a small ad near its listing. Each ad features a line drawing of a beautiful woman. In one ad the woman is winking at you. In another the woman has a long-nailed fingertip resting on her lower lip. The best one—the largest of the three ads—has a nude silhouette of a woman showing her back—she has one arm raised above her head and she has quite a curve from her waist to her hip. The drawing doesn't have an ass crack. The sketch ends right where her ass crack would begin. You tore the page from the phone book and later on, at home, you cut each of the three ads from the page to study them. Each ad says that the service is outcall only. What does that mean? Can you call and ask what that means? Does outcall mean they call you back after you call them first. Your next step—and you know that this will occupy you for a number of weeks and maybe even longer—is to crease the page of every public phone book that you find so that it opens to the page with the phone numbers and ads for paid escorts.

You have forty dollars and you are going to buy at least three new magazine titles (two girl titles and one homo title), and you're going to bring the magazines to the park and you're going to plant them alongside a path that runs through the small wooded lot adjacent to the park. You're going to sit on a bench near the path and watch and wait to see what happens when someone finds these pornographic titles. You've done this before, but not in a long time.

In Psalm 65, God says, "Have leisure and know that I am God." That's your favorite sentiment from the Bible.

You don't care who finds the magazines. It could be some older kids playing hooky and smoking cigarettes in the park. Or it could be a little kid walking to school all by himself. It could be one of the young women who jog through the park before they go off to their jobs, or one of the old retired couples who start their day with a walk along the path. Someone will find what you have left to be found, and you will watch what they do when they find it. They will react in some way, and you will see that reaction. Someone is about to find a dirty magazine in the park.

When you were nine, you asked your father—a year before he took off and left you and your mother alone—how to make friends. He said, "Be friendly, but don't be too friendly. Act too friendly and they'll think you're a queer." You asked your mother what a queer was. She told you to ask your father. You knew by the way she said it that you shouldn't ask him either. So you looked the word up in the dictionary. Then, the next day at school, Glenn Draggen called you a queer. But you knew the meaning of the word and you knew that you weren't one, so it didn't hurt you.

And if a cop catches you littering the park with your pornographic magazine, you'll say, "Officer, look at what was left here by someone." And you'll hold the magazine up by one of its corners. You'll make like you just happened to see it on the ground and that you're just as sick about finding a dirty magazine in the park as the cop is. "This dirty magazine shouldn't be in the park with all these kids around who could find it." You'll say, "I have a little niece who plays here." But if the cop knows better, if the cop sees you, Todd Tugman, plant the pornography in the park (like it is Arbor Day for hard-ons), then you will come clean immediately. If the cop knows that you are the one dropping pornographic titles and maybe some old sex toys along the path through the woods adjacent to the park—a path favored by kids before and after school, a path favored by young jogging working women, a path favored by strolling retired couples in tracksuits—and if the cop somehow knows that you have more pornographic titles in your car and even more at your apartment, and even more at a self-store facility in Ampersand Falls... If all that, then you will confess immediately. You will say, "Officer, I have had a breakdown. This is my pornography. A voice inside my head that I have always been able to ignore told me to plant this pornography in the park in plain sight of kids, joggers, and old people. I know that it is wrong, but I did it anyway because I couldn't keep myself from doing it. Because I thought it would be thrilling to plant this in the park and watch some unsuspecting person find it. I wanted to see what they would do."

***

You were eleven years old the first time you saw a porno movie. Seeing a naked woman wasn't a surprise to you or anything new, because women look the same to you whether they have clothes on or not. You see them the same way. That is, you notice the same things about them: the size of their breasts, if their faces are pretty, the shape of their hips. But seeing a naked man for the first time when you were eleven years old was a shock because the man in the video looked nothing like what you thought a naked man would look like. He was muscular and hairy, and though you had seen muscular and hairy men without their shirts on, you had never seen a muscular and hairy man without pants on. You had never seen a penis before except for your own, and this man's penis in the porno movie looked nothing like yours. It was bigger, of course. You had expected that. You knew somehow that some men are bigger than others and you had a feeling that your own penis would still be small even after puberty struck. But this man's penis was also very veiny. And just at the moment that you noticed how prominent the veins in this man's penis were and how those veins appeared alive under his skin, the woman that he was about to do it with said something like, "I love your veiny cock." You turned off the television and quickly ejected the videotape from the player. Your heart was racing and you began thinking about when you could watch it again.

What you want to do next is rent a video from the store—a PG-13 romantic date movie—and record over parts of it with a triple X scene. You read about some teenager who did it to some kid's video. You think that it's wrong to expose an innocent kid to something like that in his own home, but you don't think it's wrong to prank some married couple who are playing it safe by renting a movie that fades out to morning when the hot kissing starts. In order to do this without getting caught, you have to get the movie out of the store without renting it—because then there'd be a computer record that you once had possession of the tape. You don't know how to get a video out of the video store without renting it. There's a security turnstile that you have to walk through in order to exit the store. A buzzer will go off if you have a videotape that hasn't been demagnetized for rental.

***

Every Friday night from midnight to 2:00 a.m. you listen to your favorite radio show, "Dr. L. Frank Luvin's Intimate Advice." You've tried to call in a dozen times or more, but you always get a busy signal. Finally, your call is answered. It's not Dr. L. Frank Luvin. It's a call screener named Barry, who asks, "What's your intimate issue?"

You tell him that you can't get erections when you're with a woman, only when you're alone.

"Good," he says with a nervous laugh. He sounds gay. "I mean, not good for you, but a good topic for Dr. Luvin. Don't you think?"

Before you can answer he says your call is next in the queue, and he puts you on hold. Suddenly you hear the show through your telephone.

It's Dr. Luvin's voice, but what he's saying on the telephone is not in sync with what you hear on the radio. There is a brief delay between the live show and what is broadcast.

Then Barry's back on the line. "What's your name and where are you from? Give me an alias."

You say, "Tug, from Ampersand, Massachusetts."

He thanks you again for holding, and reminds you that you're next in queue. "Turn off your radio," he says.

You press record on your tape machine so you can record your call. You take the phone into the bathroom and undress and sit on a dry towel on the toilet. An erection is beginning to form, so you stand up to look at it in the mirror.

Then Dr. L. Frank Luvin's voice is on the phone. "On the line from Ampersand, Massachusetts, we're talking to Tug. How are you, Tug?"

You say, "Good."

Dr. Luvin says, "Can you tell us why you called the show tonight, Tug?"

You tell him what you told Barry. The words that you had rehearsed are coming out just the way you wanted them to. You feel good about having said it, and you can't wait to play back your call later on.

"Hmm," Dr. Luvin says. He has a heavy voice and he talks slow. "I don't want to say that this is a common issue, but I want to tell you, Tug, that you are not the first and only man to experience impotence in such a way."

The mention of the word impotence surprises you. "I'm not impotent," you say, talking over Dr. Luvin.

"I'm sorry, Tug, but a consistent failure to become aroused is impotence. Now I realize that you are not entirely impotent, but the only way to discuss your sexual dysfunction is to treat it as impotence. OK, Tug? Do you follow that?"

You say, "Yes."

Dr. Luvin asks you how often you've had this experience and when did it happen the first time. You tell him in so many words that it has happened every time.

"What do you mean, Tug, by every time?"

You explain that three times you have been with women who were willing to have sex with you, but that you were unable to get an erection.

"So you have never had intercourse?"

You don't answer.

"OK, Tug," he says. "Let me ask you a few quick questions."

He asks you how old you are and if you have any health conditions. He asks you if you've had any homosexual experiences. He asks you if you like pornography. He asks you how frequently you masturbate. He asks you if you have any hobbies. You have ready answers for each of his questions and you wish he could go on forever asking you these easy questions. He seems to like talking to you. He chuckles at some of your answers. But then he asks you what he calls the big question. "Tug," he says. "Do you think you know why you've experienced such a hard time—no pun intended there—why have you had such a hard time getting aroused with your partners?"

In spite of the fact that the word "partners" sounds funny to you, you respond as quickly to this question as you had to his previous questions because you know the answer. "It's because they were all dogs."

He says nothing in response. You hear your voice over the phone and then again on the radio in your bedroom. You don't know what to say next, but he isn't saying anything. "I can look at a pretty woman in a magazine or in a movie and get an erection. I can think about certain pretty women that I've seen at the mall or at work and I can get aroused. But those women don't want to be with me. So I went with the women who would go with me, and they weren't pretty. And no matter what, I couldn't get hard."

"Tug," he says, a tone of disappointment in his voice. "The most important thing you can do when dealing with an intimacy issue is to accept responsibility. You can't blame situational impotence on your partners."

Hearing the word "partners" again rubs you the wrong way. You don't like the way he says it. You don't want to hear what he's going to say next. You want to hang up. But first, as loud as you can, you yell into the phone, "Go fuck yourself." You hear it through your phone before you hang up, but you don't hear it echo from your bedroom. Instead, you hear Dr. L. Frank Luvin say, "We seem to have lost Tug."

***

Next day you buy a secondhand VHS camcorder at St. Vincent DePaul, and you watch *A Tale of Two Titties* through the viewfinder. You pretend that you're the cameraman on set and you're shooting the action live. Everything is small through the viewfinder, but you feel like you're in the movie. It's hot and you get a really hard boner. Because you can't see your cock, it feels bigger in your hand. So much better than sitting in front of the TV. Why didn't you think of this before? The charge on the battery only lasts for twenty minutes—not long enough to get off. You set the battery up to recharge and search for another title to watch through the viewfinder. You load *Kickstand Divas,* and press play. Fast forward. Rewind. Freeze-frame. Single frame advance. It's a bit hard to coordinate. Everybody masturbates, Dr. L. Frank Luvin has said that many times on his show. But nobody, you think, masturbates more than you.

Chapter Three

Seens (sic) from the *Life* (pt. 1)

He remembers sitting in a baby swing in a warm, wet diaper. He remembers staying in that swing until the wet diaper goes cold. Then he cries.

***

A half-dozen adult toys lie on a small folding table beside the unmade round bed. A red velour curtain hangs behind the table, and a video camera on a tripod is pointed at the still-life pattern: six new dildos of varying length and color, a string of anal beads (still sealed), a red butt plug, a pair of nipple clamps, and a tube of flavored lubricant (cherry vanilla).

Mammon leaves Kira alone in the motel room with Wax. She sits on the bed, stares at the toys, picks up the largest of the dildos. The empty box beside the dildo says fourteen inches. She turns it on, looks to Wax for his reaction. The humming dildo bounces in her small hands.

Wax looks away, stares out the window at his rental car—a silver Mustang. The humming stops. Wax turns around to see that the dildo has disappeared. Not in her hands. Not on the table.

Mammon enters the suite. He's wearing an expensive-looking black leather jacket unzipped because his gut is too big to zip it up. He's followed by a camera operator and the sound technician, new guys that Wax hasn't met yet. Kira removes the humming dildo quickly, switches it off, and places it back on the table.

"I told you to leave this shit alone," Mammon says to Kira. "I don't want you cumming this stuff up before we shoot. You can't wait five fucking minutes?"

Kira grabs the dildo and makes a show of wiping it clean on the hem of her robe.

***

Once he demonstrates that he can climb out of the playpen, the playpen is turned upside down. The floor of the playpen becomes its ceiling. There is one advantage to the overturned playpen: he can lift the playpen a little bit and move around the room, like a turtle carrying its shell. Then he discovers that he can also escape the playpen—which seems to be the objective—by propping up a corner of the pen with a few large building blocks and rolling himself under the padded railing. Whenever he manages to get free from the playpen, he searches throughout the house for his mom. He wants to present himself to her. "Look, Mom. I got out."

Childhood happens too fast. He should have paid closer attention, made an effort to remember more. The memories he has now are feelings, not fact, but still true. The biggest truth: he loves his toys more than he loves his parents. The reason he loves his parents is because they give him toys—and because they make him feel guilty for getting everything in life for free. He loves his friends' toys more than he loves his own toys. He makes friends so he can play with more toys. His friends' parents must love them more than his parents love him because they give them better toys than he gets.

***

CONNIE COLES (ACTRESS): One time Wax said to me, "I've learned a lot from porno actresses, yourself included." I said, "Thank you so much for saying that." He said, "You may think I don't remember you from *Fox Hole*, but I do. Chick Soldier Number Three—am I right?" I said, "Wow, I'm unbelievably flattered that you remember me." And he blushed. I made Wax Williams blush. I couldn't believe that he had remembered me and made a point to let me know. Sweet guy.

***

Childhood happens slowly. Time crawls. He is six forever. He is seven forever. He is always too young. And he never does anything. There is never anything to do. They never go anywhere. No vacations. No day trips. His parents take him to a few movies, and he goes bowling once. They don't rent bowling shoes for him. He bowls in his socks, saving his parents one dollar. He is the only kid at the bowling alley bowling in socks. He does okay in school. He likes to read, but he likes television better than books. He has only one best friend: Rollie Mignon. He likes candy. He wets the bed. He is good at saving money. And when he has enough to buy something that he wants, he is good at spending it.

***

DEE-DEE SHARP: Wax bought big things. Cars, boats, dirt bikes. He gave expensive presents to new friends. He gave jewelry to his costars and to the girls who worked in the back office at the Hacienda. He traveled, gave anonymously to charities, and even made investments in the stock market. He put his money back into the economy like you're supposed to do.

TED ROMLING: Every hero has a hometown, and Wax is no exception. Ampersand, Massachusetts. He was born there and grew up there, just like his parents. Coincidentally, Lyle spent a few years in Ampersand when he was in grammar school. I tried to get Lyle to start his operations on the West Coast. Everyone's working in the Valley. Talent's available. Good people looking for work. But he and Wax wanted to work in Ampersand. They each had a comfort level there. Even though all those years Wax lived more or less full-time at the Hacienda he never visited his parents, and they never sought him out either. I'm sure they knew where he lived. It's a small town.

***

Growing up, little Lyle Mammon watches *The Ed Sullivan Show* faithfully. He doesn't care about the circus acts or the hippie rock 'n' roll bands. He watches for the comedians. He loves Alan King, Buddy Hackett, the young George Carlin, Richard Prior, the button-down mind of Bob Newhart. In school he is always a cutup, the class clown. He has an answer for everything, and none of the teachers or the football players or even the principal can get the better of him. He knows how to crack a joke so the yolk of the joke hits the intended target square on the forehead. He delivers the punch lines knockout style. But like any good comedian, he always gets a few laughs along the way to the punch. That is delivery, and he has delivery. He feels in his heart that he is supremely suited to be a successful standup comedian and he focuses all his energy on this goal. Maybe he isn't cut out to be a Johnny Carson or a Bob Hope, but he is a funny bastard, and he could be a Marty Allen or a Mel Brooks.

***

LYLE MAMMON: If you're an Ampersand local, you'll remember the Hacienda Steakhouse, a great restaurant—once the greatest restaurant. Its doors closed many years ago, after the Route 2A bypass lead those hungry for steak around Ampersand and through Ampersand Falls. Now the Hacienda is my home, my offices, the worldwide headquarters of my enterprise. I bought it for a song, but I spared no expense in renovation. I kept half the kitchen, half the lounge, and half the dining room. I tore up an acre of parking lot and hired a landscape architect to lay in curvy berms of brown mulch and little green shrubs and red rosebushes. Inside, we have state-of-the-fucking-art studio space—basically a series of bedroom sets where my starlets work by day and billet at night. We've got an editing bay for film, video, and digital. We have a hundred dubbing stations, copying VHS—still a very popular format—and burning DVDs. There are also a few well-appointed office spaces, a server room for the web content, and a climate-controlled basement storage and shipping facility for mail-order fulfillment.

RENEE SALMON: I hated everybody until I was fifteen. All the girls used to make fun of me and tease me and the boys tried to squeeze my tits. Then

I met Johnny. He had black eyes and a heavy upper lip. His chin was pointy and his nose was flat, but I thought he was beautiful. He had thick eyebrows and a thick neck and wide shoulders. He turned me out. He's responsible. He was the first boyfriend I stole from my mother. She came home from work early one day and heard us fucking in the living room. She dragged the garden hose into the house and snuck up on us and sprayed us good.

***

Wax can always tell when his father is coming home. His car's transmission slips a gear when he accelerates coming around the corner onto their dead-end street. Once the car is in the driveway and switched off, the engine knocks and clicks for maybe thirty seconds, like it is trying to start itself up again.

***

LYLE MAMMON: I was a one-man band for the first few titles we produced. I found myself challenged, but in short order I developed a host of new competencies: videotape editing, sound editing, accounting, casting, connecting a half-dozen duping machines together and running them round the clock, scriptwriting with Ty Boyce. This is how you do it. You read up on a subject. Go to the library and get a how-to book. Read the manual that came with the ten VCRs you bought. Forge ahead. DIY. Figure it out as you go along.

HERM JOYCE (GENERAL CONTRACTOR): The Hacienda Steakhouse used to be a pretty popular restaurant until they built the Route 2 overpass and buried the rotary that used to connect the old Route 2A to Route 2. Couple businesses up Route 2A folded, like the Hacienda. There just wasn't enough out-of-town traffic anymore. Mammon bought the Hacienda and hired me to convert it for office use and a residence for him and Wax.

LYLE MAMMON: I basically had the kitchen, main dining room, and lounge cut in half. One half I kept as is, and the other I converted into six bedroom suites. Wax and I occupied the two largest suites, and I let female talent reside in the other suites. Most of the girls we started using were all based in Los Angeles. So they'd live at the Hacienda when we were shooting. They'd stay for a few weeks. Shoot something with Wax, and then we'd squeeze in some other work for them—girl-on-girl stuff usually.

TED ROMLING: Each bedroom suite was built for filming. Beds were on platforms, and ceilings were rigged for lighting and sound. There was office space on the second floor of the Hacienda, and that space was also renovated to make it usable to shoot movies. The basement served as warehouse and fulfillment center. Mammon moved the giant sign into the main lobby, so we all kept calling the place the Hacienda.

***

The three girls Mammon has with him are tanned and toned. One is tiny, one is tall, and the third one looks tired. All three have newly minted chests, which Mammon paid for, and they are about to begin extended residencies at the Hacienda. He wishes he could do them all but, alas, his pecker doesn't work so good—hasn't in a long time. The heart is willing, but the blood doesn't flow hard.

So he orders takeout from three places in town: pizzas, Chinese food, a dozen double cheeseburgers and boxes and boxes of French fries. He smokes some grass with the girls and gives them wine and watches them pig out. What he wants to do is tickle them all until they piss themselves.

***

DEE-DEE SHARP: Mammon's only five foot six, but he presents himself much taller.

VAL THE TEMP: The placement coordinator at the agency called me in for a confidential meeting. I'd been living in Ampersand for almost a year, and I'd had a few short-term assignments. I wanted to find something permanent, so I told the agency that I only wanted temp-to-perm positions. The placement coordinator—I don't remember her name now—told me she had an opportunity in Ampersand Falls, excellent salary, full benefits, et cetera. But she said the position was within an industry that I might object to. I couldn't imagine what she meant. She said that the firm marketed adult materials. I didn't understand what she meant—I guess I'm slow. She finally said, "They make pornographic movies." I *was* taken aback, to be honest, but there weren't any other options open at the time, the money was better than any place else, and I figured, what the hell. Four years later, Mr. Mammon still calls me "Val the Temp."

***

Dear Mr. Mammon,

My name is Holly Offer and I'm writing to you because I would like to begin a career as an adult entertainer working for your video production company. I am presently nineteen years old and have been sexually active for the past three years. During this time, I have had more than a hundred lovers and have engaged in the entire gamut of sex acts, including lesbianism, sodomy, multi-partner penetration, and bondage and discipline, to name but a few. I have been videotaped engaging in sex and find the process very stimulating. It's possible you've seen one of my videotaped performances, as I featured briefly in an amateur video that has been sold under the title "Gorillasuit Callgirl." If you are not familiar with this videotape, I would greatly appreciate an opportunity to personally present a copy to you in your offices at your earliest convenience. Though the production values are not very professional and my true talents are underrepresented in this tape, I think there's enough there for you to see that I have unlimited potential as an adult entertainer. Thank you for your time and consideration.

Yours (and really I mean yours),

Holly Offer

***

TY BOYCE: I am Lyle Mammon's amanuensis. He hired me to transcribe dirty dictation. Plus I have some ideas of my own. Over the years I have developed some expertise at the double entendre. And I am a tireless pursuer of the koan-like single entendre. You don't have to know a lot about sex to write porno screenplays. And you don't have to be a pervert either. I tried kidding myself that writing porno was an opportunity to see my sexual fantasies acted out. But, in the end, they weren't my fantasies at all. They were the fantasies that I thought would make for good porno movies.

***

The policeman tells him that the park is closed at night. He says, "You gotta go home."

He means to start walking home, but he doesn't move.

The policeman asks, "What's your address?"

He doesn't know.

The policeman stands. The policeman is tall. He stares at the policeman's uniform, stares at the blue-black gun in its polished leather holster. Bullets in bullet holders on his belt. He stares at the chipped black nightstick that hangs from the same belt on the opposite hip.

"I'm going to have to bring you to the station."

He feels tears coming to his eyes. He's getting arrested because he doesn't know his address. At the station they quiz him about his street. What's it near—the school, a church, the stores downtown? Are there big houses or small houses on his block? What's the last name of his favorite neighbor? They give him a pamphlet to read that has a story about a little boy named Billy Robertson who got lost and didn't know his way back home. Nobody could help him, not even the police, because he didn't know the name of the street that he lived on. Billy Robertson didn't even know the name of the town he lived in or the name of his home state. He feels sorry for Billy Robertson, and he feels ashamed to be just like him.

The policeman says, "Your parents should have drilled it into your head."

Another policeman says, "Your mother's on her way."

***

LYLE MAMMON: I first thought that I would finance our enterprise with a series of small loans from close friends. But I didn't want to be beholden to anybody. I gave up my life savings to Wax's mother. I knew we could earn that back quick enough. But I didn't want to do that while working out of any debt.

***

Wax empties his small toy box into a fresh pillowcase, closes it with a twist tie, and loops it onto the handle end of his aluminum baseball bat. "I'm running away," he tells his mother. She leaves the kitchen and comes back with her purse. She gives him a handful of change, mostly dimes and nickels. She tears a postage stamp out of a book, slips it into his shirt pocket. "You know our address," she says. "Please write us once you're settled in."

***

About a month after they finish shooting *DormitOrgy*, Mammon says to Wax: "You need a girl to practice on, and I know just the one." One becomes five. Five older women who serve as teachers in bed. They teach Wax what to do and how to do it. But all he can think of is Renee.

***

ROLLIE MIGNON: Wax couldn't play little league because his family didn't have any insurance. I didn't know a lot about it then, but I think back on it now, and see how ridiculous it was. Mrs. Williams worked at an insurance office, and she could have easily gotten insurance for the family. But she didn't want her employer to know that her husband had a job that didn't provide insurance. And they also could've gotten insurance for Wax through school. I remember they used to give you forms on the first day of school every year to bring home to register for insurance through the school if you needed it. And his mother used to talk about not having insurance all the time, reminding Wax of what he couldn't do. Couldn't have a skateboard. Couldn't ride my minibike. Couldn't go swimming at Lake Fortunate. She'd say, "If you break a leg, we'll end up in the poorhouse."

TED ROMLING: Orson Welles said there are only two things he never believed when he saw them in a movie, sex and prayer. Welles didn't live long enough to see Wax and Renee in *Divine Thrust.* He would have been a believer.

LYLE MAMMON (ON RENEE SALMON): She is always game and she possesses a cast iron pooty. Actually, we have a lot in common, Renee and I. She's a head turner and I'm a stomach turner.

RENEE SALMON: I'm more cerebral than folks know. I have an ass so my mind can dance. And I have a pussy so my mind can fuck.

***

He pees the bed until the fifth grade. He remembers the cold rubber sheet that he has to sleep on. He remembers the sting he feels peeling the dried piss lint from beneath his foreskin each morning.

***

Mammon calls for quiet on the set and then starts to sniff at the air above the tangle of naked girls. He pinches his nose, says, "Who smells?"

The only non-blond—a petite brunette with toyish implants raises her hand. She gives Mammon a loopy smile, keeps her hand up. Her hair is matted. Hungover, she looks.

"What's your name, beautiful?" asks Mammon.

"You haven't told me yet. You said you wanted to fuck me first." The other girls giggle. The girl still has her hand raised.

"Your name," he booms, then pauses. "Your name is 'Go Take a Fucking Shower.'" Mammon points toward the bathroom. The girl rises from the flesh pile and steps carefully across the large bed. "I want you to smell like fresh lettuce when you come out of the shower," Mammon shouts at her back. "Wax Williams is to eat your pussy in less than half an hour. Show some consideration for Mr. Wax Williams. I am relying on your professionalism. Use soap."

***

He gets his tonsils and appendix removed six months apart. It's like that whenever his dad gets a job with insurance. Both procedures require overnight hospital stays. He does not wet the bed during either stay. He is proud of this. But his mom is furious. She doesn't understand why he can stay dry overnight in the hospital but not at home in his own bed. "If you keep on wetting the bed, we'll have to bring you the hospital again to have your tinkler removed."

***

Todd Insulin: Mammon disdained the production values of his competitors. He especially hated the hollow sound and bad speaking voices in porn. He studied how Hollywood mic'd their sets and used that technique.

***

Mammon is looking at some vintage girly photos from the 1970s and he holds the magazine up for Wax to see a woman with teardrop-shaped breasts. "Women with tits like that don't take their shirts off anymore," he says.

***

His dad's tattoos are blurry green. He has a rifle wrapped in ivy on both of his forearms. He never gets a close look at them. Mrs. Williams always makes her husband wear long sleeves because she doesn't like the sight of his tattoos.

***

Uncle Tom's Tavern is set in a modern-day racist bar where the rules of the plantation still apply, particularly if the slave girl is hot and the big black stud *likes* to get whipped! Order a jug of moonshine and take one of the dark ladies upstairs. (Wax had been scripted to perform in blackface, enslaved as he was to his career in the pleasure biz. But Mammon had the bright idea to apply blackface on Wax from the waist down. "Because he's black below the waist! Get it?")

***

He makes every effort he can against growing bigger. He wants to stay small, to take up less space in this world. It would be easier that way to stay out of the way, to ask for nothing. For a time, it seems, he does not grow. But then this ploy—a Peter Pan scheme—backfires on him. His parents notice his lack of growth and act, as always, with the requisite amount of concern.

"He's stunted," Mrs. Williams says. She blames her husband's smoking.

Mr. Williams lights a cigarette before responding. "I would guess that it might be the cooking around here. Boy needs a decent meal."

His parents seem to be of no use to each other. They couldn't be unhappier together. They get nothing from one another and give nothing to each other. Wax doesn't know why they stay together. Other parents get divorces. When will his? He always worries that they will get a divorce and that neither will want custody of him.

***

Val the Temp: My first day on the job, Mr. Mammon introduced me to everybody as his new backscratcher. He was so nice and everybody was so nice. All of the furniture in the office was new. My work area was near a window, and I could look out into the woods behind the Hacienda and see all the way up to Lake Fortunate.

***

Picked on, needled, teased. He's a good target because he doesn't fight back. He doesn't fight back because he feels he'll only get it worse next time. Most of his tormentors give up after a time. They get bored with the way he absorbs their abuse. They want fresh meat, unpunished peers.

***

Todd Insulin: Wax's stardom in the world of adult films coincided with porn's largest growth spurt in public consumption. He was immediately in demand on the tabloid talk show circuit. But he didn't bite. He was invited to sit on symposium and porn panel discussions in the world of academe. He refused all but a few public appearances. Those rare outings were fan-centered meet and greets—convention autograph sessions. But he begged off the high-profile events. He kept silent in the press, worked often, didn't seek publicity, and didn't need to work hard to sell a lot of product.

***

Penmanship is his hardest class. His mom won't let him practice using pens. All he has are nubby pencils. She gives him her old pencils once they're too short for her to use.

***

MRS. WILLIAMS: My husband was not a romantic man but he was sweet in some ways. Whenever he brought flowers home for me, he'd say, "These aren't for you." He'd say, "I bought these flowers for the little table beside our bed." He worked in sales and had a sense of humor.

TED ROMLING: Sissy Punsky was no taller than a twelve-year-old. All of her features were upturned: her nose, her breasts, her eyes. Because she was so short, she aimed herself up at whoever she might be conversing with. Mammon dubbed her "Ragamuffin" and signed her up. She was game. She was a bit of a changeling, a sleeper beauty that you might overlook on first sight. A bitsy figure with famined eyes. And it wasn't until we had been on set for nearly six hours, blocking close-ups and walk-throughs, and shooting some extra foreplay to compensate for a quick, very un-Wax-like premature ejaculation, that I recognized her beauty. And it appeared that Wax was really hot for her.

***

He always says please and thank you. Even to other kids. He doesn't mind school very much, in spite of the teasing. He knows the school day will end at three o'clock. He knows that he'll be able to go home at three o'clock and do what he wants to do in the empty house. Three o'clock is never such a long wait. Morning recess at ten o'clock, lunch at noon, and an afternoon recess if all the boys and girls behave. Please let it be three o'clock. Thank you, three o'clock.

***

TED ROMLING: An early casting mistake we made was Betty Yeun in *Barn Buster*. She was a pretty girl; lovely, in fact. But the problem with Betty was her tongue, which was canine in length and would not stay in her mouth.

She had some kind of condition. There must be Latin name for it—glottis fucking majora. Rare. In the thousand or more women I've used in my work, I've never seen anything like it. During sex, her tongue would just loll from her mouth, flopping like a wet flag in a humid breeze. She looked like she was going to gag on it. Scared the holy shit out of Wax. He kept asking her if she was all right. We were able to edit around her tongue in most of her scenes. But it was hell.

***

A typical morning finds him mopping up the pee from the rubber sheet on his bed, wringing out the top sheet, hanging it to dry over the radiator in his room, and then spraying harsh-smelling disinfectant over the bed.

***

DEE-DEE SHARP: Jared Washboard was so named because his abdomen was overdeveloped to the extreme. That was about all he had going for him. He was one of those muscle guys with a small head. He compensated effectively by wearing his hair long. But when his hair began to thin, he opted for a clean-shaved 'do, and that tiny cabeza of his could no longer be overlooked. Mammon didn't want to use him anymore. Jared took it well. He accepted a few body only roles, and even did a few gay-for-pay gigs. But he made a quick exit out of the *Life* after he hooked up with some rich widow that he met at one of the Indian casinos in Connecticut.

***

Two teasers sit behind him in homeroom. Sixth grade. Assigned seating. Alphabetical order. Silent classroom. You're only supposed to say "present" when attendance is taken. No talking. Face to the front. Stand and put your hand over your heart and face the flag to say the Pledge of Allegiance. Sit quietly through morning announcements. Stare at the intercom speaker. Stare at the clock. Wait for the bell to ring at 8:00 a.m. to start the day.

Two teasers maintain a dialogue every morning in his ear.

"How come his hair's so short?"

"How come he rolls the bottom of his pants?"

"How come?"

They talk in low voices, back and forth.

Assigned seating. Alphabetical order.

He keeps his mouth shut, stares at the clock, waiting for the bell to ring. Stares at Mr. Keaney's bald head, bent over his morning paper.

Ray Worth and Curt Youngen. They're friendless except for each other. Always together, always teasing him. Their hair is long, stringy, parted down the middle, greasy looking. They smell like cigarettes. They smoke in the morning before school. Sixth grade and they smoke. They live in the same apartment house on Route 2. No fathers. Just mothers. No brothers. No sisters.

"Why doesn't he turn around and talk to us?"

He remembers advice from his dad: "If you have trouble with two guys, go after the big one first. The little guy won't do anything when he sees you go after the big guy." Ray and Curt are exactly the same size.

***

LYLE MAMMON: I was a cutup in school. Very first day, the teacher told us to get up to say the Pledge of Allegiance. I raised my hand. "Yes, Lyle," she said. I said, "Ms. Fucklee, how do you do that?" "Why, Lyle, you don't know how to salute the flag?" "No, Mrs. Fucklee. I never learned," I said. "Just stand up, face the flag, and put your hand over your heart," she said. "Mrs. Fucklee," I said, "Can I put my hand over your heart?" I remember her face got as red as her lipstick. What a blusher she was. She had thick lips and big eyes and black hair. Her sweaters stretched tight across the peaks of her bosom.

TED ROMLING: The girls I found to play the roles of hot office workers in *Naked Guardian Angel* were perfect. Wax had scenes with three of these women in addition to a final scene with Renee Salmon, the titular naked guardian angel. The girl in the bondage scene was named Eloise Hunt. She refused to work under anything but her own name. She was stunning. From Florida, I believe. Bikini model. Blond. A real blond—collars matched the cuffs. Nineteen, I think. She was one of about ten or twelve girls who wanted to do just one movie. They all wanted to work once with Wax and that was all they were interested in.

RENEE SALMON: I came up with the premise behind *I Was a Teenage Sperm Donor.* You know the old joke about the girl who runs into the sperm clinic with a mouth of jizz and says, "I want to make a donation"? That's the funniest fucking joke.

TODD INSULIN: Simply put, Mammon wouldn't use any performers who did not come to him first. He didn't bust any of his girls for working with another production company if he had no current work for them, but if a girl wanted to work for Mammon, they had to get their start with him. They had to lose their video cherry working for him.

LYLE MAMMON: After Wax's first few features took off, we were approached by some mainstream magazines for stories. I had offers of a few thousand dollars from one men's magazine—$2,500 advance with $5,000 paid upon publication—for Wax's diary. I took the money and gave it to Ty Boyce and told him to whip something up. They had the right to edit what we delivered, but I figured that would be a good thing. They also offered to write the thing for us, but I couldn't let them do that.

RENEE SALMON: My mother used to always say, "Have your fun, but don't be a whore about it." She also said, "We're not here for a long time, we're here for a good time." Wax was good for me. It was so good with him, I almost thought I could be monogamous. Some nights, we fucked until we glowed.

LYLE MAMMON: I am always on the lookout for musicians to score our features. What I've wanted for a long time is a bass player who can really climb trees; a bass man with rhythm who plays the thing like a lead instrument. I tried taking a guitar player and putting a bass in his hands and telling him to play the thing like he's Jimi Hendrix. Didn't work. What I usually do is take my little kiddy keyboard and pick out a five-note sequence and tell my bass player to just keep playing that over and over on his bass. Every once in a while he'll throw in an extra note or two. I tell him to play it until the people on screen stop fucking.

ROLLIE MIGNON: Wax's mother wasn't a very good cook. All she ever served were burnt roasts and dried-out chickens. She overboiled her green vegetables until they were gray and she made her mashed potatoes from a powdered mix. I would invite Wax to dinner at our house, but his mother never gave him permission.

LYLE MAMMON: Wax's parents' house—they used the money I gave them to put up vinyl siding. The contractor they hired used the wrong kind of nails—the kind meant for interiors—so all the nails rusted and left little orange dots on the siding.

TODD INSULIN: Renee Salmon—in her early work—had the whole virgin-whore dichotomy thing down pat. Now she's just a whore.

***

The Wax reaction shot—the female gaze of awe, wonder, a little fear—becomes ubiquitous and a central part of each of his films. Jennifer Laine's takes are among the most memorable. In *The Wrong Schlong* she takes one look at Wax's cock and an expression of determined sacrifice spreads across her face.

***

VAL THE TEMP: When people find out I work at the Hacienda, they always want to know if I've seen any funny business. I tell them no, truthfully. Sure, I see the tapes and the other products in their boxes, and sometimes I see one of the trade magazines left open on the table in the reception area outside of Mr. Mammon's office, but that's it. Only once did I see any nudity around the office, and it occurred because I came back to the office after 5:00 p.m. to get something that I'd left behind. I went upstairs to my work area and saw two nude women and a photographer taking pictures in the office. They didn't see me because I turned on my heel as soon as I saw them. I found out later that they were shooting photos for a new catalog—they wanted to give the men who order from our catalogs the impression that everybody working behind the scenes at Mammon Films Ltd. is a beautiful nude model. They also shot photos of nude models pretending to work in the warehouse and in Shipping/Receiving.

***

He becomes a solid B-caliber tennis player, and Mammon has a court built behind the Hacienda. He probably could be better if his lateral movement weren't hampered by what is between his legs.

***

LYLE MAMMON: Jenny Laine? I discovered her on the mouth side of a glory hole in a gay bar in Key West, Florida. That girl loved sucking cock and she was so good at it that the gays couldn't tell she was a girl. When I told her I was impressed, she told me about a small business loan that she had repaid in blowjobs.

***

Rollie Mignon has a book called *Dick Johnson's Dirty Dictionary.* It contains an alphabetical listing of over one thousand dirty words and their proper definitions and synonyms. Still, it is thin for a dictionary. Wax knows it is a joke of a book because the cover shows a cartoon picture of a boy in short pants with a big bar of soap sticking in his mouth, foamy suds running down his chin. But it is Rollie's primary guidebook in life. He is committed to learning the contents of this profane dictionary by the end of summer. The regular dictionary has some words that you aren't supposed to say, like rectum, penis, vagina, anus, glands. But the words that Rollie really wants to know can only be found in *Dick Johnson's Dirty Dictionary.*

***

ROLLIE MIGNON: I found *Dick Johnson's Dirty Dictionary* at a flea market that I went to with my mother and aunts. This old-timer was selling paperback books, four for a dollar. Most of the books had their covers torn off. I don't even know what brought me to this guy's table. I wasn't interested in books. But I saw the dirty dictionary and knew I had to have it. I picked up three other books that were about the same size and put the dirty dictionary second from the bottom in my stack. I didn't think he'd sell it to me because I was a kid. The guy didn't even look to see what books I had. He only wanted to see that I had four books. Then he asked for my dollar.

***

From Dick Johnson's Dirty Dictionary:
Foreplay: a largely female concept that places emphasis on the prelude. But not to worry: any lucky male can master the art of foreplay. All you need to know how to do is count to four. E.g. as you begin to kiss the female, count to four. Be sure to do your counting in your head, not aloud. Don't rush your count. It is imperative that you count to four properly: one... one thousand; two... one thousand; three... one thousand; four... one thousand. Once you get to four, place your right hand upon her left breast. If she pushes your hand away, begin counting again. And note that this could be a sign that your female companion might be really *into* four play and that you might have to double your counts at each juncture. After counting to four a second time, place your right hand on her left breast.

***

LYLE MAMMON: One of my favorite lines ever is a voice-over line that Ty Boyce wrote for *Hades' Ladies.* Wax is doing Eve-Lynne Knelt about as hard as a guy can, and you hear his thoughts in a voice-over. He says, "A girl this wet couldn't be telling lies."

***

He keeps an ear cocked for new-sounding words that seem to have something to do with sex. He knows most of the common curses—the ones that his dad uses, like shithead, and piss, and asshole. And he knows other ones from older kids in school. Fuck. Motherfucker. But it's hard sometimes to know if the word you've heard is a dirty word. He won't use a dirty word unless he knows exactly what it means. You could look very foolish if you use a dirty word in a way that doesn't apply.

But Rollie is fast becoming a compendium for dirty language. Kids seek him out at recess, in the lunchroom, on the bus after school. "What does snatch mean?" they ask in a confidential manner. Rollie answers their questions with authority. Most of the time he doesn't even need to consult his thumbed copy of *Dick Johnson's Dirty Dictionary.* He knows the book backwards and forwards.

One time on the way home from school, Jennifer Mills approaches Rollie and says that she wants know the meaning of a certain word. But she won't say the word out loud. She wants to look the word up herself.

"No fucking way," says Rollie. "You can whisper it to me."

Jennifer says she doesn't want to get that close to Rollie.

Rollie laughs. "I showered last week."

She says she'll whisper the word into Wax's ear for him to tell Rollie. Rollie agrees to indulge her because she's one of the prettiest girls in school.

She says to Rollie, "If you tell anybody that I asked you about this word, I will tell Principal Wormer that you brought a dirty book to school."

"I don't like to be threatened," Rollie says.

Jennifer says, "I'm just saying, don't tell anybody."

"Okay, okay."

She cups her hands around Wax's right ear. He feels his face begin to get hot and he feels a cold tingle across his shoulders and up his neck. He hears Jennifer's lips opening. He hears her inhale and then exhale. She closes her lips again, then opens them to whisper, "Smegma."

***

TODD INSULIN: Wax has no true rival in the business. The only guy close is Guy Lee, and he's just a Wax epigone. If there were no Wax Williams for Guy Lee to look like, Guy Lee would be a mere porn functionary. A pretty boy who gets some second banana parts but certainly not a leading man.

***

"Guess what I found in your room?" his mother says. He knows that she isn't talking about what she has found. She is talking about what he has hidden. A *Penthouse* magazine. One of Rollie's. He can tell that she expects him to be contrite, ashamed. So that's how he acts.

***

TED ROMLING: When Mammon was looking for new girls, he'd write up a casting call ad and place it in a few of the free weeklies in New York and New England. He called it gathering wool "ATTENTION ADVENTUR-

OUS YOUNG LADIES. Dare to take your wild side to new levels. Adult video producer seeks new talent for narrative XXX features. Dancers, actresses, lovers of *Life*." He discovered a few major talents from similar ads, and he always thought that he just might strike gold again.

ROLLIE MIGNON: My mother is Portuguese. She used to cook all day long. When she wasn't cooking, she was baking. Our house was always filled with warm, spicy smells. When Wax's mother cooked, their house would just smell like the inside of a hot oven.

***

Exterior ejaculations always chill him. He doesn't like doing it, but it's a big part of the show, has to be done. The girls can fake it, but a guy can't, especially not Wax. You have to show the camera. Have to prove that you got off.

***

He sits with his parents in the cramped living room watching TV. His mom and dad argue about what to watch. She likes police shows. He likes comedy shows, variety shows. It isn't that the living room is small—not compared to the other rooms in the house—and it isn't that the room is overfurnished—there is only a couch, a recliner, and a hard-back rocking chair pointed at the television—it is that the bulky furniture is too big for the room.

***

TED ROMLING: Jennifer Entebbe is widely believed to be the ugliest girl to ever have appeared in an adult film. Her face was like a retraced doodle. A gap-toothed, freckle-faced, flat-chested girl with shit for brains and a blotchy purple tattoo on a wide ass. She was funny-legged, like a rag doll. She had a crooked smile, unattached earlobes, and red hair.

DEE-DEE SHARP: Her professional name was Monica Juice. Her real name was Pamela Yendt. She was cartoon buxom, with unreal measurements that

I can't remember anymore. Something like 52-25-38. She had her bosoms powdered and kept a neatly trimmed beaver. A round, dimpled ass. I can't say why Wax decided to fall in love with her, since most of the folks who had his ear then—including myself—warned him against her. She wasn't evil, just very manipulative. She worked a guilt trip on Wax, or something. He had a practice of dating the girls he worked with. Something he started with Renee. He was good to them all—flowers, expensive dinners, trips.

ROLLIE MIGNON: It was as if his parents wanted him to be a geek, judging from the way they dressed him and made him wear his hair. They wanted him to be the object of everybody's teasing. He was victimized by a ballpoint pen that exploded in the pocket of his blue oxford shirt. He had to keep wearing that shirt to school, even though the stain didn't come out. And then his parents made him use a pocket protector in grades three through six.

***

He usually goes for the semimystical chicks who could go with or without. Ones who can make do, who don't put up a fuss every time something goes wrong. Ethereal brunettes with dark eyes and small teeth, quiet ways. Stoical blonds who work out with free weights and keep their pubes trimmed sharply to tight triangles. Anyway, it is just sex and getting along in life without being alone. Being able to wake up at 3:00 a.m. without being scared shitless. You need someone warm sleeping next to you. Dreaming their dreams as you dream yours.

***

DEE-DEE SHARP: Irene was a pretty girl, but she showed too much of her gums when she smiled. Mammon liked that. He thought that it made her look younger. She was self-conscious about it, and she kept herself from smiling on camera.

TED ROMLING: She was one of those people who show more bottom teeth than top when smiling. Still, Irene has an engaging look about her. Kind of loopy, off-balance, but you'd have to say sexy.

***

His mom doesn't like the idea of a teenage boy being alone in his room for any length of time. She knows what adolescent boys do when they're alone, and she won't have that going on in her home. She insists that he leave the door to his bedroom open at all times. He mostly complies, but he forgets every now and then. So she has his dad remove the door to his bedroom. Now the only place he can go for privacy in the small house is the bathroom. But he isn't masturbating. No. Through no fault of his own, he discovers masturbation late. He's almost sixteen the first time. All that time in the bathroom is spent carving things out of soap with a fingernail clipper. No lie. His parents figure he's in the bathroom whacking it for hours on end like any other teenage boy. But not him. He's nicking bars of soap and carving little figurines. He carves dogs, cars, a little teapot, cartoonlike people. He whittles a gun like a convict in a prison escape movie. He'd like to carve from balsa wood, but his Mon won't let him have a knife. Soap is an okay substitute. It's easy to work with. He discovers that he can cover up any mistakes with a little water. He just runs a wet finger over any erroneously whittled portions of the soft soap and fills in cracks and smooth edges with wet shavings from another bar of soap.

***

LYLE MAMMON: I didn't know anything about telling a story. So I studied TV shows, especially soap operas, to see how people acted out scenes, and how scenes built on one another. I learned that a lot of scenes were just about characters coming and going—entering and exiting a scene. And how people reacted when characters entered and exited. I pointed this out to Wax, but he seemed to know it already.

WAX WILLIAMS: Aneetha Diggs was altogether too thin when we met her. She was all sharp shoulder blades and bony hips. Her neck had a regal line, but it was obscured by a permanent shrug. Mammon took one look at her and said, "There ain't nothing wrong with that girl that fifteen hundred dollars worth of silicone won't fix." Then he said, "Me likes what me sees." She was a waitress. Some rib joint in Virginia off Route 95. I can't remember the name of the town. She quit her job before Mammon ordered dessert, and she traveled with us back to Ampersand. A week later she had her implants, and then we shot *Screw Loose.*

TODD INSULIN: Wax Williams' first effort as a writer/director was a forty-minute Super 8 titled *The Vault.* The premise was simple. Wax was the president of a small-town bank who accidentally gets himself locked into the walk-in vault with three of his lovely tellers. Dramatic tension comes in the form of dwindling oxygen supply. The doomed foursome decides to spend their final moments in orgy. Wax fashions a crude bed of crumbled hundred dollar bills, and in turn he humps each of the tellers. They fuck till they can breathe no more—then they die. The story of *The Vault* can serve as a metaphor for Wax's circumstance and experience in the *Life.* Like the bank president, Wax was locked in the *Life* with no option for escape. Like the bank president, Wax made the most of his situation.

***

Wax's mother keeps a ledger of expenses related to her son. Clothing. Food. Doctors' bills. Toys. Sporting goods. Everything. Because little boys aren't free. Wax sees the ledger on the kitchen table one morning before breakfast. She must have left it out after a late night of accounting. But he doesn't open the ledger and pretends that he hasn't noticed it when she comes in to the kitchen to retrieve it as he eats his cereal.

***

LYLE MAMMON: It came as a surprise to Wax that people, women in particular, had more than one opinion of him. If Ted Romling's polls were to be believed, results showed that 82% of the women surveyed said that it was highly unlikely that they would engage in sexual intercourse with Wax Williams. Of that 82% population, only 23% cited marital fidelity as their primary reason for their response, while the rest of the highly unlikely population, the other 59%, expressed simple trepidation—fear, really—that Wax's outsized penis would bring lasting damage to their vagina and/or uterus. One woman stated that she believed sex with Wax Williams might compromise her ability to bear children in the future. A number of women confirmed a general curiosity to see Wax Williams' penis in person and to touch it. One response: "I would touch it. I would hold it and squeeze it. I would stroke it. Swing it. Feel its big heft. I might take part of it into my mouth. But I would never take it between my legs."

***

He touches her left tit softly. She responds with a warm exhalation, shifts more of her weight onto him. This response feels good. He feels her warmth. He reaches his right hand to the arch of her pelvic area and she exhales again, louder this time. Wax is glad he's read that stupid book of Rollie's.

***

TODD INSULIN: A girl can have natural beauty and she can be game, but there is no such thing as an automatic porn star. I'm thinking of Rebecca Chimney. She appeared in *Kickstand* with Wax, a biker flick with, of course, a famous clubhouse gangbang. Beautiful girl. After *Kickstand* she had good scenes in perhaps thirty other XXX titles, but she just couldn't develop a fan base. She had breasts that made you think of nursing babies. They weren't sex-inspiring things. She tried to sex herself up with tattoos and piercings, but it didn't work. She claimed to be nulliparous, but those boobs of hers were just too nurturing in their aspect. Poor girl.

***

Inside the small, trophy-filled office, Coach Dunkin puts a hand on his shoulder. "What's the matter?" he asks. "You sick?"

"I am," he says. "May I go to the nurse?"

Coach Dunkin writes up a hall pass for him to go to the nurse's office. Before sending him on his way, Coach Dunkin says, "Don't let what those boys said bother you. You still got some growing to do."

In the nurse's office he rests on one of the small cots. The nurse takes his temperature and asks him if he'd like to take some aspirin.

He says no, and begins thinking about what will happen next week during gym class. He doubts that his hair will grow back by then.

***

Dee-Dee Sharp: Mammon likes licked lips and vacant eyes with loads of mascara and thick liner. He likes a flat sheen on a girl's forehead, lots of neutral base, concealer. He likes hair pulled back tight to show a widow's peak.

Ted Romling: Wayne Notches is an irredeemable hillbilly with a king-size hellcock as thick as your arm. His face has a squeezed from both sides look—it's wider in the back and front than in the middle. His ears rest flat in the concavities of his skull. And he isn't a nice guy. But he always shows up for work and he always works when he shows up. He's recently converted to the Church of Latter-day Fags.

***

The girl sitting in front of him is turned in her seat, staring at his shoes. He is afraid that she is going to say something mean about them, since the shoes his mom brought home were very different from the shoes the other boys at school are wearing.

The girl finally speaks, asking, "Are those orthopedic corrective shoes?"

He doesn't understand the question. Sometimes when people speak to him—new people especially—it takes him a while to register the words they say. It's like he has to translate everything they say. He asks the girl to repeat herself, which she does without the type of frustration his mom and dad seemed to have with him. The girl asks her question the exact same way the second time, no change in inflection or volume, but slower this time.

"I didn't want these shoes," he says quietly. He thought now that the shoes looked like they came from an old movie, like they should be worn by a boy who lived forty years ago. "My mother brought these home for me last night."

"She didn't take you to the store to try them on?"

He knows that this is the standard practice in buying shoes and clothes, but he has never once tried anything on in a store before it was bought for him. And he never is able to point to a shirt or a pair of pants that he wants. His mom picks out all his clothes. He has no say in the matter. "I wanted a pair of boots with a zipper on the side, but these are the shoes my mother got for me."

The girl nods once slowly, then turns around to face the front of the class. He taps her on the shoulder. He wants to tell her one more thing—that his shoes aren't the corrective kind—but the girl doesn't turn around.

At home that night, he tries to tell his mother that the shoes are too big. But she says that doesn't matter. "You'll grow into them," she says. "Won't you?"

***

Naked Escape: Two lusty beauties escape from a female correctional facility without even the clothes they had on their backs. In the wilderness outside the prison they discover a camper, played by Wax Williams, pitching a tent…literally. Turns out he's a full-grown man lost in the woods since a Boy Scout trip fifteen years ago. He's naked, too, because he grew out of his uniform.

***

TY BOYCE: Mammon always has me draft the plot capsules that appear on the video box before scripting the movie. He's more interested in the copy on the video box than he is in the shooting script.

WALT WILLIAMS: Not long after we got that letter from the gym teacher, I got a new job with Sears and Roebuck, selling washers and dryers. It was retail, not showroom, but I had health benefits for the first time in a long time, so the wife was happy about that.

MRS. WILLIAMS: It was a good plan. Dental. Major medical. No deductible for hospital stays. Low copay for office visits and annuals. Good prescription rate. We decided to catch up on Wax's shots and the like.

ROLLIE MIGNON: They took Wax to the dentist and then they took him to the orthodontist. They took him to an allergist. They took him to the podiatrist.

WALT WILLIAMS: She didn't like the look of his toes. She never had, since he was an infant. She thought his toes were too short.

***

Mrs. Williams orders Wax into the bathroom and tells him to take his sneakers off. She gets down on the floor on her knees and begins inspecting his feet. She doesn't like what she sees. She calls to her husband to come to the bathroom. "They're not right," she says. "Are they?"

Mr. Williams shrugs.

"The toes are too short," she says.

"I think it's that his feet are wide, and that makes his toes appear short."

"No," she says.

"The boy's still growing."

"If we don't get his feet looked at now and get them fixed, we'll only have to get them fixed later on. And that'll be when we don't have insurance again."

Wax doesn't know what she means by "get his feet fixed."

"I'm taking him to the podiatrist," she says. "It can't hurt."

After his parents leave the bathroom, Wax looks down at his feet, stretches his toes.

***

Dear Mr. and Mrs. Williams,

I am your son's physical education instructor and I am writing to tell you about a concern I have regarding your son's physical development, which you may already know about. I am not a physician, but I do have a master's degree in physical education and I believe that your son may have some type of puberty disorder that has affected his development. Your son does not appear to have any pubic hair, and his penis and testicles are well below average in size compared to other boys his age. I would like to strongly suggest that you consult a physician to see if he requires treatment for a medical condition. Please feel free to contact me during school hours if you have any questions.

Regards,

Coach Ronald Dunkin

Consumer Profile

In Houston

You are laughing with her, enjoying the big drinks, exchanging compliments. She tells you that your suit is nice, and you say how much you like her hair. But you keep getting the feeling that she's being a wiseass, that she's getting a big kick out of you. You ask her if she wants another drink.

"Sure," she says, but she insists on buying. "You bought the first three," she says. "It's my turn."

You'd bought the first four, in fact, but you don't see any sense in correcting her. "I'll get this one," you say, and you tell her that it isn't coming out of your pocket. "I have an expense account."

Her eyes light up. "Oh," she says, all giggles. "Do you pad it?"

You give her your biggest smile, the one you use on new clients. "Of course," you say. "But it's tricky." You tell her then about the unspoken ceiling on expenses. You explain to her how you have to guess what that ceiling is, stay just below it and claim just above it. "The company is happy, and I stay home three nights a week counting my money."

Again she giggles. "So, you're out and about four nights a week?"

"Something like that."

Her eyes go for yours, and she says, "What a life you must have."

This is her fourth or fifth wiseass remark. You are starting to feel a little uncomfortable with her. You decide to ask her in a serious voice if she's putting you on.

She places her hand on yours and says, "I thought we were both putting each other on."

You have to laugh at that as you feel her hand squeeze yours. She leans forward and kisses you on the cheek and whispers, "Why don't we make this one the last one."

You drink up your drink fast—so does she—and make for the other end of the lounge. The elevator is open and empty. You get in holding hands. You press the button for your floor and the doors close. You put your arms around each other and kiss—but not for long. The doors open at the next floor—garage level—and into the elevator steps an honest-to-God cowboy, with grimy dungarees, leather chaps, boots with spurs, and a dusty black Stetson. He is carrying a saddle over his shoulder. He has a lump of chewing tobacco under his bottom lip. He tips his hat to you both and presses the button for the twelfth floor. The elevator starts up again and you come out of the bowels of the hotel to get a big view of the Houston skyline, such as it is.

"Houston," you say, taking her by the waist and turning her to face the glass back of the elevator. "What a city. Today I saw an A-frame bait and tackle shop next door to a seventy story steel and glass skyscraper."

With that, the cowboy turns to you and says, "Excuse me, folks. I couldn't help but overhear." His voice is craggy but clear. He sounds like a smart man to you. "I can tell you that once upon a time there were no zoning laws in the city of Houston. You could put up any kind of building you wanted, anywhere you wanted."

You say, "That makes for a pretty uneven skyline."

The cowboy laughs and turns back around to face the elevator doors, whistling something. When the elevator stops at his floor, he turns to tip his hat. In the hallway he starts to whistle again.

***

Up in your room, she turns the TV on while you fix drinks. She doesn't make a fuss when you tell her that she'll have to switch gears to bourbon. "That's all I got up here," you say. "Nothing sweet."

"That's OK," she says. "Just add water and lots of ice."

She is sitting at the foot of the bed. She takes her shoes off, starts flipping through the channels on the dusty TV. "Not much selection."

You tell her she can order something on pay-per-view, which she takes to mean porno.

"No," you say. "I wasn't suggesting…"

"Of course you weren't."

"Really. I don't watch the stuff."

"Never?"

You tell her you saw enough of it when you were in college. "Never really liked it."

"I want to say that I don't believe you for even a second."

"It's just all the same. Like Westerns."

She doesn't understand what you're trying to say.

"Every Western that Hollywood ever made is exactly the same. Every porno movie ever made is exactly the same."

Your voice, which had been quiet in the bar and which you had been trying to preserve for your presentation in the a.m., is rising.

"Can I order you a porno?" She has the menu up on the screen. She scans through the titles, which she reads with fake giggles of pretend disgust. "Have you ever heard of Wax Williams?"

Of course you have.

"I want to find one of his."

"You know a lot about porno movies?"

She considers the question. "I live alone," she says. "I spend a lot of time online."

You interrupt her to tell her that you, too, live alone, and to tell her that you spend a lot of time online. You want her to know that you have that in common, if nothing else.

"You live alone. You're online all the time. And you don't look at porno?"

"I might look at sites that have naked women on occasion, but I don't go to sex sites."

"You're like a *Playboy* man?"

"I'm not a subscriber… anymore."

She laughs her laugh from the bar. "I love it when you try to be funny."

And only half looking at the TV but with both hands on the remote, she orders up her Wax Williams movie, *The Well-Hung Jury*. She reads the synopsis aloud, "Wax Williams is foreman of a jury of his near-peers in this highly stylized porn noir classic. The defiant and deviant double-D DA is played by six-footer Rhonda Schwonda. The lovely Juliet Hecht plays the sublimely supine pubic defender."

You groan and start humping the television. Bourbon gives you energy.

"I won't make you watch it," she says, stepping closer to you than she has been all night. And she says something about only needing to see the first five minutes of a Wax Williams movie to be satisfied. She takes her drink from you and sips a little from it. You look over her shoulder at the TV. She keeps talking, but you're only half listening to her. You take the glass of bourbon out of her hand with the idea that you will kiss her, and you realize that she's introduced a new topic: reincarnation.

"To tell the truth," you say to her, dropping right into her first short pause. "I really don't believe we come back again. But I don't think the people who think so are necessarily wrong."

She takes her glass back and steps away from you, walking around the bed to other side of the room. She's holding her glass of bourbon with both hands. She asks you if you believe in God. You nod your head, adjust the volume on the porno—nothing's happening yet on screen. Wax Williams still has his pants on.

"And do you believe there's a devil?" She says this like she is a lawyer and you are on the witness stand, like she is cross-examining you.

"Sure," you say, just to keep the conversation flowing.

She drinks what's left of her bourbon and comes toward you, unbuttoning her blouse. She's laughing. She says, "You and me."

She takes the drink out of your hand and unties your tie. You kiss again, both of you putting a little more body into it. You start going around and around the room together, biting and pulling at each other, losing your balance on purpose. You're banging against the walls and knocking her into the furniture, until finally you land on the bed.

Her breasts are air-conditioner-cold under your hands. You kiss her belly. Your tongue goes in her navel. "I'm going down on you," you say. You start rooting and roiling with your tongue working. She's sweet and blond and you are in heaven.

Five minutes pass. Ten minutes pass. She's really getting into it, bucking up and down and letting out with these little sounds. Your tongue feels like a boxer's arm that's thrown too many punches, but you're still working, pausing only to come up for air or to tell her a dirty joke.

"Please," she says, tugging at your ears. "You have to stop." Gentleman that you are, you comply. You come up beside her and put your head next to hers on the pillow. Her cheeks are bright red and there's sweat on her forehead and upper lip.

"When was the last time someone went down on you like that?"

"Never," she says, trying to sound sad and worn out. "Everybody always wants to do me ass backward."

She laughs then, but you don't. You ask her, "Do you?"

She nods and closes her eyes. She laughs again, and this time you laugh with her.

"Roll over," you say.

She rolls over and you start at it. It is difficult at first. But then it is the easiest thing.

She says, "The thing is, you either like it or you don't."

You say, "Do you like it?"

She says, "Yes."

"Hell," you say, surprised by your pleasure. "I like it too."

You finish before Wax Williams on the television, so you watch. The two women lawyers are sexually servicing the sequestered nine-man jury, all with cocks of ten inches or more. Wax Williams in a courtroom ménage a trois. The criminal on trial is never seen from the front, nor is the judge. The judge is represented only by a gavel that is a teak phallic object. No witnesses respond to cross-examination.

A few hours later you are at the desk in your robe, doing some last-minute work on your presentation. She is asleep under the messy blankets.

She wakes up and says, "What are you doing over there?"

"Work," you say.

"Work," she says. The wiseass edge to her voice is gone completely. She is talking like a little girl. "Why don't you come back to bed with me."

"I can't," you say. "I have this work to do."

She sits up Indian-style in the center of the bed. It's a pretty sight, but you tell her to get back under the covers before she catches cold.

"But I want to catch cold," she says, still using her little girl voice.

You ask her why she'd want to do that.

"Because I don't want to be warm," she says. "Because I want to be cold."

You don't say anything.

"Come back to bed with me," she says.

"No," you say. "I have to do this work."

Then she starts crying and talking crazy. She tells you that if you don't come back to bed with her, everything between you will be wrong. She tells you that work is one thing and the rest of life is something else. She tells you it's good to catch a cold if you don't want to be warm. "Just please come back to bed," she says. "I'm saying please."

You leave the desk and go to her. You put your arms around her. "Don't cry," you say. But her crying won't stop. She sobs harder, shaking in your arms. You start to fill up because crying is contagious for you. "Don't cry," you say. And just when you think you can't keep back the tears any longer, just as you're about to lose it and start bawling like a baby, she stops with her crying and starts laughing.

***

You wake up in the morning and have your showers and a nice breakfast from room service. You eat together in silence, but it isn't at all awkward or uncomfortable.

You get your things together and leave the room for the elevator. The doors open and she steps in first. You press the button for the ground floor and start going down. At the twelfth floor, the elevator stops. The doors open, and standing there is the cowboy from the night before. Only now he's wearing a three-piece suit and carrying a briefcase instead of his saddle. He's got on a three-hundred-dollar necktie and a pair of very expensive-looking boots. He's wearing the same black Stetson, but he's dusted it off. He steps in and tips his hat. He says, "Good morning," then he turns to face the elevator doors.

You feel her take a small step closer and reach for your hand. You give her hand a squeeze. You think about turning to look out at the Houston skyline in the daylight, but you don't. You try to think of something to say to either her or the cowboy, but nothing comes to mind. And though you can't say for sure what's going on inside her head, you have a pleasing feeling that she is thinking the same things you are. But you don't say anything and neither does she.

Chapter Four

Seens (still sic) from the *Life* (pt. 2)

BEN BETTIS: One of Wax's best money shots I ever got was in *Lovers' Knot.* Wax and Renee. She performed oral on him for three-quarters of an hour. I did the scene in one shot. I just kept rolling, no cuts, and that's just how it went into the film. No edits, start to finish. Perfect. Renee brought him to the point of climax a half-dozen times before she finally let him unload. I can still picture the way I caught the natural light within the long, translucent ribbon of jism that connected Wax's shining cock to Renee's flinty chin.

***

His mother schedules him for a complete physical with Dr. Johnson. She gets his name out of the big directory that came with the materials from their new health insurance provider. She selects Dr. Johnson because his office is in a new building not far from their neighborhood. Wax will be able to walk to the appointment after school lets out.

Mrs. Williams visits Dr. Johnson first. She wants to deliver the note from Coach Dunkin to the doctor. She wants to make sure Dr. Johnson gets the note. She believes that Wax might not give the note to Dr. Johnson.

***

LYLE MAMMON: Wax likes sweet girls who are a bit dense. In our business—and I have to say this must be true in the rest of the world—dumb girls are usually very nice and smart girls usually have a mean streak. Maybe that's a sexist theorem—forgive me. But add one more exponent to the equation: beauty. All the women who passed through my employ and all of the women I take notice of in the world outside are beautiful. So maybe I should say *dumb* beautiful women are usually very nice and *smart* beautiful women are often mean.

***

Mammon doesn't see the difference between his videos and the ones made by the new wave of female porn auteurs. He says, "They just have their couples fuck slower and the woman gets on top more and gets eaten out more."

***

TED ROMLING: Lyle Mammon is actually a talented director. He has a good visual sense and he works well with his actors. Mammon is certainly not without plotting abilities, though his specialty, and what has earned him a reputation as an innovator of form, is his knack for lesbian plot twists. He makes crude little storyboards for each scene—mostly just the master shots with side sketches of potential close-ups. He knows how to block a scene quickly and he uses his technical crews economically. He shoots lots of coverage so he can cut his movies for the softer hotel market.

***

When the girl returns to the set—the movie is *Sinfulenza*—Mammon asks her again what her name is. She feigns perturbation, pouts, and reminds Mammon that he has yet to bestow a name upon her.

"What's your real name?" he asks.

She seems to struggle with the question for a moment. "Hillary," she says finally.

Mammon says nothing. He relishes every and all naming opportunities. Porn nomenclaturing—Lyle Mammon gives names to all the pretty girls and big-cocked studs who seek work as sexual performers in a videotape milieu.

"Do you want to know my last name?" she asks.

"You have two last names, my little doll," says Mammon. "Hillary Dillary-Doll."

Hillary claps her hands quickly. Exhales in an exaggerated way. So much happiness with her new name.

And Mammon says, almost singing, "God gave names to all of the animals and I'm naming all my girls."

Hillary strips off her robe. "I'm Hillary Dillary-Doll," she sings.

"All right, Hillary," says Mammon, beginning to direct his newly named starlet. "I want you to look at the dot I drew on the wall over there, not at the camera. Then I want you to blink just once, slowly, then look out the window. If you can remember to do so, you can part the curtains ever so slightly. But remember, when you look out the window just stare straight ahead like you can't see anything because complex and conflicting thoughts are running through your mind."

"Thoughts?" she asks.

"Yes," says Mammon. "Conflicted thoughts."

The look on her face turns blanker. She shows him the slow blink he's after, but he knows she won't be able to replicate it when the tape rolls. "You feel two ways about Jock . . ."

"Jock?"

"Jock is the name of Wax's character in the movie."

"I forgot that," she says, looking again at her script.

"You love him, but he keeps on hurting you. He has other women on the side. You're just like all the other women in his life. You thought you were special because he told you that you were special."

Still a blank look. New tact. "Have you ever felt two ways about something?"

She's trying hard to think. Her eyes are big.

"A love-hate relationship," Mammon prompts.

"I love pancakes, but I hate that they're so fattening."

"Exactly. Look out the windows and think about pancakes. Count to ten thinking about how good pancakes are. When you get to ten, start thinking about how bad pancakes are and count to ten again. Can you do that?"

"Yes, I can."

***

LYLE MAMMON: I am like Henry Higgins in reverse. I discover proper fair ladies and teach them how to be sluts.

***

The treatments have the effect of speeding up time. Is that possible? Maybe it is a function of all the catching up he has to do. The growth spurts are very painful. He endures most of the pain at night, while he tries to sleep. He is kept awake by the sound—real or imagined—of popping cartilage, muscle tearing, growth plates grinding. He lies as still as possible. He is growing so fast it hurts. His dick is growing. Needle-sticking pain in his dick.

***

LYLE MAMMON: Dr. Johnson's crazy concoction was an unscientific mixture of human growth hormones, steroids, natural herbs, vitamins, and some crazy shit like freeze-dried bull semen, ground rhino horn, pineal gland from an elephant. Electrolytes. Salt. Powdered oxygen. Liquid oxygen. A variety of dietary supplements—portions of freeze-dried NASA meals meant to be eaten only in zero gravity. Cell expanders. Cell dividers. Cell hardeners. Ginkgo biloba. Extract of panax ginseng. Cayenne fruit pepper. Yohimbe. Talmax root. Copper enzyme. Muira pauma. Canine bone meal. Velvet deer antler. Gypsum. Mahogany sawdust. Cement mix. Vitamins D, E, and a host of the B complexes.

***

"You'll be getting hair there soon enough," Dr. Johnson says during an extended examination. "But your dad probably already told you that."

Wax shrugs, shakes his head, "No."
"Well. He'll be telling you soon enough, I'm sure."

***

WAX WILLIAMS: I don't, as a rule, watch my own movies. It makes me feel uncomfortable, seeing myself in the act. I did enjoy watching *DormitOrgy* because it was my first sex. I remember that I was having difficulties sorting through my fantasies at the time, trying to enact the best ones, to put my hands in all the places they'd been wanting to go, and to make sure I was pleasing Renee. I remember Lyle telling her that she should fake it if it didn't feel good, but I knew that I would be able to tell if she liked what I was doing.

***

The nurse with the tight uniform—the one who performs oral sex on him in Dr. Johnson's office—isn't a nurse after all. She is a doctor, actually. A doctor pretending to be a nurse. She's been following Wax's treatment and growth, and she thought a taste test needed to be done.

***

TODD INSULIN: I don't believe an accurate record of Wax's treatment exists now—if one ever did. Dr. Johnson was a quack. He wasn't a scientist. He wasn't a very thorough doctor. He kept spotty notes and fudged a lot of Wax's charts. Remember, he had to be able to bill all of this to the Williamses' medical insurance. He had to spend so much time fictionalizing a treatment regimen for Wax that he had no time left over to record what he was actually doing. What went into those big horse pills he gave Wax? Who knows.

COACH DUNKIN: Wax's story also involves baseball, don't forget. The national pastime. Wax was a natural. A first-ball, fastball hitter. He sat dead red every at bat. Line-drive hitter. Power to the opposite field. Able to take a pitch. Walked a lot because he didn't see many good pitches. His plan was simple. He would distinguish himself as the premier third baseman in New England high-school baseball. He may have missed out on Little League, but he'd make the most of high-school ball. He would play in the best Cape Cod league. Recruiters would pursue him from all across the country. They'd be impressed by his baseball skills. They'd respect his work ethic on and off the field. He'd get a scholarship to a good school. Full boat. He'd leave his unhappy home and focus on books and baseball. He'd play a few years of college ball. Then the minors. He'd be happy if his playing days ended in AAA. That would be success. But I like to think he was meant to be a big leaguer, and he would have worked his ass off to get there.

***

Gagging down a dozen pasty capsules a day. He knows that his penis is supposed to get longer in puberty, and though this new length is more than he expected, he doesn't realize exactly how overgrown his penis has become until that first after-practice shower with the varsity baseball team.

***

DUPER DAN: I was hired to run the video duplication system and to keep the warehouse organized. I do more than just dupe tapes all day, but Mammon called me Duper Dan one day and it stuck. I've begun editing raw tape and mixing sound. I've been taking night courses at Wadsworth, mostly computer graphics and web design. Working at the Hacienda is the best job I ever had.

***

Then the development of a thewy torso. He's never had such energy. It seems as if he is growing inside and out. His muscles seem to be lengthening and getting harder. He lifts and lifts, but he doesn't get bulgy, which is fine with him. His chest and shoulders become very well defined. His waist slims and his ass becomes rounder. It is like a second puberty, but this time it's the real deal: inches and inches. He starts to look different. He grows to a strapping six feet two inches. His shoulders get broad, square. His waist and ass are narrow. His legs are well muscled but not at all bulky. He works out incessantly, but he opts for flexibility and suppleness over bulging strength.

***

TODD INSULIN: Wax wore a mask of sorts when he performed, and he was sure to never let anyone see underneath that mask.

***

At first Mrs. Williams disbelieves what she overhears one of Wax's teammates say about him. The same things had been said about her father when he was alive. Namesake. Named for. Named after. The older and the younger. A sort of junior. Francis Wax Hartnett, her father, and Wax Hartnett Williams, her one and only son. Grandfather and grandson who never met. What rubs off with a name? They used to say that her father kept his tucked into his boot. Her father was a barber—a giant of a man, a head taller than all his customers. He sang bass in a real barbershop quartet and wore a handlebar mustache. He used candle wax to keep each curl perfect and in place. He was Ampersand's only barber for thirty years, and then the albino set up shop right across the street, with a new electric barber pole lit from within spinning up, up, up. Her father had his chipped barber pole scraped and repainted, but that was useless. Everybody in town wanted to go to the albino barber.

***

DEE-DEE SHARP: Don't get me wrong. Mammon is a sexist pig. I don't want to say who he was talking about, but one time at an awards ceremony he pointed at an actress who works for a rival studio and said, "Something tells me she probably smells bad between the legs." I told him he was sick. And he said, "I think she stinky where she pinky." And you have to laugh at something like that.

***

It's shallow of him, he knows, but he likes artificial breasts. They look good, and he likes the feel of them. The girls with implants are easy to spot and growing in number. More have them than not. The ones without implants will work a few films anonymously to bankroll their tit jobs. Then they become female leads. How can he fault them for their augmentations? After all, wasn't his cock enlarged through artificial means?

***

TED ROMLING: Wax is the ne plus ultra—the ultimate, nothing beyond him, nothing greater. His loss will affect the porn industry in myriad ways. He brought people into the stores. A new title from him got people interested. They'd go to their local adult superstore to buy his new tape, and they'd pick up another tape or two, maybe a novelty item—a new toy for the wife.

***

Heidi Degrees has a sullen but sexy look, plus she has large breasts on a small-shouldered frame. The room is messy, smelling like a hangover. Wax wishes he'd met her before the shoot. But it doesn't matter.

***

COACH DUNKIN: The other boys on the team didn't want to shower with Wax once they got a load of him naked. I can't say for sure, but I think it was some of the same guys who had teased Wax in the shower back when he was a freshman. But that's not why Wax had to quit the team. The problem was his size was getting in the way when he played. He couldn't move laterally, and I think it hurt his swing, too. Whatever medication they were giving him, must have deadened his quick-twitch muscle fiber. He lost bat speed.

***

Mammon sees to it that his girls have abortions instead of children. This is no *Life* for children. But he wonders about names for babies. It isn't so easy.

***

ED GRAUBS (CO-OWNER, SUNRISE VIDEO ARCADE): Operating an adult superstore in Ampersand, Massachusetts—the birthplace of Wax Williams—is both a blessing and a curse. We get the pilgrimage types every now and then, folks who travel across country to drive by Wax's boyhood home, and we get the creeps who skulk around the Hacienda hoping to see a porn star coming or going. They often end up in our store, as if we're somehow affiliated. Like we're the Wax Williams souvenir stand, or something. I'm sorry. Ampersand is no porno mecca.

***

The odd little lady at the laundromat gets him thinking about his mother. Not for any specific reason. She doesn't resemble his mother at all. But Wax assumes that she is a mother to someone, and he has a mother of his own and he hasn't seen her for what seems like a very long time.

***

Through the nipple. Under the muscle. Textured saline implants.

***

ART STYE (CO-OWNER, SUNRISE VIDEO ARCADE): Lady comes in one morning asking if we have any jobs available for a cleaning lady. Place is a fucking mess, so I hire her. Minimum wage. Twenty hours a week. At first we just had her clean the office in the back and behind the counter. She is a cleaning machine. Then we set her loose on the sales floor, vacuuming the aisles and cleaning the video/DVD shelves and the magazine racks. Customers don't seem to mind. They don't pay any attention to her. She doesn't cramp their style, or anything. They shop around her. Then she asks if she can clean the booths upstairs. I say, "Be my guest." Turns out she's Wax Williams' fucking mother.

***

She finds that it is easier to clean the booths immediately after they are vacated. If she waits even a few minutes, the booth becomes occupied again and that means double the mess to clean up. Often the videos still have time left on them when the men vacate the booths. She never looks directly at the videos as they play. And she never looks at the nude pictures on the covers of the magazines or video boxes when she dusts. It is easy to keep her stare elsewhere. A lady doesn't look.

***

RENEE SALMON: I did an in-store at Sunrise one Friday night. I was signing copies of *Vaginamite.* Pretty good crowd showed up. Some familiar faces. Fan club types. I recognized Mrs. Williams right away. Wax has her nose and eyes—a pretty woman for her age. She kept staring at me. She knew about me and Wax, that was clear to me. I wasn't about to let her stare me down. I gave her the hairy eyeball right back. From what Wax told me about her, she wasn't much of a mother. Sort of a cold woman. He didn't have any horror stories about her. He said she couldn't cook very well.

TODD INSULIN: Adult video aficionados enjoyed his sleepy-eyed look. One reviewer made note that Wax's face went nearly white when he came. He was probably oxygen deprived. All of the blood in his body was in his penis.

***

"Forget it," says Wax. "The girl's as dry as a bone."

"Lube her up," Mammon calls out.

A set-dresser, Alan Dudley, appears with the required lubricant, which he neatly applies to the indicated area.

"Should be called lubri*can,*" says Mammon. "Because it makes it so you can."

Bonnie Bell seems to be genuinely responding to Alan Dudley's clinical touch, but then she goes cold again just as quickly when the tape starts rolling. Wax assumes a kneeling position behind her, hard enough for entry, but meeting a dry wall of pink flesh.

"Come now," says Mammon. "Command her rear. Have at her ass."

***

LYLE MAMMON: We're a lot alike, Wax and I. Except he's handsome and has a very large penis, and I'm what you would call funny-looking and not so big in the lap area. He's a stud, and I'm a dud.

***

He examines his predicament and traces a line of responsibility back to his parents. At first, he blames his mom and dad for what is between his legs. When he was young and it was smaller than he thought it should be, he blamed their genes. And when it gets big—too big—he knows it's due to the medical treatment they forced him to undergo.

***

TED ROMLING: Boobs and pubes. It's a really simple equation.

LYLE MAMMON: No lie, the girl had a cold hole. I only fucked her once, but she made my dick cold as a popsicle. But she was sweet, kind even, compared to most of the other girls. Cold hole, warm heart.

***

After he is off the baseball team, Wax's mother gets him a job at the old candy store. The candy man's name is Clifford Noziglia. Before he opened the candy store forty years ago, he tried to sell jewelry. He got robbed the first day he opened for business, so he sold his remaining inventory and bought enough candy to fill his shelves. His young customers are thieves, too, but they don't have guns and they only rob him by the penny.

"Watch him," the candy man says, pointing to a boy with Down Syndrome who enters the empty store loudly. "He steals."

"I think he's retarded," Wax says.

"He steals," says the candy man, slapping an open hand on the counter.

The store remains empty for the next ten minutes, then Rollie stops in to say hello to Wax. The candy man disappears into the back room, closing the door behind him. "You watch the kids," he says. "I'll watch *you*."

Rollie laughs. "He's going out back now to make some more candy." And he makes a masturbatory gesture.

***

LYLE MAMMON: Wax drove up the price for any costar willing to take him on. The girls called it hazard pay.

***

Something is wrong with the third prescription that Dr. Johnson gives Wax. After taking only one pill, Wax begins to cramp. The pills are big, but he never has any trouble getting them down. After vomiting all night, Wax goes to see Dr. Johnson. He doesn't have an appointment, but he has to see him. He walks by himself to the clinic. He spots Dr. Johnson smoking a cigarette with one of the nurses in the back parking lot. "Doctor, I'm not doing so well."

"Let's get you inside then and have a look."

Wax follows Dr. Johnson into the clinic and up the stairs to his office. The doctor has missed not one but two belt loops. This is something that Rollie would laugh out loud at. Wax simply smiles, sick as he is, and also intent on maintaining a mature level of behavior at all times, now that he is sixteen.

Wax lies on the examination table. He gives Dr. Johnson the bottle of pills. After breaking one of the capsules open and tasting the gray green powder inside, Dr. Johnson says, "I forgot to sugar the pill, Wax. I'm sorry."

***

He also realizes that his cranium is increasing in size. He notices when loosening the adjustable straps on all his baseball caps.

He keeps a weekly appointment with Dr. Johnson, Wednesdays, four o'clock. His ejaculate is examined closely.

***

LYLE MAMMON: I never understood the appeal of Mary Algae. I don't know why Wax liked her so much. Like a lot of the girls in the *Life*, she had a great body but not much face. She had less face than most. She wasn't ugly. It was more that she always wore the wrong expression on her face. Or no expression, or too much expression. We get very few letters from customers that are critical of the girls, but just about every bad letter we ever received was about her. It just wasn't fun to watch her get drilled.

***

Make an effort to become lost in the act. Become oblivious to the video eye. Ignore the crew. Feed off their silence, their quiet breathing. Their awe.

***

TED ROMLING: Porno business has the closest, most symbiotic relationship with its customers. We know what the people want and we give it to them. There's nothing that we won't put on video, and there's nothing that they won't watch. The only way porno would ever go away is if everybody in the world went blind.

DEE-DEE SHARP: Kendra Bourbon always wore her hair done in a knot standing up on the top of her head, what the boys on set call a blowjob knob.

TODD INSULIN: I interviewed Wax on the set of *TrainSexual Adventures* and found him to be very well spoken. His head worked well, unlike most of the other adult performers that I've conversed with. He was able to take words out of his head and put those words in his mouth and say them in the right order. I appreciated that quality in him. But I also like people who get lost in their sentences, who try to weave complex thoughts through sentence fragment after sentence fragment.

TED ROMLING: He had his suitors, Wax did. Women and men, worldwide. Ardent one and all. Most of them wealthy and some of them, in fact, beautiful. They trekked to Ampersand once word got out about the Hacienda.

Wax had a taste for German wines and European clothes. He carbo-packed on pastas the evening before video shoots.

DEE-DEE SHARP: Mammon calls himself the Sultan of Twat.

***

A little luminescent dollop of Wax's still-warm spooge clings to Jenny Cleft's pretty lips. She turns to face the camera, twinkle in her eye, to say, "Showered in jism."

Mammon says, "Cut," then throws a towel to Wax. "Can you go again… twenty minutes?"

***

LYLE MAMMON: The name of the midget who accidentally shot me in the knee was Hector Min. It was a real gun loaded with blanks. It hurt like hell and did a lot of damage—powder burn, mostly, and a wound that looked like a bullet hole. Wax somehow knew that we had a first aid kit on set. He cleaned and dressed the wound perfectly. We would have continued shooting after that, but Hector drank a whole bottle of wine to calm his nerves after the gun discharged. He passed out, and we couldn't do the scene with our midget asleep under the table.

DEE-DEE SHARP: Wax took a string of confectionary lovers after Renee finally broke it off with him. They were on-again off-again for years really. Mostly Wax took up with his costars or girls that Mammon sent his way. Girls that were always a little more aggressive than him, but at the same time girls who wouldn't challenge Wax or come between him and Mammon.

***

The Nude Private Dick: Wax Williams is a well-endowed private detective hired to uncover the mystery surrounding the disappearance of several beautiful women from a Southern California nudist colony. Wax goes undercover… sans clothing. He collects a few clues and gives all the nudists an eyeful. After a few promising leads turn into nothing more than sexual liaisons, Wax cracks the case. An evil dwarf (played by Hector Min) has lured the women to his cave in the hills with false promises of eternal youth. Though the dwarf is heavily armed, Wax clobbers him with his big dick, frees the girls, and then each girl gives Wax a thank-you fuck.

***

TED ROMLING: Wax Williams was a professional straight away. He learned his vapid lines. Hit his marks, sported wood on cue. He didn't come too soon. He was simpatico. He had success fast not just because he had outsized genitalia, but because he had charisma, star qualities. He distinguished himself from others of his ilk through his bearing. He was the eighth wonder of the world, as Mammon has said many times. The rednecks and musclebound jimbos who work in this business couldn't hold a candle to him...no pun intended on Wax's name.

***

He is recognized everywhere he goes. On airplanes. Hotels in foreign countries. Malls in Florida. Sporting events. Good restaurants. Everybody must watch porn.

The girl in the bed tells Wax that her name is Tabootha.

She is nude already. She is pretty. A redhead, very slender. Wax runs his hand along her quiet curves. "Did Mammon give you a last name?"

"He said I didn't need one."

***

Cable access show in Manhattan. Wax is nude and so is the woman interviewing him.

She asks, "What's it like seeing yourself having sex on the TV screen?"

Wax says, "It's like putting on a mask and looking in the mirror."

"Next Question: Is your dick so long you can suck it?"

"It is. But I don't."

"You're just like that old man from Nantucket," she says.

"I have brought it to my nose, touched my forehead with the tip of it."

But some mornings—many a morning—Wax wakes curled in a fetal ball, the head of his cock in his mouth.

***

TY BOYCE: Mammon wanted to write a memoir entitled "Cuntstruck." I was to ghostwrite it. We set up a series of interview sessions about a year back. He ended up canceling all but two meetings. He drank throughout both sessions—vodka tonics. He rambled. Started strong both times, but ran out of steam quickly. We kept drifting into other business: script ideas, feud genealogies, health issues, insults he'd wished he'd thought of when they would have counted, missed opportunities to fuck good-looking women that didn't know any better. But he had his lyrical moments. He said, "Cuntstruck I was, stars in my eyes." I told him, "You can't call the thing 'Cuntstruck.' Bookstores won't put it on the shelf."

LYLE MAMMON: I guess I was always cuntstruck even when I was a little boy. I remember looking up girl's dresses, and giving nickels to this girl in my neighborhood so she would let me look at her hoo-hoo. I gave her a nickel every day for a week, then she asked me if she could see my pee-pee. I told her I'd show it to her for a quarter. She gave me a quarter, I unzipped and whipped the little pecker out.

***

He wakes up alone at 3:00 a.m. and wants a snack. A female snack. There are five or six girls making their home at the Hacienda. The sound of his door opening in the dark night is an invitation heard in their sleep. Nude beauties make their way to his suite. Along the way, one knocks lightly on Mammon's door. He wakes quickly, finds a loaded video camera.

***

Every time they drive by one of those storage facilities on the highway—the ones with the orange garage doors—Mammon says, "People are going to be living in those spaces in a few years. Mark my words."

***

Sex in Storage: In this pre–AIDS era pseudo-docudrama, a hearty population of "clean" men and women are living in government-protected storage—let out only to procreate for the state. But they get to fornicate for the fuck of it behind the orange doors.

***

LYLE MAMMON: Cathi Rears backed into the *Life,* so to speak. She was interested in ass work only. I understand that she was married to a man who refused to penetrate her rear entry, so whenever she got the hankering for some backdoor loving, she would drop by the Hacienda. She wasn't pretty in the face, not that that mattered, given her specialty. She fell out of the ugly tree and her face hit every single branch on the way down. She never shut up and she had an annoying voice. She was a flat-voiced, nasal yacker. There were also some rumors that she may have stolen some items from the other girls. I remember Dee-Dee saying once, "When it comes to Cathi, believe the worst."

***

"So you're friends with Marianne Strand?" Carole Nuller asks.

"Yes," Wax says.

"She's very embarrassed about what happened after the prom," she says, giggling. "I know I'll sound like a jerk, but I'm just gonna come right out and ask you. Is it as big as she says?"

***

Her name is Tia Eccles and he tries to put her at ease by teasing her about how good she looks. He is the old pro now, and she's the neophyte. She won't admit that she's beautiful. She'll only go so far as to say she knows that she's cute. "Pretty," he offers. "No," she says firmly. He takes her hands to signal that he is conceding, but on his terms. He says, "You may not be beautiful yet, but I predict that you will be a world-renowned beauty in less than a year."

***

DEE-DEE SHARP: Nobody was ever taking care of Wax. They always made sure he got to shoots on time and that he got all of his immediate needs taken care of. But nobody made sure he had a life beyond all the work he was doing, the movies and the conventions and the strip clubs. Especially after he moved out of the Hacienda. Really, it was sad. Follow Wax back to his practically unfurnished apartment. See how he lives. No place to sit. Nothing hanging on the walls. No bed. He's sleeping in a sleeping bag on the floor in the living room. In the kitchen there's a stove, a microwave, a fridge. But no table or chairs. He eats standing by the sink.

KEN BETTIS: I am a survivor in this business. I was working a hotel shoot in Daytona, Florida, once when I backed off a third-floor terrace trying to line up a tight from-under shot. I fell something like forty feet to the hotel pool area. I didn't hit water, but I stood right up, laughing my ass off, bleeding a bit from the mouth because I nearly bit my tongue off. The crew brought me to the local hospital where I was treated and released. No broken bones.

***

He lives between now and eventually. He wants freedom from the *Life*, showing off his cock and fucking women who make him hate himself. Some day soon.

***

ART STYE: I'm the one that found her body. I kept noticing guys were heading upstairs to the booths and then coming right back down. I figured some crazy dude might be up there, rough trade scaring away the paying customers. But I get to the top of the stairs and I see her on the floor, her legs sticking out of one of the booths. I don't know how long she'd been there that way. Ambulance came, couldn't resuscitate her.

RENEE SALMON: I happened to be in residency at the Hacienda the week Mrs. Williams died, shooting seven movies in seven days. Wax was out of town. Nobody knew where. I went to her service at the cemetery. There were only a few women from her church and Wax's father, who has Alzheimer's and didn't seem to know what was going on.

***

Then Mammon gets right to it. "I'd be lying if I said I was surprised that you filed suit against me."

"There's no lawsuit."

"Some lawyer of yours has been hinting."

"That's my new accountant. He tells me I've got enough money."

"But you're mad that I have more." Lyle Mammon looks like a man who is lying. Trying to wrangle himself out of something that he doesn't feel guilty about but that he knows is wrong—for him that is equal to honesty, coming clean. He says, "Wax, I haven't cheated you, and you know that." He says, "I am not a thief." He says, "I'm a man who met up with a boy with a tremendous cock, and I rode that cock to the bank."

Wax says, "Why do you have so much more money than me?"

Mammon says, "We made equal profits on the movies we made together. The books tell you that. You don't need an accountant to show you that. But my money went in other directions. I put my money into other projects and made more. You spent yours or gave it away."

***

TED ROMLING: When she was growing up, the boys in school called her Icky Vicky. She wasn't icky anymore. Mammon dubbed her Victoria Garden, and he always made sure she wore flowers in her hair.

WAX WILLIAMS: Women seem to come and go in this *Life.* They work a few scenes, bank the money and then hit the road to feature dance at the bigger strip clubs in the best markets. Videos are just a steppingstone for them.

RENEE SALMON: One thing that always hurts me to see is when a guy can't get any more work because his gear isn't reliable. That's just about the only reason a guy gets kicked out of the *Life.* Once it happens once, it happens twice. Once it happens twice, he doesn't get a third chance.

LYLE MAMMON: Quickie Hickey earned her slutty sobriquet for her claim that she could orgasm immediately upon the point of penetration. Her moans were perfect, and they're often used to this day in overdubs for girls who don't give good voice to their pleasure.

***

One day Wax arrives at the Hacienda to find Renee lying on a table in the banquet room, her nude body covered in flesh-colored frosting and a lit phallic-shaped candle stuck in her navel. He hasn't seen her in six months. It's his twenty-third birthday, which he had forgotten all about.

"Blow me," Renee says.

"Very funny."

"Make a wish. I'll make it come true."

Wax approaches the table and extinguishes the candle with a wet pinch of his thumb and index finger. Suddenly the lights go up and he sees that the room is filled with folks from the production company—his costars and members of the crew: Duper Dan and the guys who work in the warehouse and shipping department. Mammon leads them all in a loud but warm rendition of "Happy Birthday."

***

Wax buys some land in western Massachusetts. Like all of his major purchases—cars, condos—he pays cash. His plan is to build himself a roundhouse to keep the devil out of the corners.

***

Silence, Exile, and Cunnilingus: Wax directed and cowrote the script with his longtime scribe, Ty Boyce. This literary romp follows a young American professor as he misspends a research vacation on the Emerald Isle. Beautiful location shots—acres and acres of purple heather and green rolling hills. The professor finds a load of Irish lassies to enact sexy scenes inspired by the fiction of James Joyce.

***

He looks at the sorry note he's written for her and is sure that he's misspelled every third word. He's written too much. The note should have simply said, "Fuck you, Renee. I'm sick of your shit." He crumples the note and looks around her shitty apartment for something to break, something meaningful to her. He wants her to come home to find something of hers broken to shit.

***

TED ROMLING: Hundreds of women sought to work with Wax. Amateurs and professionals. Whores and neophytes. The most popular actresses in adult film lined up to star opposite Wax Williams. It was a rite of passage for the young ones, and something about which the older ones on the way out could always reminisce. The very length of him caused fainting, seizures, hallucinations. One of his first costars, Amanda Lamancha, had difficulty breathing after a particularly long scene. "I think he punctured a lung," she said. A doctor was called to the set. Amanda was examined. In fact, her lung wasn't punctured, she was merely hyperventilating.

***

Mammon is in possession of a video of two pretty youngsters fucking. The boy is fifteen, maybe, skinny as hell, squeaky voice, slender dick. The girl has tits, but nothing in the way of hips. Her lower torso seems three years less mature than her top half. She could have passed for sixteen, but she is shooting so hard for nineteen that she comes off looking thirteen, fourteen. No hips, no ass, and skinny legs are the giveaway. She is a child. The label on the tape—handwritten—says, "Statutory Tape." After ten minutes of painful-to-watch intercourse, Wax finds himself concentrating on the crew shadows on the headboard of the bed the teens are fucking on.

***

Renee tries hard to recall something memorable about even one of the string of identikit lovers Mammon has set her up with. She isn't distressed by the commonality of their faces, their physiques. She is just frustrated that they aren't enough to make her happy.

"Some guys don't give you much to go on. It's like they don't want to be remembered, which, to me, is retarded. I could never figure it out. A guy fucks me and I want to totally haunt his shit for the rest of his days. I want to be in his thoughts when he's working up a bone for the woman he marries."

***

VAL THE TEMP: I was opening the morning mail for Mr. Mammon when I came across a large envelope from an attorney in the Midwest, I can't remember which state—Iowa, Illinois, Indiana, one of those. I did what I was supposed to do, read the first and last paragraphs of the letter and underline anything that I thought Mr. Mammon should pay attention to. I don't remember exactly what the contents of the letter were, but it was about a boy who used one the company's penis pumps and had had a terrible accident with it. I could hardly bring myself to look at the photographs in the envelope. That poor boy.

Consumer Profile

Bidet

The plumber asks you what is wrong with your sink. If he just takes one look at it—filled with gray, stale-looking water, the stopper sitting on the counter beside the soap—he will have his answer. He doesn't have to be a detective. He doesn't even have to be a plumber. Everybody knows a stopped-up sink when they see one. But he isn't looking at the sink. He is looking at you—specifically at your chest, trying to discern the outline of your breasts through your heavy sweater.

"It won't go down," you say, backing away from him just a step.

"You lose something down there?" You take this as an accusation. The plumber wants to put the blame on you because he's buddies with the landlord. You decide not to answer him. Instead, you try to excuse yourself from the bathroom, telling him that you will be in the room at the end of the hall if he needs you for anything. But he keeps standing in the doorway, blocking your exit. It seems like he is staying in your way deliberately. "Just need Mr. Snake," he says, showing you a tightly wound blue metal coil.

When he opens his toolbox, you see a dozen or more miniature bottles of vodka. They are mixed in with his tools, right out in the open. You can't believe that he hasn't even tried to conceal them. Most are empty and look like they've been in his toolbox for a long time. The tiny bottles have a rusty look to them, like his tools. Their labels are all peeling off. What you find most curious about the little bottles is the fact that the empty ones don't have their caps. You wonder what he does with the caps. Does he throw them over his shoulder for good luck? Does he save the caps in his shirt pocket so he can count them up at the end of the day to see how many he's had? Has he swallowed the caps?

Before he lets you pass, he says, "Your hair. You wash your hair in the sink?"

The suggestion is ridiculous. You would never wash your hair in this or any bathroom sink. The thought of it gives you a sick feeling. You picture your nose touching up against a caked-on gob of leftover toothpaste as you try to angle your head under the faucet.

The plumber smiles at you then, lifting the toilet seat. For a moment, you are certain he is going to begin using the toilet in front of you. But he is merely satisfying some professional curiosity he has with the seat. He makes the bathroom seem smaller. You have stood side by side with Robin in the bathroom a hundred times and have never once felt crowded. You wish Robin were with you now. She has a way of dealing with guys like this plumber.

The new proposal you are working on is the same as the last one. You have greater hope this time because Neal, your boss, has been told that something might give this time around. You are asking for five thousand dollars from the state for a testing program that will help place teenagers who left high school before graduating into entry-level technical jobs. You'll probably get two thousand, three if you are very lucky. What you have so far isn't any good. There is a tone you need on these things that you know is missing from this proposal. You have to plead a little, and you need just a touch of urgency. This reads like a cross between a letter to Santa and a term paper.

Just to hear words, you switch on the radio. You keep spinning the dial every time you land on music. You stop for a moment when you hear a woman's voice say, "He has taken all of my panties. Even the ones from the hamper."

The DJ asks her what she is wearing, since her boyfriend has her panties.

"Right now," she says, "I just have pantyhose on."

The DJ groans. "You're begging for a yeasty," he says.

The woman laughs. There is a marked difference between the sound quality of her voice and that of the DJ's. Her voice is cut in half by the phone lines. You spin the dial quickly to the left end, toward the college stations. A small-voiced young woman comes on. She reads a list of band names and song titles in an intelligent voice that is without inflection.

From the bathroom you hear the plumber swearing. Then there are footsteps toward your room and a knock at your door. The plumber sticks his head in. His eyes go to your computer. You fight an impulse to cover the screen from him. "Snake won't do it," he says. "Have to look inside. Open the trap up."

"Okay," you say, turning back around to face your computer.

But he doesn't leave. You can't imagine why he is still standing in the doorway. Then he says, "You should use the bathroom now."

In the bathroom you look at the tops of your knees and then at the length of snake that is showing from the sink's drain. You touch it and it bounces. A scraping sound like a person gagging comes from deep inside the drainpipe. Through the door the plumber asks again if you've lost anything down the sink.

You say, "No," and tell him that you're not the only one who lives in the apartment.

You look inside his open toolbox. In addition to the little vodka bottles, you see a copy of *Playboy* magazine. The woman on the cover has no shirt on. She has her body facing away from the camera in such way that you can see most of her left breast, but not its nipple. You want to open the magazine and look inside. But as you reach to pick it up, the plumber knocks on the door.

"What?" you say.

"Nothing," he says. "Did you fall in?"

You don't understand what he means, that he is trying to make a joke. You wait a moment, then ask him if it is okay to flush.

He laughs and says, "Be my guest."

As you step from the bathroom, the plumber says, "Bet you wish you had a bidet."

You hear him clearly; still, you make him repeat himself. You want him to realize that he should not try to talk to you about such things. But you can tell by the way he asks his question the exact same way the second time that he would never understand that some topics should be kept off limits between strangers.

You say, "Why would I want a bidet?"

"I put one in for this rich lady. She watched me install it. She asked me if I knew why she wanted to have a bidet. I told her I knew what they were for. She laughed when I said that. She told me she was going to squat over her new bidet every morning and bring herself off."

***

At first you drive too fast and then you drive too slowly. But the other cars on the road seem to accommodate you. Each lane change has a logic of its own. The stoplights at each intersection are in perfect sync with your need to stop and your desire to move on. Until you come to a stop at the light in front of Sunrise Arcade, an adult bookstore. You look away from the tiny storefront, which appears no different from the other shops in the area—liquor store, convenience store, dry cleaners. Except the windows have a shiny opaque tint and the store's new awning is fitted with a backlight to make the name of the store glow brightly. The name of the store would have seemed innocent enough to you if it weren't for that backlight telling you that it is a store that sells dirty magazines and videos. You look impatiently at the red stoplight. You want to lean on the horn, though no other cars are in front of you.

You think again about the plumber and what he said about the bidet. You managed to smile at him and excuse yourself without blowing up or, worse, melting down. Now, as you drive to the office, you try to recall every little thing about him. You hadn't noticed much. You remember his shirt and his pants were the same color green and that he wore his mostly gray hair greased back. He is probably in his early fifties, you figure. His nose and forehead were red. He had a sort of rocking motion when he stood next to you. His cheeks and chin were covered with spotty gray stubble.

When you get to the office, no one is there except for Amy and Brad, two new interns. You find them in the staff room playing a game of hangman on the chalkboard. You wouldn't have given their game a second look, but you see that the dangling stick figure has been drawn with an outsized penis and the word spelled out beneath him is *D o r m i t O r g y.* You read the word twice and almost say it aloud.

All of the interns seem weird to you, but Amy and Brad are the weirdest. The girl stares a lot, and the boy does too. They make you feel the need to repeat yourself. And there seems to be some kind of romance going on between them, but you can't say for sure. They never understand anything, and their identical looks of incomprehension appear practiced. They don't want to learn anything on the job, you think. They just wanted *your* job. They want to steal your job, and they probably know enough to do that. You complained to Neal about them, but he was too softhearted to do anything. "They're just young," he said.

Knowing the answer will be a long time coming, you ask if there have been any calls for you.

Amy says, "The phone hasn't rung all morning."

"Maybe we have a problem—with the phones," Brad says. "Do you want me to call the phone company, Miss Clarke?" Brad always calls you Miss Clarke, even though you have taken the time to point out that you are only four years older than him. He just can't bring himself to call you by your first name. It is a ruse, you're sure, to make you feel old.

You sit at your desk and collect some papers that you don't really need. Amy and Brad continue watching you from across the room. You can tell that Amy has noticed that you aren't wearing any makeup. Their obscene game of hangman is fully visible from your desk. You can't stay in your office.

You tell Brad that you will be in early the next day, adding that he should erase the board before Neal returns. He disappears then, pulling on his tie like it's a noose and turning to look back at Amy.

At Neal's desk you stop to write a short note telling him that you won't be able to see him later. You had made plans for dinner, but you no longer feel up to it. There is no way you will be able to sit across from Neal in a restaurant. There is no way you will be able to bring a fork from your plate to your mouth, chew the food and swallow. You picture yourself choking on a salad, literally gagging on lettuce. You don't say that in the note, though. You write instead that you are afraid you've let your work slide for too long, and now you feel backed up.

***

Outside your building you sit in your parked car, staring up at the lit windows of your apartment. The way the plumber's shadow moves in the bathroom window makes you think he's dancing. You briefly worry that he might have been at your computer while you've been gone.

You don't have your watch on, but you figure it must be close to four o'clock. Robin will be getting home from work soon. You haven't decided whether you should intercept her at the entrance to your building, or if you should just let her go on up. It might be best to let things happen naturally, as if nothing were amiss. That way, you'll have the choice of staying in your car until the plumber is gone or following Robin up the stairs to face him again. This time you won't let anything he has to say bother you. You will fix tea for yourself and Robin, offer him some politely, and then get back to your proposal.

The sign on the side of his van reads, "Donald Elger, Plumber." Beneath that, in big block letters, it says, "Sinks, washers, toilets, showers, bidets." The word "bidets" is stenciled in slightly different lettering. It's a close match, but not quite exact in color or size. He must have added it, you think, after his rich lady.

The only thing you know about bidets is from reading *Tropic of Capricorn* your junior year. The French whores used bidets to wash themselves after sex. It seemed to you to be part of a mysterious ritual, a cleansing that couldn't have mattered in a literal sense. You remember in one scene, a Punjabi went to the bathroom in a bidet and horrified everyone in the brothel.

You slouch down in the seat of your car, wishing you had something to read while you wait for Robin. You lock your door and the door on the passenger side of the car. You close your eyes and let yourself doze off.

***

You wake unsure if you've been sleeping for ten minutes of two hours. The thought that comes first is the same thought you have each morning when you wake up. This time, alone in your car, you say the thought out loud: "I'm still a virgin." You make a mental list of who knows: Robin, Neal, your mother. Then you wonder if the plumber knows. Do the interns, Amy and Brad?

The plumber's van is gone. The lights are still on in your apartment. You hope this means that Robin is home.

As soon as you open the door you hear the sound of the shower running. You knock on the door to the bathroom, then go in. Through the steam in the bathroom, you watch Robin part the shower curtain just enough to poke her head through. Her hair is soapy and her hands are wet and red.

She says, "You just missed the shitfaced plumber."

You look at the sink. The water has gone down. There is a ring of grime around the drain that looks like coffee grounds. The plumber's rusty thumbprints are everywhere.

"He left something for you," Robin says. "On your desk."

In your room, beside your computer, you find a grey button about the size of a nickel. You don't recognize it at first, then you realize it came from Robin's big white sweater, which you know is in *your* closet now, not Robin's. You bring the button with you to the bathroom and go straight to the sink. You let the cold water run for a few seconds before you fill a glass. You put the button on your tongue and swallow it with a sip of water. Then you start laughing because Robin is whistling in the shower. Not singing, whistling.

Chapter Five

Personal Appearance

During his hiatus from video work, Wax earns his keep by making the rounds at adult entertainment trade shows, which consists of three to five shows every season. Nothing too hard. Show up, show cock, and talk up *All Doll*, which is scheduled for release shortly. Sign autographs for an hour and three-quarters. Easy. Three grand plus expenses—a good room in a good hotel, lunches and dinners for free. Lots of the same faces from show to show. Collectors. Sluts. Gay dudes. Divorcees late to porn and radically devoted to Wax as their last premenopausal crusharooney. Sign up to five items per person. Magazine covers, video stills, portraits, dildos, video boxes…

"Why are XXX video boxes so big?" A question from Wax to Ty Boyce.

"Repeat, please," says Ty.

"Why are the boxes that triple X videos come in so big?"

Ty Boyce pauses one beat, two. "Because, Wax," he says, "they grow that way."

***

Wax wanders the booths at the convention, which are set up like a maze to make sure you go in at one end and come out at the other with no chance of a detour or premature exit. There are a lot of video dealers showing amateur hour stuff on the large TV monitors that hang from the ceiling. Magazine people are hawking ad space, and chesty women are handing out their eight-by-tens to anybody claiming to be a producer of adult features.

The crowd is all too bent on coming off respectable. The men wear sharp suits and most of the women have on business outfits. Everybody is shaking everybody else's hand. The staff at the Hotel Cashpot acts like there isn't pornography on display everywhere and there aren't adult film actresses flashing tit, sitting for twenty-dollar nude Polaroids.

Wax always expects a much larger turnout of perverts and tuggers, guys with funny-smelling clothes on, scummy eyeglasses. Guys with odd walks and facial ticks just trying to get their hands on the dirtiest fucking thing that's out there. But it's just never the case. Mostly the attendees are collectors, amateur enthusiasts, and connected dealers trying to hook up with the right swingers, the ones with money and/or access to young bodies. There is an ass grabber making the rounds to keep things interesting. He's striking about every five minutes, and he isn't differentiating between male and female asses.

Wax stops at a laminating booth where you can have your favorite nude photos preserved for two dollars each, the selling point being that you could come on the laminated photo more than once. The hawker wears a straw boater, a red bow tie, and garters on his white shirtsleeves. He must be sixty. Armed with a flesh-colored, penis-barreled squirt gun loaded with an ejaculate substitute (shampoo mixed with cream rinse conditioner is Wax's guess), he spurts a few squirts onto a laminated centerfold, wipes it clean, then holds it up to the crowd. "Just clean her up—one, two, three—and she's ready for your next date."

Wax moves on, browses more tables, trying to move through the crowd carefully, not wanting to be recognized. He doesn't want to bump himself into a conversation with a fan or an unwanted sales pitch. Whenever he gets that sidled-up-to feeling, he picks up his pace.

One of the more popular booths has authentic private investigator sex-surveillance photos. The photos are not pretty, most shot from some distance using a telephoto lens. Ordinary people—private citizens—having sex in hotels, in cars, behind shopping malls, in libraries. Blue dots cover faces and smaller blue dots cover identifying characteristics like tattoos, scars, unique piercings.

Wax says to the guy working the booth: "This stuff isn't really pornography."

"Then call it erotica," the guy says.

"It's not that, either," says Wax.

"But I'm not looking for a fight," says the guy.

Wax moves on, thinking, *It's not porno or erotica if the folks involved aren't trying to make something pornographic or erotic. It's just sex, and that's nothing to look at.*

***

TED ROMLING: I wasn't surprised to find out that Wax was doing personal appearances after he announced his retirement. It made sense to me. He needed money to hold himself over until *All Doll* came out, and the truth is, I think Wax always liked doing meet-and-greets. But once he started cranking out features, the roadwork was reduced to four or five appearances crammed into three months, with maybe a week to ten days of R 'n' R in the middle. Not all strip club appearances. Wax'd do the conventions and some in-stores. It became very lucrative for him. I bet personal appearances accounted for more than a quarter of his income during years two and three of his career. And he didn't have to make too many appearances. He hit select cities: Las Vegas, New York, Miami, San Francisco. Mammon almost never traveled anymore. He had to stay back at the Hacienda. Look after the business.

ERIC B.: There are only a few adult male performers that aren't repulsive. Wax Williams and a few very new young guys who've been doing the videos for Mammon that Wax would have done if he weren't in semiretirement.

JON Z.: Today I had him sign my copy of *DormitOrgy*, box *and* tape—nobody ever thinks to have stars sign the tape itself, but you have to. Wax was very polite to me and he was also very nice to the other people in line. But I can tell that he doesn't suffer fools gladly. I saw that he spotted the rude people in line and he was a little cold with them. Sure, he signed their gear and thanked them for coming to see him and all that. But he didn't go out of his way to connect with them, like he did with me today, and like he did when I saw him last month in Atlantic City.

COLLECTOR ONE: There are precious few official nude Wax Williams portraits in circulation. This is Mammon's doing. He controls the incunables market, releasing limited edition prints to his favored collectors. He's done the same thing to a smaller extent with small distribution videos. You can find pirated copies of all these materials, but the quality is really lacking and they are not collectible—no original labeling, specious production standards, grainy videos dubbed from dubbed video dubs, and bad printouts of poorly scanned photos.

LYLE MAMMON: So Wax signs a few hundred pictures of himself and charges these folks $18 per photo. Do I have a problem with this? Yes, I do. I paid for the photos that he's hawking. Every time we'd do a photo session, I'd pay for everything—the photographer and assistant, studio time, prints and negatives. And then when we'd sell them, I'd get half of the total sales. I did some math to figure that each photo cost me approximately three dollars. We'd sell them for—as he does now—eighteen bucks. Wax got nine and I got nine. But really I only got six. I never complained about that arrangement back when we worked together—notice how I said worked together, not back when he worked for me. I figured my six bucks would have been zero dollars if I had never met Wax. I looked at those three bucks as my cost of partnership.

***

Up in his hotel room, Wax turns up the heat as high as it will go, but he still feels cold. He collects the small soap bars from the bathroom and begins carving with a new pair of nail clippers he bought at the store in the lobby. He uses the needle from the hotel's complimentary travel sewing kit for detail work. First he carves a fire engine, then a spotted Dalmatian dog, and then a fireman's hat. Since he is a convention attendee, the pay-per-view porn in his room is playing for free. He scans the menu of movies until he finds one of Renee's, a new one called *Sweeping Beauty.* He selects it with the remote and stretches out on the bed to watch. He becomes happy when she appears on the screen, dressed as a servant girl in a low-cut dress made from dingy rags. She sweeps a dirty floor into a fireless hearth. Her face is still beautiful, and he sets to carving a bas-relief profile of her into his last bar of soap.

Before he can finish, there is knock at his door. It's Ty Boyce. "I wanted to let you know that some old friends are also in town, working the convention," he says.

"I figured," says Wax.

"The Handles are here, Joel and Eva. They're having a soiree after hours on day two of the convention. Advance showing of *All Doll* for retailers. They have inquired about your availability to make a personal appearance."

Wax considers the request briefly, then says, "Why not."

"They'll be happy," Ty says. "I can hear Joel saying, 'That's so grand of Wax.'"

"Who else is here?"

"Janna SayQua is here. She'll be at the Handle's party, too. Lyle's here, of course. I haven't seen him yet. No messages from him. Eva Handle says he's been very low key about this convention. He doesn't have anything else to sell—just *All Doll*—but he's letting them run the show."

Wax says, "They thought they were running the show when we shot the thing."

"Also," Ty says, "have you heard anything about the gangbang?"

"What gangbang?"

"Renee is scheduled to film a gangbang here at this hotel later this week, after the convention. And there's a rumor going around that you'll be in it."

***

RENEE SALMON: People always ask me if Wax Williams was the love of my life. I tell them that he was the love of *this* life for me. And maybe he was the love of a past life, too, because we have a past together. We just never had a future. The older I get, the more I realize that everything I do is guided by my past lives. We are born and born again. Sex is the connector.

SHEILA K.: The special viewing section was worth the fifty bucks. Wax's tent was so much better than the other ones. His had better lighting inside and it smelled nice. Like incense. Like cinnamon toast.

COLLECTOR TWO: Almost all of the private viewing tents at the convention are occupied by starlets. Mostly very newly minted ones. Their tents are about instant photos and air kisses. No photos in Wax's tent. He's been known to hug some of the ladies in line, but only when he's got his robe on. He's the only male performer who sets up a tent. The lines outside his tent are always the longest.

TANYA K. (SHEILA K.'S SISTER): What I like about Wax the most—aside from his unit—is the sweet attitude he has. It's like he doesn't belong here at this sleazy thing. This sleazy, sleazy show with all these bimbo cunts and whack-offs. He's above it all—though he doesn't act superior. And that's the way he seems in the videos, too. Like he's the one guy in the room who isn't on the make, and like he wouldn't be a porno actor if it weren't for the fact that he has to because what else can he do with himself and his big unit.

SHEILA K.: They limited the number of viewers in the tent to six at a time. That meant, to me, that Wax was always the seventh person in the tent, which is a good use of numbers, good numerology.

ERIC B.: I remember thinking that there should have been a security guard in the tent with Wax. He could have really been exposed to danger in the tent with so many strangers—and there were some real freaks at the show. If I had what he had, I'd be afraid of what people might do to me. He has so much to lose. He should be more protective of himself.

TANYA K.: I was surprised that Sheila and I were the only girls in the tent during our viewing. The guys viewing with us didn't seem queer at all, but I don't know what they were doing there if they weren't. I mean, if I was a guy and I had a normal-size unit, I wouldn't pay fifty bucks to go stand in a tent and look at some naked guy with a big unit.

SHEILA K.: We had five minutes in the tent and Wax was totally nude most of the time. He had a robe on at first—just a hotel terrycloth robe, but the white of it was glowing in the lighting they have inside the tent. He opened the robe slowly and all eyes fixed at his waist—and below. His big unit did a slight swing side to side as he pulled the robe off his shoulders. My heart was in my throat, and I could feel my face getting hotter. My cooch was getting so wet. I was glad I was wearing a thong because, very casually, I was able to hike it up just a bit to give myself a tight camel-toe wedgy in the front that pressed right on my clit.

JON Z.: I had heard that the viewing would be with Wax's cock inside, like, a long glass box. But I guess they only have to do that in certain states. So I was prepared to see him on view in a box, like a mausoleum-type thing. I was caught off-guard. I haven't seen a naked guy standing in front of me since shower time in high-school gym class.

TANYA K.: He's so tall and his legs are perfect. He has such a tight set of buns. Lots of guys go to the gym and focus on their chest and abs and arms—all upper body stuff. Wax is built right from head to toe, and I was thinking that it's very smart of him to develop his legs so good since there's such a focus on him below the waist. Everybody's always looking at his big unit, so he was smart to get his legs worked up so good.

ERIC B.: In a way, the viewing was too long. I became uncomfortable about midway through when the two women we were viewing with started moving around. They were a distraction. I think we all should have stood still until Wax put his robe back on and left the tent. These women—they stepped behind Wax and looked at his ass, which I thought was very odd. And they looked up close at his feet and hands, and at his cock, of course.

TANYA K.: The music was just right. The other tents all had bad porno music on. Wax's tent was playing some light piano music with nature sounds in the background—running water from a little stream and birds singing and crickets talking back and forth. It made for a nice mood, relaxing. It was just loud enough to drown out all the sounds of the convention outside the tent.

ERIC B.: I kept looking at his face. I didn't want to have him see me staring at his cock. I wanted to make eye contact with him in the tent because I didn't earlier in the day when he was signing my stuff. He seemed just as shy as me. But he had asked me if I was going to stay for the special viewing. I told him yes, though I hadn't planned on it, and I didn't even have enough money to go. I ran from the autograph session to the ATM in the lobby of the hotel, and I took out enough money to get in line for the special viewing.

LYLE MAMMON: I know the guy selling tickets outside of Wax's tent. His name's Marty Flynn. Used to do a little work for Ted Romling whenever he was in Vegas. Marty is not a smart man. I've heard it said that he'll watch a TV even when it's off. Anyway, Marty is surprised to see me standing in line—or maybe he isn't. He probably knows enough to know that I'm on the outs with Wax. So when my turn comes, I ask Marty if I can buy six tickets and go in alone. The fat chick in line behind me gasps. "What a great idea," she says. Marty says about the same thing, and he sells me six tickets. I give him an extra hundred bucks for being a sport, and he ushers me inside.

WAX WILLIAMS: I could hear Mammon outside the tent, talking to the ticket collector. He didn't sound like himself. He was subdued. He had a file folder under his arm. He was wearing an *All Doll* baseball cap. "Every good story ends in court," he muttered. "Looks like that's where we're headed, Wax." I thought he was trying to tell me that he was planning on suing me. But he was shaking my hand so energetically, and it seemed that he wanted to turn the handshake into a hug. He looked like he was about to cry.

***

"Wax. This is bad. We've got a lawsuit on our hands. Fucking kid blew his cock up. This is so bad. We're getting subpoenaed. They want to take depositions."

The file folder contains a letter from an attorney representing an eighteen-year-old boy who injured himself badly while using the Wax Williams Length-MaXXXer System—a penis pump manufactured and marketed by Mammon Films Ltd.

"Look at the pictures, Wax," Mammon says in a weeping voice.

In the photographs—six pages of black and white photocopies, three photographs on each page—the head of the boy's penis is torn almost entirely from the shaft. The hair on his thighs and scrotum and belly is matted with blood.

"They claim we didn't provide adequate instructions for proper use of the product."

"I thought it came with a how-to video," Wax says. "We shot a video, Lyle. Me using the thing. Me showing another guy how to use it."

"They claim that the video had no instructional value. They claim it was included to add prurient interest."

"Is this kid still alive?" Wax asks.

"He's suing us, so yeah."

The talk outside the tent became hushed when Mammon entered, the folks next in line trying to overhear as much of the conversation as they could.

Wax scans through the letter trying to find a dollar amount. "How much do they want from us?" he asks Mammon.

"Ten million."

Wax wonders if he'll be responsible for paying half of whatever the court awards. If that is so, he'll be back in the business again for sure. His exit strategy, still only half-formed, will have to be abandoned. No way he could retire.

"What do you think he'll settle for?" Wax asks.

"We're not going to settle," Mammon says, tears gone from his voice. "No fucking way. We settle with this douchebag and every fucking needledick who bought the thing will be suing us. No, no, no, Wax. We fight this thing."

Marty Flynn sticks his head inside the tent, whistles quietly. "Time's up."

***

LYLE MAMMON: Nobody likes to be the bearer of bad news. What made telling Wax about the lawsuit even harder was the fact that I had no solution to offer. I couldn't tell him how we could fix the problem because I didn't know what to do next.

SHEILA K.: I think that the vibe in the tent was just right because it was warm inside and the light was a little glow of black light above and soft floor lights pointing to where Wax was standing. It had a dreamlike quality.

TANYA K.: Leaving the tent was like coming out of the theater after a matinee—the sunlight is blinding. You're in the tent with Wax and the music and the mood lighting. And you step out into the auditorium with all the other people and the other tents and booths and there are posters for new porno movies hanging up, and you realize how special those moments inside Wax's tent were.

SHEILA K.: I wanted to go to the special viewing a second time, but my sister said no.

TANYA K.: We did stick around after our special viewing to watch the women in line behind us come out of the tent after their special viewing. The looks on their faces. I imagine that's how we looked when we came out of the tent—all lost and looking like we just had sex.

JON Z.: I'm not gay, and I never have been and I won't ever be gay. I'm just not and I think that it's wrong. But I like Wax Williams. I like his movies and I like the magazine work that he's done in straight porno mags—I won't buy the gay magazines that run his pictures. I came here today because I wanted to meet him. To see him up close. He shook my hand after he signed all my shit. He didn't think I was a weirdo, and I could tell that he liked me. I'm not crazy enough to think that we're going to be best friends, and if I ever go see him at another trade show he probably won't even remember me. But he was nice to me today, and I bet he will be nice to me again if our paths ever cross in the future.

SHEILA K.: In the end, when all was said and done, the whole thing just made me horny. My sister and I had only booked one room in the hotel and that wasn't going to work. I had to check into my own room afterward because I wanted to be alone with my new Wax dildo.

TANYA K.: I felt the same way—except I didn't buy a dildo. I wanted a real man. I didn't want to do myself in a hotel room.

ERIC B.: I can't wait to write in my journal on the bus ride home. I want to write about what I saw and I'll probably post something tonight at Wax's web shrine. What will I say? I'll say he shook my hand and the autographs he wrote for me are perfect. He used a silver marker and he signed in the exact spot I wanted on all the pictures. He made a very big E for Eric when he wrote, "To Eric with my sincere regards, Wax Williams." I'm also going to write about the lack of security in the tent and even at the signing booth. I'll be careful about how I describe the lack of security—I don't want to give anybody any ideas. But Wax is so willing to put himself out there, to be there with his fans. Something bad could have happened to him. Any of those women could have dropped down on their knees and taken a bite off his cock. Someone could have bitten it right off.

GENE DOERR (OWNER OF A THREE-STORE CHAIN OF ADULT BOUTIQUES IN CENTRAL OHIO): The release party for *All Doll* was expected to be the highlight of the convention. Lots of excitement around that movie for a couple of reasons: it has been about a year since the last Wax Williams feature release, the Handles have a good track record for producing edgy stuff with high production values, and the new girl who was playing the doll was attracting a lot of attention. It's going to be a guaranteed seller and it will bring folks into the stores and they will invariably buy another tape or two, maybe even a novelty.

ELAINE DOERR: The invitation that we got for the *All Doll* party was the only reason we came to the convention. We were going to skip this year, but we couldn't miss that party.

JOEL HANDLE: We had special invitations printed and we got them to our retailers a few weeks in advance of the convention. Somebody got a hold of one and made a bunch of counterfeit invitations, which I'm told were getting sold at the convention.

LANNA SAYQUA: This is my first convention. I'm loving it. Everybody seems to know me already, and *All Doll* hasn't even dropped yet. I've been so busy. My spread in *International Pink* is out next month. I have three other features ready for release once *All Doll* is out. I'm hitting the road this summer, feature dancing at select gentlemen's clubs on the East Coast.

JOEL HANDLE: We know *All Doll* is going to be big. It screened well with reviewers at all of the trade magazines, and we've got over twenty thousand paid pre-orders. We took our time with it when we were editing. We created this shot of the doll exploding in the lab and we intercut it as counterpoint to the deflation sequence.

JANNA SAYQUA: One reviewer complimented me on my melismatic moans.

DEE-DEE SHARP: In addition to their suite on the top floor, the Handles had reserved the suite opposite theirs and rooms on either side of both suites. Basically, half the rooms on the top floor. The doors to each room were wide open and the party moved freely from room to room. That made it harder to check invitations. Lots of crashers wearing tourist T-shirts in the hall.

EVA HANDLE: Everybody with an invitation to the party gets an *All Doll* goody bag, which contains an *All Doll* baseball cap, an *All Doll* baby T-shirt for the girls and an *All Doll* hooded sweatshirt for the guys, a three-minute video preview of the feature, and the latest catalog from Mammon Films Ltd. The girls' goody bag also comes with a brand-new barbie doll. And the boys' goody bag comes with an inflatable sex doll.

JOE WHEELER: I lent Joel and Eva the remaining transparent dolls so they could display them at the party in Vegas, alongside one of the dolls that was actually used in the film.

JOEL HANDLE: We had a gelatin sculpture made in the shape of a sex doll. It is cherry flavored but virtually transparent—just a little pinkish. People will love it and we'll let them start gobbling it around midnight.

CORA KNIGHTLY (SENIOR CURATOR, WAVERLY ANTIQUE DOLL MUSEUM, PUEPTON, NEVADA): We get lots of requests to install remote exhibits of our collection. Typically from schools, the Girl Scouts and from trade associations that stage conventions in Las Vegas for female-owned and operated companies—the ladies who sell cosmetics or craft materials out of their homes. The Handles were the first vendors from the adult entertainment convention to make an inquiry with us. My board of directors was inclined to refuse the request, but the Handles were willing to pay us triple our standard rate, and they paid to insure the exhibit while in transit and on display.

LYLE MAMMON: I wasn't really in a party mood. But I had to go. Some of our best clients were going to be there. I had to make an appearance, thank our retailers for their business, talk up *All Doll.* All I could think about was the lawsuit, the photos of that kid. I locked the letter and the photos in the safe in my room at the Cashpot and headed upstairs. I gave the DJ a hundred bucks to let me hang out behind his setup. It wasn't as loud back there, and it was up on a small riser, so I could see out over the party.

EVA HANDLE: Mammon was not his usual mock-avuncular self at the party. He looked like a ghost with nobody to haunt. I didn't know it at the time, but I guess he was depressed about the lawsuit. He usually tries hard to be the life of the party. But he was very quiet. Instead of talking too much, like usual, he was drinking too much. And that just made him sleepy.

BEN BETTIS: The Handles' suite had two walls of large sliding glass doors that opened onto a beautiful deck. But it was too windy to let anybody outside. There was a triangle-shaped hot tub that was stocked like a fishing pond with a half-dozen naked women—local strippers that Joel hired to put on a show for the invited guests. Their job was to maintain a high giggle quotient and to bring an eruption to the party every so often by kissing each other or enticing someone new into the hot tub. They were posing and playing for everybody to see, bobbing up and down in the hot tub, all wet shoulders and tits. Beyond them you could see the neon lights of Vegas, blurry but bright in the steamed windows that formed a corner behind the hot tub. I wished I had my video gear with me. The scene would have shot well.

***

Mammon watches the hot tub girls closely. He tells the DJ that there are two kinds of lezzies: the kind who fuck girls because it turns them on and the kind who fuck girls because it turns men on. "I like both kinds," Mammon says.

***

GENE DOERR: My wife and I, we don't swing. Sure, we earn a good living selling adult videos and sex toys, but we're one hundred percent monogamous. Which is okay, of course, with our colleagues. Going to a party with porn stars and producers and other adult-oriented retailers doesn't challenge our monogamous lifestyle, and by the same token, nobody at the party held back their lifestyle pursuits on our account. What I'm trying to say is that we planned on leaving the party before it turned into a flat-out orgy, which is where most people at the party seemed to be taking things.

JOEL HANDLE: One thing that prevented the party from going completely over the top was the fact that there was still one day left to the convention. Everybody had responsibilities of one kind or another the next day, so they could only overdo it to a certain extent. And every once in a while, when things threatened to get out of control, I would remind folks that they had work to do on the convention floor in the a.m. "Hate to be a party pooper, but don't forget that you're on duty tomorrow."

ELAINE DOERR: Going to a wild party really gets a married woman charged up. You don't have to partake. You just have to be receptive to the energy. You see a young handsome man and woman meeting for the first time and you bear witness to their attraction for one another. You watch them as they dance. You watch them step into the hot tub together, nude, and they begin kissing, and maybe they're touching each other under the bubbling water line. You are there in that moment with them and you are with your longtime lover and what you have to do is steal a bit of that new lovers' energy and bring it back to your room. Which we did. It's not that different from watching a triple X movie with your spouse. Same principle.

JANNA SAYQUA: Wax arrived a little before midnight. I knew that he was there before I saw him because I heard people buzzing about it. "Wax is here. Wax is here." Word must have been spreading through all of the rooms, because the party started moving into the hallway.

***

"You're a fucking doll," Mammon says when he sees Janna. She sits on his lap, kisses him on both cheeks. "Oh, Lyle," she says. "I'm so happy to see you." She is chewing grape-flavored bubblegum. She has the whole pack in her mouth, so she has to chew with her mouth open. She drinks champagne inexpertly, watches herself on one of the flat-screen televisions that is playing scenes from *All Doll.*

***

BEN BETTIS: Some Hollywood party people in attendance. Familiar faces, but nobody of special note, not even B-listers. A whole slew of party girls like the ones in the hot tub, but not paid to be there. There was also one semi-famous artist who is known for painting abstracts that are very phallic.

JOEL HANDLE: There was a tension between the retailers and the performers. Both groups seemed to think that the party was for their benefit. So you had the retailers waiting for the performers and the assorted hot bodies—invited and uninvited—to do something outrageous... something pornographic to make the party a real porno people party.

EVA HANDLE: The party was chaos. But I like chaos occasionally. Lyle kept getting drunker. He said to me, "We're all guilty of our disaster." And then he said, "That's Shakespeare—*King Lear.*"

LYLE MAMMON: It was a great party. If you like piss-warm beer. Wax came. Wax went. I don't remember.

DEE-DEE SHARP: When Mammon drinks, he's the human equivalent of a self-basting turkey. He sweats out the alcohol quickly, but then he, like, reabsorbs the alcohol that he has sweat out and soon every pore in his body is drunk.

JOEL HANDLE: I didn't want a really good party to devolve into another game of keep Mammon away from Wax. They were both invited to the party. They're adults. They have their own relationship. I had my film. It was going to drop big. I don't give a fuck if they back into each other at the wet bar. Luckily, Lyle passed out at the DJ's feet round about the time that Wax arrived.

***

Wax steps off the elevator and the party greets him loudly. His presence registers immediately on the entire floor. He hears his name spoken over and over again, sounding, in total, like a suppressed roar. He had planned on avoiding a noticed entrance. Over the loud dance music he hears his name being said again and again. Different voices. Same name. Wax Williams. Whispered, delivering the news of his arrival. And sometimes said loudly. Whooped. Hollered. WAX FUCKING WILLIAMS.

A little dude pushes through the crowd and thrusts his hand at Wax. He shakes the little dude's hand, feels how cold his own hand is by comparison. Then more hands appear in front of his face. A few women throw tight, low hugs on him.

He sees Dee-Dee Sharp—the first familiar face. He wants to ask Dee-Dee where Joel is, but he thinks it might be rude, like he was looking past her.

***

Dee-Dee Sharp: Wax looked good. His hair was as long as I've ever seen it. He was wearing a new leather jacket, black. He looked good. Kissed me on the top of my head. He gave me a wonderful hug. People don't know this, but a lot of times Wax will tuck his dick up into his shirt instead of into his pants. It's true. So whenever I hug him, I lean my chest and shoulders into his six-pack abs and try to cop a feel. He's on to me, though, so he never lets me hug him for too long.

***

Party mission: find Joel and Eva. Talk to the guy they want him to talk to. Meet the faces that he will meet. Everybody wants a quick picture. There are only three other men in the room who are over six feet tall.

A girl hands her cell phone to Wax. "My girlfriend loves you. Say hello." He says hello into the phone, hands it back to the girl.

"Where's Joel? Where's Eva?"

But nobody seems to know who he's talking about. He asks one of the topless waitresses where he can find the Handles. She seems puzzled by the question. So he describes Joel. "Short man, small glasses, uncombed hair, corduroy pants, probably a sweater on."

The waitress points to a closed door inside the crowded suite at the end of the hall. Then she hands him a tall glass of champagne, kisses him on the lips—a Happy-New-Year-type kiss. The partiers closest clap their hands and raise their drinks to toast the kiss. They hold up their glasses to clink with his champagne glass. He sips after each clink, automatically, and the glass goes empty. He turns to look back at the elevator. He's not halfway to the Handles' suite. The waitress swaps his empty glass for another full one, kisses him again. Then a few women nearby line up to kiss him. The drunker ones grip tightly around his neck, trying to pull him down deeper into their kisses, which have gone from "Happy New Year" to sloppy French. The men at the party begin to peel away from the group surrounding Wax, and so he's able to quicken his pace down the hallway. The women match Wax step for step as he makes his way toward the Handles' suite.

Inside, the party is louder. At the center of the suite is a u-shaped leather sectional. All of its cushions are on the floor. The men and women on the floor appear drunker than the ones in the hallway. A few of the men are sleeping and two of the women are nude. Wax steps carefully between supine bodies and at last he stands in front of the only closed door in the room. His sense is that Joel and Eva are on the other side of the door, so he knocks and enters.

"So glad you could come," Joel says, and Eva, standing beside her husband says, "I knew you wouldn't miss this."

On the unmade king-size bed are a few boxes of *All Doll* videos and DVDs. There's an open laptop on the small round table near the floor-to-ceiling window.

Wax knows he needs to say something more than hello, so he says, "Quite a party."

Joel says, "This movie is going to sell a million copies."

Wax thinks how much Joel sounds like Mammon, then he hears—as if on cue—the toilet flush. But the man who emerges from the bathroom is not Lyle Mammon. Joel makes a quick introduction. "Wax. Want you to meet Sean Bothers from the Gloss Corporation."

Wax read an article about Bothers a few months ago in *Adult Video Showcase*, an industry trade magazine. Bothers had come to Gloss from the retail music industry.

"Wax," Bothers says after turning their handshake into a shoulder-bumping half hug. "I've heard from many, many people that *All Doll* will be your last film."

Wax nods, sees in his periphery that Joel and Eva are also nodding.

"And though it is certainly a loss to the industry, your retirement presents us with an opportunity to market this film in a special way. Your swan song. Your parting shot. You see what I'm saying?"

Joel and Eva take position standing behind Wax as Sean Bothers speaks. They each have a hand on Wax's back, and Wax senses how badly they each want to answer Bothers' question.

"He's done it all," Eva says. "Nothing left to prove."

"Needs to seek new adventures," Joel says.

"Wax," Bothers says. "Wax, I need to have an assurance from you that *All Doll* will, in fact, be your last film before I make a commitment to stock this film in all of my stores..."

"Wax," Joel cuts in. "Sean's firm operates over seventeen hundred adult superstores in North America."

"I need your assurance, Wax," Bothers begins again. "I need to know that you won't be coming out with a new title next month or the month after that."

"Right," Wax says.

"You can only have one swan song," Bothers says with conviction. "From what I've seen, *All Doll* would serve perfectly as your swan song. It's a movie that could sell strong for a good six months. Maybe even a year. But it will be just another dirty movie if you decide to make a comeback in six weeks and try to sell another title."

"This is my last," Wax says with no equivocation.

Sean Bothers extends his right hand again for another shake of Wax's. He has a hard smile on his face. He looks fiercely happy. His hair is gelled. His eyebrows appear to have been weeded or waxed into shape. His eyes examine Wax's face, plainly looking for a smile returned. Wax smiles finally, turns to show his smile to Joel and Eva. They smile at the sight of Wax and Bothers. Their smiles show relief, something else.

"I want a picture," Bothers says, producing a disposable camera. "A grip and grin for my office. My little wall of fame." He tosses the camera to Joel. "Hold that button on the front to warm up the flash."

Bothers still has a grip on Wax's right hand. He's pulling Wax closer to his side and preparing to reach his left arm around Wax's shoulder once Joel Handle has the flash warmed up. Eva stands behind Joel. She seems to want to step into the photo, but she's keeping herself in check.

"Eyes and teeth," Joel says. The flash fills the room. Joel advances the film and takes another shot as soon as the flash is ready again.

"Okay," Bothers says. "I have only one more request, Wax."

Anticipating the request, Wax takes off his coat. Joel and Eva exchange a quick look. Eva takes the camera from Joel. Wax unbuttons his shirt and his cock drops out, bouncing forward and hanging over his loose belt. Bothers and Joel Handle exchange surprised looks. Eva snaps the picture.

***

Back in his room, Wax checks the heater to make sure it's on full. He unpacks a rubber sheet from the bottom of his suitcase, lays it on the center of the bed. The champagne from the party is just a headache now. He's thirsty, but he's afraid to drink a glass of water so close to bedtime. He stretches a top sheet across the rubber sheet, tucks it in neatly on both sides of the big hotel bed. It's been two weeks since his last accident, but he doesn't want to take any chances.

He fills the oversized two-person tub in his bathroom and gets in slowly. He resists the urge to close his eyes. He feels tired—weary—but not ready to sleep. He tries to recall a few of the faces he saw earlier in the tent. All eyes. Mouths agape. Stillness is what he tries to project when he's working a special viewing. He makes himself a statue, a display. He wants to be still again, in the warm bathwater, now that he's alone and the day is done. But he feels the cold of the room on his shoulders and he's afraid he'll wet the bed if he goes to bed now. He sinks himself chin deep into the tub and watches his penis break the surface of the water. He reaches with his left hand and brings it underwater. He begins to think about a few of the women at the party, feels himself begin to get hard. If he whacked off now in the tub, he might pass out and drown. That would be a fitting end for him, he thinks. Dead in a hotel bathtub in Las Vegas, his very last ejaculation floating around his ears.

Recalling Mammon's photos of the injured boy, he steps out of the tub and forces himself to pee. He's still half-hard, so he manages only a few drops. His penis feels cold in his hands. He remembers something Mammon used to say. "Only cure for the way you feel is a blanket and a pillow. If that don't work, find yourself a whore." Wax would choose the blanket and the pillow.

Once in bed under three blankets, he restarts Renee's new movie, *Sweeping Beauty*. She's being undressed out of her rags by three nude blond women who Wax believes are meant to be angels or fairies. Renee stands in an oak tub in the center of the room she was sweeping earlier. The blond angels are soaping her. He should be immune to this stuff, but he's not. The sight of Renee is a turn-on, but the thought of her doing a gangbang next makes him realize that he's still cold and suddenly very tired.

The last thought to cross his mind this night: there are a lot of hours in the day.

Consumer Profile

Single File

You begin your story on the plane with a writing exercise. You take a familiar, timeworn phrase and substitute a key word in that phrase. Model phrase: All politics are local. You write, "All sex is local." And you underline it. You have, now, a theme. Your story could have started a hundred different ways. The plane's as good a place (setting) as any. Your writing plan is to contradict the inherent wisdom of this new axiom. You are certain the events of tomorrow will help you do just that: All sex is *not* local.

You're headed to Las Vegas. You are a preapproved participant in what has been billed as the world's largest gangbang. Renee Salmon, star of over two hundred full-length adult features, is going to have sex with as many as one thousand men, depending on how many show up and how many of those who show up can prove that they're not diseased and can then obtain and maintain an erection. You will be one of those men, you're sure, as you took the precaution of preregistering on Renee Salmon's website, and you obtained the required (and clean) DNA PCR test for HIV and a clean RPR test for syphilis. The erection part is another matter. It's been a while.

You will not be paid for your time or services. In fact, the whole thing will end up costing you over a thousand dollars, totaling airfare, hotel, meals, and all of the other miscellaneous charges that you have agreed to and the ones that will pile up along the way.

You plan on writing about your sexcapade. Yes. You plan on seeking publication under a pseudonym. You figure you can write as well as the next dumb fuck, and you know you can damn well write better than any of the idiots who will be with you in line. You're not sure if the event will be covered by the press. You hope not. You want your story to be the only thing written about this gangbang. An insider's exclusive. You majored in journalism your first two years of college but later switched to computer science. Your dream was to be an action journalist, travel the world and take on action-packed writing assignments. You learned enough to know how to put together an article. You learned the inverted pyramid. You learned about vetting and corroborating sources. At the gangbang you'll get quotes from a number of your coparticipants, conduct follow-up interviews with the video distributor—Renee's look-alike sister, Eva Salmon-Romero, and her husband, director Paulo Tomas Romero—and maybe you'll even try to get a brief interview with Renee Salmon. But once the writing is done, you don't know exactly how you should go about approaching media outlets with your story (a nerd's eye view) of the world's largest gangbang. Media outlets are starved for content—right?—particularly the electronic media sector. Your story would be sensational and you would work all the angles. But this isn't the first (or second) video gangbang, and none of the others were covered on TV or in regular newspapers. Perhaps it's not newsworthy.

Just before landing, you start writing about yourself from the second person point of view, and it makes you happy. It's the distance (perspective) that will make you part of the story but also removed from it. Then you begin seeing yourself as the guy sitting a few rows up. You're a lot alike, you and this guy. You're both about the same age, same height and build. The guy in front of you is a little better dressed. A little better put together in a fashionable sense. Newer clothes. Better haircut—or maybe just better hair. Better job, more than likely. Better car. Better house. Probably a better ex-wife. Life would be better if you were this guy, you think. But you don't write that or dwell on it for too long.

Vegas is weird. You knew that it would be. You can't believe the heat. The Hotel Cashpot (your taxi driver called it the Hotel Crapshoot) is loud, even though they don't have a casino, just a dozen rows of slots and video poker crammed into a narrow room behind the lobby. It seems all the guests (your characters) are there for the gangbang.

Your room is small and it has two double beds. The TV is bigger than the one you have in your apartment. The room has a sliding glass door that opens to a balcony overlooking the little pool at the hotel next door. You're on the third floor. The gangbang is going to be held on the seventh floor. Tomorrow. You fall asleep without unpacking or eating dinner.

Next morning, you take the stairs up to the seventh floor. There's an un-uniformed security guy standing on the landing at the seventh floor. He asks if you're here for the event and you tell him yes. "Sign in Room 701, and then get in line," he says. He's not unfriendly, just all business. After you register, you look at your randomly drawn number, 463. You think of a long, long line at the deli. But it's good that you've drawn a high number. You'll get to see more of the event as you wait your turn.

You survey the line as it begins to form. It's a very straight line and the guys are quiet. But it's early, and these punctual participants (early birds like you) are clearly the good citizens of the gangbang. The outlaws, degenerates, and wackos—all of them keeping their own schedule—are sure to arrive later, adding, you hope, color (conflict) to the content of your journalistic endeavor.

Each man is handed a sheet of paper upon arrival with a short list that is titled "Gangbang DOs and DON'Ts": DO have your certified HIV test—dated within the past ten days of this special event. DO sign your release form and make sure you have valid photo identification that will confirm that you are least 18 years of age. DON'T smoke in line. DON'T drink alcoholic beverages in line. DON'T behave in too loud or boisterous a manner while you are waiting in line—we're all guests of the Hotel Cashpot, and we are subject to their rules of decorum.

You hear someone say that Renee Salmon is in Room 725. You remind yourself that your assignment is to use words to draw a mood map of the event.

The guys immediately ahead of you and behind you are a safe group. No real scaries, you're relieved to see. Regular guys. Guys like you. Porn buyers. Unhappily married. Divorced. No girlfriend or prospects. Late twenties. Early thirties. No studs, but most of them in fairly good condition. None of them really ugly, but none of them could be called handsome. In fact, not very many of the guys waiting in line with you are handsome. Some of them are downright funny looking. Many are short. A couple of them are fat—big guts, manboobs, heavy legs. They don't appear to be self-conscious of their size and shape. There are a few young, musclebound guys. *Prison muscles,* you think, *Penitentiary physiques.* There is a midget in line, too, a square-shaped three-footer with a rolling walk. He struts up and down the line, drunk, making a show of himself, trying to fire up his taller gangbang cohorts.

The line moves slowly at first. It feels like the thing hasn't gotten started. You don't feel like you're part of something that is underway yet. You feel like you're still in the preamble of it all. It seems like things could get called off at any minute. It doesn't seem like the thing's going to happen. You wonder if gangbangs are against the law. But guys are going into Room 725 in groups of three to five.

DON'T linger on the premises after you've had your turn.

You can't get close to any of the TV monitors that are showing the action in 725. Too crowded. These are guys who like to watch, and it must be a trip for them to see this gangbang (their gangbang) in the same way they've seen all of the other video gangbangs that they must have rented.

Questions go up and down the line. What's she doing in there? How many guys has she done so far? Is there a time limit when you take your turn? Few answers come in return. It's a long hallway.

You note that most of the guys who have their shirts off have tattoos. They are all much younger than you. Waiting in line is tough on them, you can tell. No patience. They're antsy, bouncing on the backs of their heels, stretching their arms over their heads. Could be they're on drugs.

You didn't tell anybody what you were going to do. You took the time off from work without saying where you were going or what you were doing. You packed your bags and got on an airplane and started writing and waiting.

A group of three frat boys with Greek letters shaved into their chest hair are surprisingly quiet as they wait. A pretty woman in a tight business suit asks if anyone's interested in pre-ordering the video—$19.95. A deluxe limited edition costing $300 is also available to participants and fan club members. The limited edition video set of the gangbang will include a companion eight-hour documentary assemblage of footage that won't make the final cut of the two-hour commercially released version of the gangbang. You place your order with your VISA.

Many of these guys waiting in line are what you would call subcultures of one.

There's a guy in a Nixon mask. A guy dressed like a gladiator. A few guys in Elizabethan garb—like they just came from ye olde Renaissance Faire. Two guys are dressed as the Blues Brothers, Jake and Elwood. All of these guys want to make a presentation of themselves, make a statement with their appearance. Extremists of many sorts. There are a lot of near misses. Some aren't as well thought out as others—like the guy who is dressed in a cop uniform but who clearly is not a police officer. He is asked to leave because he is making everybody nervous—including the producers and the crew.

One guy has a tube of lubricant with him, still sealed in its box. He explains that it's the only lube on the market that he isn't allergic to. He says he will let Renee Salmon open the package herself, so she'll know that it is clean, that it hasn't been tampered with. But then he says he'll use whatever lube and condom that Renee Salmon wants him to, even if it gives him a month of crotch rot.

The plethora of quickie chapels in Vegas makes you think you should write about your wedding one day. But first you want to write about your divorce, which should be part of this story.

One guy is sweating so much that he's beginning to make you sweat. You can't look at him he's sweating so much. He's the human equivalent of a self-basting turkey. Standing there, sweating. He looks like he might pop. Somebody should get him a cold beverage, you think, before he dehydrates and sweats himself dead.

A guy arrives dressed like a magician—top hat and cape. He is wearing white gloves. He starts doing sleight of hand, halfhearted card tricks. Others in line applaud him quietly. His audience is mostly the old farts, who all look alike. Trim golfer types wearing their retirement well. White-haired. Tanned. Jocular. Rich-acting.

You're bothered briefly that the men standing in line don't deserve the pleasure that awaits them, yourself included. They don't rate sexual satisfaction, and they know it—you know it.

You met your wife in college. She was a shy girl. She was pretty, but she dressed like an old lady because it was fashionable (or maybe it was anti-fashionable). At the time, you thought it was important to have a funny haircut, but she convinced you otherwise and told you that there was no reason why you shouldn't be her boyfriend.

One night online you had Renee Salmon all to yourself on her website. No other members signed in. You didn't know what to type. She was naked, staring from the small screen, motionless except for her slow, measured blinks. You weren't alone with her for long. Two names appeared below yours in the lounge and they began typing commands at her immediately. She came to life with their instructions. And you watched.

You duck into the men's room every once in a while to jot down notes. What are you writing? An article? A short story? A fictionalized memoir? Won't know until it's done.

A new worry now—that you won't get beyond this point. Standing in line. Waiting. Dumb look on your face. Half a day's growth of beard, itchy. Thinking of your ex-wife and then of the lawyer who handled your divorce. Both named Jennifer. Both tall. Both blond and disgusted by you. Lawyer Jennifer told you to give wife Jennifer whatever she wanted.

A few guys look like adventurer types. Lining up today at a gangbang in Las Vegas. Later this month they'll be standing on the infield of the raceway at the Indy 500. Others like them are simple Las Vegas gambler types. Card players who like the odds of this gangbang.

A guy with a microphone looks into one of the video cameras and says, "They have come from far and near." He acts like a TV newsman, but you recognize him as a porno actor named Bo Ring. His cameraman keeps him in a tight shot, then does a quick pan down the length of the line. They're looking for good quotes from the guys in line for added documentary footage. If you're asked for comment, you will comply. But you will not give your real first name or say where you're really from. And you will alter your voice slightly in pitch and modulation. You will need to be able to deny it if some friend or relation ever puts you on the spot. You will need to be able to say, "That's not me waiting in line at that gangbang."

The new guy three guys ahead of you has a funky smell. He isn't talking to anyone, but his armpits are silently conjugating a single verb: stink, stank, stunk. He looks like he might lose his nerve and back out. He has the kind of facial hair that you see on post-op female-to-male transsexuals. His whiskers are sparse but long and grow a little too regularly beneath his chin and along his jawline. Sure enough, when you're watching your video of the gangbang two months later and see this guy take his turn, you see him reach around behind himself, deep into the crack of his ass, to activate some hydraulic or inflating device to create an erection for himself.

Your wife had two best friends—one ugly and one fat. Neither had husbands, so they concentrated on you—your flaws. The fat one always seemed to show up around dinnertime. And the ugly one—she should really be called the alcoholic, ugly one—often called late at night from bars for a ride home. They both had your wife's ear and kept track of your shortcomings. The divorce was their idea. You're sure of that.

A bellman wheels a large tray of ice and towels down the line. They're icing Renee Salmon's vagina to keep the swelling in check. The wheels on the cart squeak.

You're surprised that so many of the guys in line are just naked, as if they arrived that way. At least a dozen. They just stand there, naked, waiting their turn. You hadn't planned on getting completely naked even when you took your turn with Renee Salmon. You had planned on getting by with a simple unzipping, or maybe stripping down to your boxers and T-shirt.

There is a buzz of activity at the front of the line. You try to look over tops of heads. You want to see into the room, to see the bed, which someone has said is round. But the video crew is blocking your view. Every once in a while, one of the cameras breaks away from the bedroom action to pan down the long hallway to show the line. Participants have been instructed to wave and whoop it up during these moments. So you clap and whoop. Sometimes the clapping and whooping gets rhythmic. But it always dies down quickly when the cameras turn to face the other way. Loud. Then quiet. You're thinking, *I'll never forget this,* and that is what you will say if a camera finds your face and you're asked to comment on the day or its events.

When your wife left you, you didn't know what to think. At first you didn't want anyone to know. Then you wanted to tell everyone, and admit that it was mostly your fault.

A trio of porno actors—young studs—show up four hours into the proceedings. You recognize them all, but know the name of only one of them: Jeremy Spoken. He's been in a few of Renee Salmon's videos, but the other two haven't. They walk directly to 725 and the door is closed behind them for a good half hour. Their arrival adds fuel to the rumor that Wax Williams—in Vegas for an autograph session at the porn convention—will be Renee's special guest and one-thousandth lover of the day.

Two grossly fat men—both of them 400-plus pounds—arrive together but then take up places in line about twenty feet apart.

You visited Renee Salmon's website every night to see if the date and exact location had been confirmed or changed or reconfirmed. You bought your ticket for Vegas the night you received a "hold-the-date" e-mail with instructions for participants. Your VISA was billed $349 for two nights at the Hotel Cashpot.

The line moves forward again and you can measure the distance between yourself and Renee Salmon's room by the number of doors. You do a gut check every other door. Are you meant to be here? Will you get off, or is the situation too much, mentally? There are now more than seven hundred guys in line.

DO help yourself to a complimentary condom.

Guy coming out of Room 725 says, "She blew me. She said, 'Your cock is mine.' She said, 'Weary traveler, rest your ball bag on my chin.' I didn't hold out for very long." A friend of his gives him a big bear hug and says, "This guy's got a dick as skinny as a swizzle stick."

You try to recollect some of your best bedside patter to entertain Renee. She loves to laugh and you love her laugh. Her famous giggle. She giggles in all her films. A review of her performance in *Mirror, Mirror* referred to her as the "highly risible Renee Salmon." You had to look that one up, and when you found out that it meant someone who laughed easily, you saw how apt that reviewer had been in his description of her. Your fantasy has always been to tickle Renee Salmon into a giggle fit until she pees herself. She hasn't done that yet on video. One time you wrote on Renee Salmon's blog: "Tickle squirm and tickle sweet feet and giggling shrieks and do you from behind."

Someone brings out a deck of cards. Las Vegas.

Your silliest written-down thought of the day: The room ahead with the round bed. Boudoir ultimate or abattoir finale?

Someone says, "There's guys in line blowing each other." And that's when the shouting starts. A tough-looking guy in front of you turns and gives you a hard look, as if to tell you that he is tougher than you and that he will drop you if you're one of the guys in line who's blowing guys. *Fuck him,* you think, and you give him the same look he's giving you, to signal to him that you are just as disgusted by this news as he is.

A guy wearing a white turtleneck and holding a clipboard against his chest addresses the men in line, "Gentlemen," he says. "Please keep in single file." He has a whistle hanging around his neck. The line gets straight.

You've altered your appearance in a several ways. You've grown a goatee. You've bought tinted contact lenses. You've parted your hair down the middle, even though your hair fought it. You put two large rings on your right hand. You bought three gold chains. You're wearing a clip-on diamond stud earring that doesn't require piercing. You have shaved your chest. You look like another character from the movie of your life. But your face is your face, and your name is on the list of participants that the producers are keeping. A good detective could prove you were here, but you can think of no reason why anybody would go to great lengths to prove that you have taken part in this gangbang. Who would care? Not your ex-wife. Not your dead mother and senile father. Not your sister living in Canada. None of your crazy Rhode Island cousins.

One guy says, "This line is getting longer." Another guy says, "The universe is expanding." You think about your writing exercise—all sex is local.

Ten guys up, a petite redhead is working the line. She stands in front of a heavyset black dude. She has a roll of condoms in one hand and cash in the other. She's naked, blowing guys for twenty bucks. She appears drunk. And there's another girl working the line from the back. A blond—medium build with a plain face and a waitressly manner. Nice lingerie. She's giving stand-up lap dances—at least that's all you can see.

There's a loud exchange between two guys about their deli numbers: both have numbers that say 696. Each guy says that he's number 696 and that the other guy's is number 969. Their argument is brief. Neither wants to get ejected. That's what they're calling it if you get told to leave.

Ejected. The skinny guy in the white turtleneck said, "If you can't behave in line and keep it together, you're gonna get ejected. No gangbang."

Just as you are let into the room, Renee Salmon says she wants to take a break. The cameramen put down their cameras. The sound guy takes off his headphones, lowers his foamy boom and leans it against the wall.

DON'T say or do anything to freak out Renee Salmon—that's your primary DON'T.

Renee Salmon stands up from the circular bed, a nude moving little statue of a woman. And you're in the room with her. A beautiful face and a perfect shape. Perfect skin. A tiny nose. A wide mouth. A tiny chin. Perfect implants. Large nipples—pink—shaped like plungers. A slim waist. Long legs for a petite woman. A high-sitting ass. Tiny feet. She wants a cigarette and some ice water. She puts on a short satin robe. She lights her own cigarette. You sit on the bed and stare at her, smiling. "Your moment will last longer than the others," she says, and you say, "I'll make it last forever." Someone in the room—the soundman—chuckles. Renee Salmon blows a long stream of cigarette smoke at the ceiling. You ask, "Will you smoke a thousand cigarettes today?" She doesn't answer your question as she steps past you to the bathroom.

As soon as Renee Salmon touches you, a wave of embarrassment comes. You feel the foolishness of the thing, and you feel the beginning swell of regret. Your actions are being recorded. This image of yourself, naked from the waist down, a beautiful porn star working to arouse you with her hand, is being captured and preserved forever. Are you frightened? Ashamed? You know that it is unlikely that you'll make it into the two-hour version of the event that will be sold everywhere. But it is all but guaranteed that what you are about to do will be part of the eight-hour companion tape. Then Renee Salmon's robe is off. The cameramen shoulder their cameras. The big lights circling the bed come on. You note the smell of her cigarette, her perfume. She has put fresh makeup on her face and along her neck. You kiss her right shoulder. Someone standing in the doorway says, "He's up." The condom goes on easily. Her hands are so small. "You be nice to me," she says in a breathy voice close to your right ear. "Be sweet, cause I'm so sore." You're going to fuck a porn star. But what's your editorial stance? You had meant to square away the motivations of every guy in line before your turn came. But you didn't. You gawked at them. And now you're gawking at Renee Salmon. You remember her described in a magazine article as a woman indifferent to attention, but a seeker of it nonetheless. She places your right hand on her left tit and her hand makes your hand squeeze. With her other hand she puts your penis in position to enter her. You tell yourself to enjoy these few good seconds of plunge, pure plunge. Then you begin to doubt your understanding of what you're experiencing. She does a squeezing, kegelly thing once you're inside and that's about all it takes. You think of the words "motile arousal," which you've read somewhere recently. You think of her vagina—the way you've seen it close up in her videos—and when you come it is a pouring thing.

Chapter 12

In Deposition

Complainant's deponents: Robby Rolland, who hurt his penis using the Wax Williams Length-MaXXXer System; Robby's aunt, Paulette Lucille Rolland; Robby's doctor, Nora Banner; and Robby's attorney, whom Mammon has dubbed Churchill.

Codefendants: Lyle Mammon, President and CEO of Mammon Films Ltd.; Wax Williams, adult film performer and endorser of the Wax Williams Length-MaXXXer System; Joe Wheeler, New Day Engineered Plastics, manufacturer of the Wax Williams Length-MaXXXer System; and their esteemed counsel, Anthony Vincent, Esq. (some people call him Tony but an equal number of people call him Vinnie).

Date and location of depositions: withheld

Deponent One: Dr. Nora Joyce Banner

Anthony Vincent: Do I detect an accent, Doctor? Are you British?
Dr. Banner: I am from England. That's where I was born.
Anthony Vincent: Are both of your parents British?

Dr. Banner:	English? No. My mother is from India. My father is Jamaican-born. I grew up in England.
Anthony Vincent:	Would you describe yourself as Anglo-Indian?
Dr. Banner:	I could be described that way. Am I being asked to describe myself?
Anthony Vincent:	Would you?
Dr. Banner:	I've never said Anglo-Indian before. But if I had to check a box on a form, that could be a box that I could check. Most people assume that I am black. I think of myself as a brown girl from England.
Anthony Vincent:	And what box would you check for race?
Dr. Banner:	I suppose black. I don't understand this line of questioning.
Anthony Vincent:	I'm trying to establish your identity. Country of origin is part of that. The information that I'm trying to gather here today is meant purely to establish who you are, how you came to be involved in the case. Can you confirm for the record your country of origin?
Dr. Banner:	I think that I just did that. Perhaps we could have my first answer to your first question read back. In addition, I've provided both attorneys with my name, address, medical training, license information, immigration status, passport number, and a lot more. I thought that all had been...
Anthony Vincent:	We could move this along faster—be done sooner—if you answer the questions in the simplest, most direct manner.
Dr. Banner:	I understand that, sir.

***

LYLE MAMMON: Robby Rolland's dick doctor? Oh, she was hot. Very hot. Exotic. Light-skinned black woman with a British accent. Her hair was close-cropped with little pointy tufts, and she had it dyed a yellowy blond color. Almond-shaped eyes. Full lips. She was a bit flat-chested, but she had great shoulders, a very nice neck, and a very tight ass—what I call a neat seat.

***

Anthony Vincent:	May I ask why you are practicing in the United States?
Dr. Banner:	Because my specialty is microsurgery, with a special interest in reattachment procedures. I decided to practice medicine in a place where I would be kept busy doing what I love and what I trained to do.
Anthony Vincent:	So you chose (name of midwestern American state withheld)?
Dr. Banner:	Yes. It's situated centrally to a number of key agricultural areas, and there's also an active industrial base—heavy and light manufacturing. There's quite a call for my services in this part of the world. There may be other places in the world with similarly high rates of industrial accidents, but the United States represents the place where my services have the most market value.
Anthony Vincent:	What is your understanding of the particulars of the civil action for which you are being deposed today?
Dr. Banner:	I understand that I am to present my medical findings and how I helped Robby by reattaching his penis after it became partially severed upon use of the penis pump.
Anthony Vincent:	And have you performed similar surgeries in the past?
Dr. Banner:	Yes.
Anthony Vincent:	Could you declare how many?
Dr. Banner:	How many?
Anthony Vincent:	Yes. How many patients have you treated who required this surgery?
Dr. Banner:	I anticipated this question, so I consulted my files prior to this appointment. I had performed penile reconstruction and/or penile reattachment surgeries on twelve patients prior to Robby Rolland.
Anthony Vincent:	What percentage of your work would these twelve procedures represent?
Dr. Banner:	Certainly less than one percent. Mostly my work is hands, arms, digits. Also legs, feet, some toes. I also get a lot of ears, for some reason.

Anthony Vincent: What were the causes for those twelve penile surgeries?

Dr. Banner: Industrial accidents. Agricultural accidents. Mostly unhappy events of heavy machinery meeting human flesh.

Anthony Vincent: How did those procedures differ from the one you performed on Robby Rolland?

Dr. Banner: Extent of tissue damage was not as great in Robby's case.

Anthony Vincent: How so?

Dr. Banner: Well, an injury to the penis in an industrial accident includes irregular tissue damage, a lot more pulling and twisting. Robby Rolland's injury was a straight partial severing caused by a faulty vacuum mechanism.

Anthony Vincent: Dr. Banner, please state the facts of your treatment only. Please do not offer your conjecture as to what caused the injury, whether it be a faulty product mechanism or improper consumer use of the product.

Dr. Banner: I will.

Anthony Vincent: Thank you, and please continue.

Dr. Banner: Yes. Robby's injury was quite a straight wound. It was also a comparatively clean wound. No dirt, extraneous debris, torn clothing. He'd lost quite a bit of blood though, since his penis was in an engorged state of arousal.

Anthony Vincent: If you had to rate a degree of severity for this case, how would you rate it on a scale of one to ten, with one being the least severe and ten being the most severe?

Dr. Banner: The severity of the injury is high in all cases in which a man comes to harm this serious. I can rate the degree of severity only in terms of the challenges involved in the treatment of such cases. With that said, factors like the age and general health of the patient have impact.

Anthony Vincent: Of the twelve penile reconstruction and/or reattachment procedures that you have performed, was Robby Rolland's the most severe, the least severe, or some place in the middle?

Dr. Banner: I would have to say in all honesty that his procedure was the easiest of the kind that I have performed.

Anthony Vincent: Does your work also include cosmetic surgery?

Dr. Banner: Not in the sense that I'm enhancing the appearance of a person who hasn't already suffered some physical injury. Not plastic surgery. But certainly I often perform several follow-up surgeries on patients to improve the look of their affected areas, their reattached flesh. Procedures to reduce the appearance of or eliminate scar tissue. Also, follow-up surgeries will be done often to improve function of affected areas, make improvements if therapies are not working.

Anthony Vincent: And Robby Rolland required a follow-up procedure, didn't he?

Dr. Banner: Yes. I operated a second time on Robby to sort of straighten him out. He was pointing out of direction. To the right, if I remember correctly.

Anthony Vincent: How would you describe the overall recovery that the patient has made?

Dr. Banner: He's made an excellent recovery. He is not sterile, nor is he impotent. He's regained I would guess 90% of his erectile function. He has lost some length, which is certainly ironic given his reasons for buying the pump and the claims that the pump advertised.

Anthony Vincent: Could you define how much length he's lost?

Dr. Banner: It would be hard for me say, but I would say that we sacrificed tissue that would account for an inch in his erect state. He has reported some pain during arousal since the operation. He was initially prescribed medications to curb arousal, but we do not want to eliminate the nocturnal arousals that occur in all men to ensure proper blood flow. Mr. Rolland is committed to his therapies, which have been significant. His therapy routine is draining.

***

Deponent Two: Robert Edward Rolland

Anthony Vincent: Mr. Rolland, we're discussing today the specifics of the action that you have brought against the manufacturers and marketers of the Wax Williams Length-MaXXXer System. That is, Mammon Films Ltd., New Day Engineered Plastics, and Wax Williams. I want to establish the facts of your purchase and use of the product. These facts are crucial to the civil action that you have initiated. Do you understand what is expected of you today?

Robby Rolland: Yes.

Anthony Vincent: Before we begin, I want to say that I have reviewed the photographs of your injury prior to the initial surgery, photographs taken after the initial surgery, and a series of photos taken after the second surgery, which have been submitted to the court. Your injuries were devastating, as we can see, and I want to applaud you for your courage and perseverance in recovery.

Robby Rolland: Thanks.

Anthony Vincent: Why did you buy the Wax Williams Length-MaXXXer System?

Robby Rolland: I wanted to be like Wax Williams.

Anthony Vincent: In what way?

Robby Rolland: I wanted to be big.

Anthony Vincent: Prior to the purchase, were you aware that other similar products were available on the market?

Robby Rolland: Yes.

Anthony Vincent: What made you select the Wax Williams Length-MaXXXer System?

Robby Rolland: It seemed like the best. It was the biggest.

Anthony Vincent: What made you feel that it was the best? Was it the most expensive?

Robby Rolland: It cost about the same as the others they had in the store. I thought it was the best because Wax said so on the box it came in.

Anthony Vincent: You bought the system, brought it home, and began using it. Correct?

Robby Rolland: Yes.

Anthony Vincent: Did you read the instruction manual?

Robby Rolland: It came with an instructional video with Wax using it.

Anthony Vincent: Did that videotape provide good instruction for the use of the system?

Robby Rolland: I suppose. I couldn't hear very well what the announcer was saying because I had the sound down low in my room.

Anthony Vincent: Why is that?

Robby Rolland: I didn't want my aunt to hear it.

Anthony Vincent: Was Mr. Williams' demonstration of the product adequate?

Robby Rolland: I suppose. He really couldn't fit into it very well.

Anthony Vincent: Did you fit into it?

Robby Rolland: Yes.

Anthony Vincent: Can you describe what occurred when using the product?

Robby Rolland: I started pumping and felt the thing start pulling. I had to stop after a few pumps to get my hair out of the tube. Then I started over and kept pumping.

Anthony Vincent: Did you feel any pain, discomfort?

Robby Rolland: Not at first. I just got harder and saw that I looked veinier.

Anthony Vincent: And then what happened.

Robby Rolland: I kept pumping and then I got dizzy and then I heard, like, an explosion, like "pnnish"—I don't know what happened next. I guess I passed out. My aunt said she came up to see what was the matter because she heard the explosion. And I didn't answer her, so she ended up busting into my room to see what the sound was.

Anthony Vincent: The photo of the pump shows that it didn't explode or crack. Was the sound that you heard the sound of your penis exploding?

Anthony Vincent: The doctor told me that it didn't really explode. It tore in the place below the head. It didn't tear completely in two.

***

ANTHONY VINCENT: The attorney for Robby Rolland was a Winston Churchill look-alike. Very stately. All the men wandering the halls of their firm look like statesman from a bygone era. I thought maybe some reenactment of the signing of the Treaty of Versailles was being staged in another deposition room.

***

Deponent Three:	Joseph Alan Wheeler
Churchill:	Can you state your name and occupation for the record?
Joseph Wheeler:	My name is Joseph Alan Wheeler. I am President and CEO of New Day Engineered Plastics, a plastics manufacturing company based in (name of small New England state withheld).
Churchill:	What is your relationship with the defendants?
Joseph Wheeler:	My company has partnered with Mammon Films Ltd. to produce a number of adult novelties.
Churchill:	Such as?
Joseph Wheeler:	Inflatable dolls. Dildos. Pocket pussies. Butt plugs. Cock rings. Penis pumps.
Churchill:	You produce other pumps?
Joseph Wheeler:	Yes.
Churchill:	Is there anything unique to the manufacture of the Wax Williams Length MaXXXer System?
Joseph Wheeler:	The inside of the cylinder is molded from a cast of Wax Williams' erect penis. It is about nine inches longer than the standard pump and approximately three-quarters of an inch larger in diameter.
Churchill:	The packaging says that the product is assembled in the United States? Is it produced entirely in your plant?
Joseph Wheeler:	No. We manufacture the cylinder, but we outsource for the pump and its parts.

Churchill: Are all of the product's component parts manufactured in the United States?

Joseph Wheeler: Our vendor for the pump mechanism is based in South Carolina. They hold a series of patents for vacuum pumps, but I believe their manufacturing is offshore. I want to say China.

Churchill: But the product is assembled entirely in your plant?

Joseph Wheeler: Yes. It is assembled and packaged in our plant.

Churchill: Mr. Wheeler, does your company have a formalized quality control program?

Joseph Wheeler: Yes. This particular product was tested extensively before we went into production, and each unit is subjected to a battery of tests, which includes a pressure test at 30,000 PSI. Additional QC includes visual inspection of each assembled unit prior to packaging.

Churchill: And do you track and maintain a record of products returned for defects?

Joseph Wheeler: To my knowledge, we have not received any returns on this or any product. I believe that adult novelties have a very low rate of return. If an end user purchases an adult novelty and the product fails to perform, he or she simply discards it and does not seek a refund or replacement.

Churchill: Is that a personal conjecture, or are you quoting industry research?

Joseph Wheeler: It is what I believe. Our consumers often have to overcome embarrassment and shame to work up the nerve to purchase one of our products. If the product fails to meet their expectations, I believe they simply take the loss rather than seek a refund or product replacement.

Churchill: Final question. Can you tell me the total manufacturing cost of the product, including materials, parts, and labor?

Joseph Wheeler: First manufacturing run, unit cost for my company was $2.34. That was for 10,000 units. Second manufacturing run was for 20,000 units, and since we didn't have any setup costs or systems costs, we got the per unit cost down to $2.10.

***

Deponent Four: Paulette Lucille Rolland

Anthony Vincent: I understand that you've raised Robby on your own.

Paulette Rolland: Yes. His parents aren't in the picture. I don't know where they are or what they're doing with their lives, but I made a promise to my brother to take care of Robby and I've lived up to it.

Anthony Vincent: That's very commendable. He's a very nice young man and we all feel badly that he had this unfortunate accident.

Paulette Rolland: Well, I did get a letter from Mr. Williams saying that.

Anthony Vincent: If you've shared that letter with your attorney, we would like to see it, too.

Paulette Rolland: They have it. You talk to them.

Anthony Vincent: Thank you. I am pleased to know that Mr. Williams sent a note to Robby to wish him well in his recovery, though it should not be viewed as an admission of responsibility or liability. It was a kind gesture from a celebrity to a loyal fan. That's how it was meant, I am sure, and I hope that that is how you and Robby read it.

Paulette Rolland: (No verbal reply. Waves hands to indicate that the topic is closed.)

Anthony Vincent: Ms. Rolland, we just heard Robby describe what happened on the night of his accident, but it would be helpful to hear from you in your own words what you witnessed—what you saw or heard or what Robby might have said before or after he had his accident.

Paulette Rolland: I have things that I want to say before I answer any questions.

Anthony Vincent: That would be fine with me. I assume that you have discussed this with your counsel.

Paulette Rolland: I want to say that Robby was the very best boy until he started watching the dirty videos. And I don't know how he got his hands on the dirty videos, but he did and then he changed. And this contraption that he bought, I don't know what possessed him to buy it or where he bought it. I wish I'd known he brought this into my house. I wish I could have known, because I would have busted it into pieces.

Anthony Vincent: Thank you. Is that all?

Paulette Rolland: I brought photos of Robby from the 4H and FFA that I want you to see.

Anthony Vincent: You'll forgive me my urban upbringing, Ms. Rolland, but can you tell me the 4H is and what FFA stands for?

Paulette Rolland: 4H stands for Head, Heart, Hands, and Health. He raised a prizewinning sheep when he was just a sophomore in high school. And FFA is the Future Farmers of America. He studied sheep raising with the FFA.

Anthony Vincent: I'll describe the photos: The first one is a younger Robby with shorter hair and he is standing behind a little lamb and he's making rabbit ears behind the lamb. Very funny. And the second photo is Robby with the same lamb, I assume, though both lamb and Robby look a little older and the lamb has been shorn of its wool in this one.

Paulette Rolland: That boy loved that little lamb. Used to sleep out in the barn with her the night before every competition.

Anthony Vincent: Thank you for sharing the photos with us. Since you've mentioned videos, can you elaborate on that subject?

Paulette Rolland: I found several dirty movies in his room when I was cleaning it up after his accident.

Anthony Vincent: Is several five or ten or more than that? Can you confirm a number?

Paulette Rolland: I would say there were a hundred or so.

Anthony Vincent: Note to counsel, we may need to get a list of these movies...

Paulette Rolland: Who you talking to?

Anthony Vincent: Excuse me. I was making a note to Robby's attorney that these videos might be relevant to this action. So we'd appreciate a list of the titles of these videos.

Paulette Rolland: What do you mean?

Anthony Vincent: I can take this up with Robby's counsel. It's possible that something he saw in one of those videos is partly responsible for his accident.

Paulette Rolland: How can that be?

Anthony Vincent: Well, you yourself said that Robby changed when he started to watch these movies. If that is so, my clients should be able to examine the contents of those tapes to see if we can learn more about what might have influenced Robby before he had his accident.

Paulette Rolland: Makes no sense. The damned contraption was defective.

Anthony Vincent: That is what Robby and you contend. But it is the belief of my clients that Robby misused their product, which led to his unfortunate accident. That is the difference of opinion that we are trying to resolve with this case.

Paulette Rolland: But you can't have the movies because I threw them all away.

Anthony Vincent: Thank you, Ms. Rolland, for sharing this information. This is something that I should take up with Robby's counsel. Let's move on, shall we?

Paulette Rolland: Let's finish up.

Anthony Vincent: I think we can move quickly, since you are very direct and I have only a few questions for you. Can you remember anything out of the ordinary that might have happened on the day Robby had his accident?

Paulette Rolland: No. I drove him to and from his job at the taffy plant...

Anthony Vincent: Excuse me. Did you say taffy plant?

Paulette Rolland: Yes. Robby works at Cummings Taffy Confections. He pulls taffy.

Anthony Vincent: So he went to work and came home in his usual fashion?

Paulette Rolland: Yes. And I fixed him dinner and we ate watching the news on the television in the living room. And after dessert he said he wanted to watch something in his room. I figured he wanted to watch one of his karate movies, so we said our good nights. Then about twenty minutes later I heard an odd noise from his room upstairs.

Anthony Vincent: How would you describe the noise that you heard?

Paulette Rolland: It was like a very loud popping sound, like when a light bulb blows as you turn it on. So I went up the stairs, and I could see that there was light coming from under his door. So I wondered what the sound could've been, so I knocked on his door. No answer. I knocked again and again. When he still didn't answer I tried the handle, but the door was locked. I was getting nervous when he wasn't answering. So I pushed my shoulder against the door and it opened pretty easy. It's an old house and the doors and the doorjambs don't really hold the locks anymore.

Anthony Vincent: Can you describe how you found Robby?

Paulette Rolland: He was passed out on the floor with his pants down to his knees. He was bleeding pretty bad. You seen the photos, right? Do I have to describe it?

Anthony Vincent: Why don't you say what you did next?

Paulette Rolland: Well, I could see that he was breathing, so I tried to wake him up. But he didn't rouse. The bleeding was pretty bad. I knew I'd have to call an ambulance, so I made the call. I wanted to get him dressed before they came for him. But he bled more when I tried to move him. I got an old towel from the bathroom and covered him. Then I saw that damned pump on the floor beside him. It was filled with blood. And then I saw what was on the TV. It was Wax Williams and he was completely naked and he had the same kind of pump hooked up to himself. I think I might have screamed then. I almost tripped on Robby rushing to the TV to turn it off.

***

TY BOYCE: What follows is what Lyle Mammon recounted to me after he gave his deposition. For some reason, his actual deposition file has been lost or destroyed. We all of us had our doubts as to whether this is what he was asked and what he said in response. But this is the only "record" of his deposition.

***

Deponent Five:	Lyle Mammon
Lyle Mammon:	Before we begin, may I ask one question?
Churchill:	I believe that my assistant has already confirmed that there is, indeed, an Applebee's Restaurant not far from these offices.
Lyle Mammon:	Very funny. No I have a question for you, sir.
Churchill:	Please. Ask away.
Lyle Mammon:	You got any Jews working here? I mean, I looked at the list of partners on your letterhead. You got like fourteen partners, and I don't see that any of the names are Jewish.
Churchill:	I cannot answer that question, Mr. Mammon. I simply do not know the religious persuasion of all the men and women who work in this firm.
Lyle Mammon:	Well, I'm a Jew.
Churchill:	Not that it matters, but I had assumed that you were Italian, like your attorney.
Lyle Mammon:	I'm an Italian wannabe. It's called pasta envy. Always wanted to be Italian. But you gotta be born Italian in order to be Italian. I was born a Jew. My parents were Jews. But they were bad Jews, especially my father. He was the kind of Jew that wears his yarmulke under his toupee. My mother wasn't much better. She didn't keep kosher. She swore like a trooper. She had affairs on my father. We didn't go to temple. We didn't celebrate the holidays. We weren't rich. That's the first symptom of being a bad Jew: poverty.
Churchill:	. . .
Lyle Mammon:	These are the jokes.
Churchill:	Our researchers completed a financial analysis that projects your personal net worth at close to fifteen million dollars.
Lyle Mammon:	What the fuck? Invasion of privacy.
Churchill:	This is a standard exercise in personal injury case. We

accessed only public records of your holdings and assets.

Lyle Mammon: So I got good at being Jewish. In spite of the fact that I am what you would call an unobservant Jew, I've made my millions.

Churchill: Earlier today, Mr. Wheeler established the unit production cost of the product. Can you confirm how much you paid Mr. Wheeler for each unit?

Lyle Mammon: $8.50.

Churchill: And the product sold at retail for $49.99.

Lyle Mammon: Yes. And we wholesaled it for $30.00.

Churchill: Nice markup.

Lyle Mammon: I had other costs. Such as production of the instructional video. Packaging. Warehousing and distribution. I think a lot of people bought the pump for the video, which is exclusively available with the purchase of the Wax Williams Length-MaXXXer System.

Churchill: I would like to ask you to look at a few photos and offer some comments on what you see.

Lyle Mammon: No thanks. I've seen your pictures. You want to see a Jew cry? You're trying to get me all discombobulated looking at those horror show pictures.

Churchill: Personal injury law is highly subjective. I want to make sure you've seen the evidence and understand the weight of it.

Lyle Mammon: I feel bad for that dumb fucking kid. I really do. But I don't want to make him rich just because he blew up his dick. My feeling is that that queer farmer was going to do some damage to his dick one way or another. Just so happens that he was sticking it in one of our products when he succeeded.

Churchill: Mr. Mammon, if I could break the Q&A for a moment for a comment. I'd like to say that there is a vast difference between liability and responsibility. In court we have to prove liability. With a pretrial settlement, we need only to convince the defendant of his or her responsibility. In a case such as this, once parties have agreed to participate in the deposition process, the course of resolution is almost always a cash settlement—because a settlement is in the best interest of both parties. You and your associates made a good deal of money from this product and stand to make a lot more. As I understand it, sales for this product could remain strong for several years. But if the details of this case received a full public airing in court and, subsequently, in newspapers, the facts of the case would most assuredly impact sales in the negative. Is the product unsafe? I don't think that's the question. It appears the product is soundly manufactured and has no defects. Have you provided consumers with instruction and direction to ensure the safe use of the product? That's the question. That was your responsibility to the consumer, and we don't believe that you have lived up to that responsibility.

***

Deponent Six:	Wax Hartnett Williams
Churchill:	I always like to begin depositions by thanking the deponent for his or her time. So thank you.
Wax Williams:	Thank you.
Churchill:	This is an important part of the civil process, as the testimony that we gather today from you and the other parties will help to guide us at trial, should this matter go on to court, or—and this is the preferred course—perhaps we will see a clear way to settle the points at issue that will be agreeable to both parties. I also want to commend you, Mr. Mammon, and your counsel for maintaining a private stance regarding this matter. Your celebrity and the graphic nature of Mr. Rolland's injury would make for a media circus if this personal injury action were to become public. I have to admit that, prior to taking on this case, I was unaware of your

work and your very successful career. But I polled a number of my colleagues at the firm, and I discovered that you are quite famous.

Wax Williams: Not for much longer. I've retired.

Churchill: Well, I believe that your fame will continue whether you're retired or not. But let's begin. You have licensed your name or your likeness for a number of products.

Wax Williams: That's right.

Churchill: Our researchers have documented two dozen adult products. Does that seem accurate to you?

Wax Williams: Yes. I suppose.

Churchill: Anybody ever advise you as to the risks of personally endorsing a consumer product?

Wax Williams: No, sir.

Churchill: How do these products generally come to market? Specifically, was it your idea to lend your name and likeness to a penis pump that is nearly twice the size of the next largest penis pump on the market?

Wax Williams: I don't know. I guess he...

Churchill: Mr. Mammon?

Wax Williams: Yes. He thought my name on it might help it really sell.

Churchill: So you took no part in the design of the Wax Williams Length-MAXXer System?

Wax Williams: No. A few prototypes had already been made.

Churchill: The inside of the cylinder is said to be molded in the shape of your erect penis. So how was a prototype produced without your participation in that particular feature?

Wax Williams: I guess they used one of the plaster casts that were made a few years back for the Wax Williams Mega-Dildos.

Churchill: How much have you realized to date, cash-wise?

Wax Williams: Nothing. Everything was put into an escrow account once we were informed of the lawsuit. Lyle had offered me the option of a one-time fee or a percentage of each one sold. I usually take the one-time payment because

	it's easier that way, and I don't have to hire an accountant to see if the percentage reported is accurate. But for some reason, I didn't this time. I took the percentage, thinking I'd get a check every once in a while.
Churchill:	The promotional copy for the Wax Williams LengthMAXXXer System claims that you used a penis pump when you were a young man. Is that true?
Wax Williams:	Yes. It was prescribed by my doctor.
Churchill:	Do you attribute the notable size of your penis to the use of a vacuum pump? Studies show that hyperemiation—penis enlargement via vacuum penis pump—provides short-term results at best.
Wax Williams:	I'm not sure. It was a long time ago.
Churchill:	In addition to the instructional tape that was included with the purchase of the product that you endorsed, we have footage that was edited from the final version of the instructional tape. I'd like to play a portion of that for you now.

***

Churchill points a small remote control at the television that sits on a credenza adjacent to the conference table. On screen Wax is having trouble inserting himself into the penis pump. He is able to fit not quite half his length into the long cylinder. Mammon steps into the shot. Laughing, he watches Wax struggle for a moment, and then he reads from a bound script, "As used by international adult film star Wax Williams." He looks once more at Wax, who is beginning to have trouble operating the pump action. Mammon takes it from his hands. "Put it away," he says. "Let your boner die and then we'll try again later."

***

Churchill:	We have more deleted footage of your attempts to use the product with similar results. Also, we contend that the actual demonstration that appears in the instruction video is edited in such a way that it is impossible

	to learn how to use the product. Would you say that the Wax Williams Length-MaXXXer System is a difficult product to use?
Wax Williams:	It's a bit cumbersome...

***

CHURCHILL: Mr. Williams initiated the settlement agreement. He offered to sign his share in the profits from the Wax Williams Length-MaXXXer System over to Robby. I understand that Mr. Mammon was amenable to do the same.

ANTHONY VINCENT: The terms of the settlement are confidential. I am allowed to say that no liability was assigned to New Day Engineered Plastics. All parties agreed that the product had no defects. Mr. Churchill and I collaborated on a document that provides for a shared responsibility for the license and use of the product. That is, the seller could have done a better job communicating instructions to the end user. And the consumer could have used better caution and control when he employed the product in its designed use. We crafted the language to reflect the goodwill of all parties. After the agreement was signed, we adjourned to Applebee's at the suggestion of Mr. Churchill. Robby's aunt did not join us, but Dr. Banner did—I think just to keep an eye on Robby.

Consumer Profile

Rat

Ona would talk about anything. There wasn't a self-conscious bone in her body. She would also flash her left tit at a person if she had to. She flashed both men and women. She told you that her left tit had hypnotic power. "But only at a low level," she said, "I can't rule the world with it." Kelly said that Ona was simply an exhibitionist. Then Ona said, "I'm not the one that's a porn freak." And they all turned to look at you.

Gail was a rapid blinker because she was dishonest. She wasn't even smart enough to make up lies that were believable. And she was not messed up. Ona said she was just acting messed, because she didn't have the imagination to do anything else with herself.

The second time Ona called you, you talked with her on the phone for two hours. Ona was so funny, but she listened, too. You could hear Ona exhale her cigarette smoke over the phone. You pictured Ona in an oversized robe with one of her long cigarettes pointed up towards the ceiling. You talked a bit about the other girls, but nothing mean.

Ona'd been to an orgy. She didn't partake, she said. She just watched, trying not to have any direct eye contact. It was a big orgy. Eight or ten people. And they weren't ugly. What amazed her was how quiet it all was.

She expected moaning and sex noises times ten. But, if anything, those ten people were quieter than the average twosome.

Kelly was in a good mood on the field trip to the museum. You were all impressed by how well she knew her way around, and then she let you look through one of her sketchpads. You had a five-minute giggle fit standing in front of a six-foot-tall marble sculpture that looked like a giant vibrator. Gail stepped up to it and pretended to hug it. She said, "How phallic can you get?" Then Ona shouted, "Wax Williams." Everybody turned to look at you.

It was supposed to be an informal group without a leader. But about midway through the first meeting, Ona took over. Which was a good thing. Groups that don't have a counselor to move things along can get bogged down on little things. But that hadn't happened yet.

Ona didn't swear. "Swearing is for men," she said. "It shows they have no vocabulary." She wanted the group to adopt a no swearing rule. Mostly everybody agreed and tried not to. Ona seemed pleased. When one of the girls would slip up, the others would look to Ona for a reaction. They expected her to go off, but she would always let it slide in a way that seemed forgiving.

Gail was the one that would always bring up the topic of sex. It got so everybody waited for her to get it going. She threw her head back when she giggled at their questions. But she didn't know everything. She always said, "You guys are a bunch of pervs."

They all said you were mysterious. You'd never been called that before. But before, all the people in your life knew everything there was to know about you. Now, everybody was new. It can be hard for you to show people what kind of person you are. You can never tell what people will think of you after you let them know something personal about yourself. It's best to just keep them guessing.

The overnights came every two days after the second week. They hooked you up to a heart monitor and a brainwave monitor some nights. There was a video camera high up on the wall above the narrow bed. Sometimes the room was too hot and sometimes you were freezing. You never got the same room twice. When you woke up from a dream it was hard to know where you were and if you were actually out of your dream yet. There were long questionnaires in the morning before breakfast. They took blood three times a day.

Ona made the best T-shirt. She used three packs of iron-on alphabets to make it. The girls all read it aloud when she showed it to them: *I am still a virgin. if i should die a virgin, would the first man to discover my dead body please give me a good and proper fucking. no matter how cold i am, bust my hymen.* The T-shirt was a gift to you. Ona told you to wear it until the offer was no longer valid.

Kelly was the one who realized the medication was affecting her sense of smell. Then everybody noticed it. And worse, it gave you all a smell. And it didn't matter how much perfume you put on. Nothing covered it. You all smelled the same. You all smelled like the medication you were taking. Which proved how powerful it was.

Jeannie didn't think the program was working for her. She felt the same way she always did. She said that even when she started to feel okay, she'd start thinking about how it used to be, and then that would make her feel like her old self. Later on, Ona said, "Maybe Jeannie's the placebo—she doesn't smell like the rest of us."

Five teenage girls who are strangers to one another cannot be thrown together and be expected to get along every minute of the day. It won't happen because it can't happen. You were more skeptical than your mother. You wanted ownership of your recovery, sure, but you weren't convinced that what amounted to a summer day camp for horny teenage girls was the right place for you.

You moved to Ampersand with your parents the summer you turned fifteen. They had no idea about the house's previous occupants. It wasn't until the first day of school. You were waiting at the bus stop, and some fat boy told you that Wax Williams used to live in your house. He said, "Wax Williams grew up in your house—he does porno." You had been able to dismiss the fat boy with a hard look, but soon you realized that everybody in your new school knew that you lived in Wax Williams' old house, and somehow that had become your new identity.

Sometimes the old women from the other study would wander into the day room. There was one, Mrs. Grieves, who always said, "There's caffeine in the decaf." That's all you ever heard her say.

Ona called you one day laughing her head off. "I just saw your planetary double," she said. "Your absolute look-alike," she said. "And he's a fifty-year-old Chinese guy."

The video camera was for everybody, but Kelly always wound up taking control of it. On one of the first overnights she snuck the camera into your suite and started taping Ona's every move. Ona loved the attention. She ate it up. She insisted that Kelly follow her into the shower and keep the tape rolling when she put in a tampon. The two of them acted like they were drunk or on drugs. They wouldn't include Gail, even though she kept trailing after them. When Ona burst into your room and jumped on you in the bed, Kelly shouted, "Hot lesbian sex."

You were the prettiest one in the group. Gail was kind of harsh looking. Jeannie was a little overweight, but sweet looking. Ona had the best body and the best clothes. Kelly didn't know how to put her makeup on right. She always ended up making herself look younger, which should not be possible.

Ona said the best way to get something out of your system was to rat on yourself. "It doesn't matter who you tell," she said. "Just tell somebody. Another person has to know about it before you can get over it and move on to the next thing."

They all had questions about your ex-boyfriend, Eric. You wanted to tell them all how weird he was. But when Ona saw his picture and said he was cute, everyone agreed. You couldn't think of a way to describe how he was weird that wouldn't sound like you were really the weird one. You didn't think they'd get it. You looked closely at Eric's picture when it came back around to you. You wanted to cry—it seemed like they all expected you to—but you couldn't make any tears. You told them he kissed good, left it at that.

Everybody in the group had your phone number, and you had theirs, but the only one who ever called you was Ona, and Ona was the only one that you ever called. You didn't know if Ona ever called any of the others. You didn't ask.

Gail said to you, "Don't get too buddy-buddy with her," meaning Ona. She said, "Ona's a lifer." But she wouldn't explain what she meant by that. It had something to do with the way Ona seemed so comfortable with the doctors, and how she tried to talk like them all the time.

You wanted to talk more in group, but your voice would always start to fade after a while. You'd get this choked, pressured feeling, and your glands would ache. The sound of your voice always bugged you. You just wanted to be quiet and listen to the others talk. They all had more interesting things to say, anyway.

Gail laughed at Kelly when she didn't know what a sixty-nine was. Ona said, "Leave her alone. She's only fifteen." You all got quiet then. Gail and Ona stared at each other until Jeannie, who hardly ever spoke, said,

"Six licks nine, and nine sucks six." You all laughed hard for about ten minutes over that.

In bed at night and unable to sleep, you worried. Worried that you would wake up in the morning and be a little girl again. Then worried that you should have been a child longer—a weird feeling of unfinished games. A recurring dream. A worry that you hadn't played enough with certain toys. You worried about books you should have read twice and kid movies that you watched too many times.

You loved shopping with Ona. Ona was good at figuring out what things would ring up to with tax. Once when you were at the mall, Ona pointed to a mismatched couple. The girl was gorgeous and the guy was very ugly. "Beauty and the Beast," she said. "He must be a master of hypnosis or have a really big dong."

The thing that got to you about Eric was that you could never blame him for anything. It was all his mother's fault. He was so into keeping things organized and in perfect order because his mother had made a neat freak out of him. His room was ridiculous, with all his stuff kept just so. He had all these shelves with his trophies, old model airplanes, baseball caps, and the little things he'd saved from his childhood. It was like everything was on display. He didn't like you touching any of his things.

Ona wanted to rat on herself. It was after the group was over, and she treated you to coffee. She kept squeezing your arm. "I sent away for a vibrator," she said. "It came yesterday." She said she brought the vibrator up to her face and pressed it to her cheek like the lady in the ad. Then she found batteries for it in her father's flashlight.

Ona liked playing the devil's advocate. She was good at it, too. She could see a topic from three or four different points of view. She deserved a TV talk show of her own. She got everybody to say things they didn't expect, and it wasn't just getting the other girls to rat on themselves. Most of the time it was positive. Gail tried to do it every once in a while, but whenever she did, it came off like she was badgering.

You would just hang up the phone when Eric's mother answered. She never gave him any of your messages, anyway. If his mother got to the machine before Eric, she'd erase your calls. You were sure that Eric knew this, but he didn't do anything about it.

All the questions were multiple choice. You could never give your own answer. Most of the time, the answers you had to choose from didn't come close to the way you wanted to answer. Gail said, "They already know the answers they want." She said she always gave the wrong answers because she wanted to mess with their results. Ona said, "Your wrong answers are figured into their results beforehand. They know you lie, Gail."

The day Jeannie quit the program, Gail talked about her. Everyone just listened. Jeannie's little brother died when they were both really young. He had cancer. The family was never right afterwards. Her mother drank. Nobody would ever talk about her little brother after he died. They never even visited his grave. Jeannie thought that if anything were to happen to her, if she ever got sick and died, her mother and father would just forget about her, too. So she tried to seduce her English teacher at school one day, but he turned her down and told her she shouldn't behave that way. Then she tried to get him in trouble, but another teacher had overheard everything Jeannie had said to her teacher, and she ended up just looking foolish.

Kids used to come up to you in the hallway at school and ask if Wax Williams had left anything behind when he moved away. One girl came up to you when you were opening your locker and said, "Wouldn't it be weird if you had his old locker, too."

The ad for nude models that Ona answered was for an amateur camera club. She tried to talk you and then Kelly into going with her. It paid eighty dollars an hour, and the men there just did it for a hobby. Sometimes their wives were there in the little studio. Nothing sick went on. You didn't have to do anything you didn't want to. You and Kelly both said, "No way." Ona only went twice. She said it didn't excite her like being sketched in the nude did.

Eric's mother had mouse feet. You would be alone with him in his room or in the TV room, and she'd appear without a sound. You'd be kissing or just about to kiss, and there she'd be. There would never even be any sound of footsteps. You'd just suddenly realize that she was there. She'd give you a look, and say, "Hi." Which meant, "I caught you."

Ona got bored with the group. All she ever wanted to talk about was this guy in her exercise class. One day Ona asked Gail why she didn't do something to correct her overbite.

You told yourself to just ride it out. "Contain yourself," the voice in your head said. "Don't act out." You knew how to be normal. You could look at normal people and see how they behaved, and that made it easier for you to be yourself. You weren't horny all the time—probably no more than any other girl your age. What threw you off was seeing another person do something that you couldn't comprehend.

Gail said she had an ex-boyfriend that used to make her look at pornography. She was trying to rat on herself. She thought she had to be shocking. She also said he had a gun, and that he etched her name and his with a heart onto a bullet and then fired the gun into the ocean. Everything she said had to be far-fetched. Like something from a movie or one of her books.

At one group meeting nobody talked at all. At first it didn't seem weird. There had been other times when it took Ona a while to get the ball rolling. But this time nothing happened. They all just looked through magazines. Not one word passed between them. The room was so quiet. The only sound was Kelly coughing every few minutes.

One afternoon you shot a game a pool against yourself in the empty rec room. You made a good break, though nothing fell. You sunk two stripes in a row, then a solid, then another stripe, then a nice run of four solids. You caught the stripes up to the solids, and the eight ball started looking bigger. You remembered how your father used to take you to the pool hall on Sundays. He'd toss his wallet onto the table and say, "It's all yours. Just don't scratch on the eight ball." You used to be so scared of that black ball. Then one day your father gathered the eight balls from every rack in the hall, spread them out for you on your table, and told you to sink them all. Sixteen eight balls on one table. You never scratched on the eight ball again.

Kelly disappeared for three days and you all thought she was history. She turned up at her father's house in Maryland, and he shipped her back. After that, her mother would wait for her in the hallway during the group meetings. None of the girls were allowed to sign themselves out anymore after overnights.

They didn't like it when you asked them questions. And they lied. Early on, when the shape of the pills changed, they said it was the same medicine. Even though the pills were bigger, they said it was the same dosage. They said the active ingredient was the same, but they added some kind of multivitamin so all the girls would have the same iron level. Ona said that was plausible.

Ona was the one who started the mud fight. They had moved the group meeting out to the courtyard on the first warm day. The grass was a little squishy in places, and the sky was kind of gray, but you found a semidry spot and sat down. You were all talking like you used to in the beginning. Gail had a letter from Jeannie that she read to everyone. Ona reached behind her and got a handful of mud, which she threw straight up into the air. When it landed on everyone, you all went after Ona with mud in your hands. You smeared her face and butt. Then it became a free-for-all. You piled onto each other and rolled off into the mud. When it started to rain, you all danced around in circles, holding muddy hands.

It was at the midway point in week eight that you got fed up. It never would have dawned on you to quit, like Jeannie had. But Ona told you the tests were going to get weird in the last few weeks. That's when you decided to rat yourself out to Ona and tell her that the videos they found in your bedroom weren't yours—they belonged to Eric. He had a bunch of Wax Williams videos and he wanted to watch them with you at your house. When you got caught, your mother thought you were some kind of porn freak. You said to Ona, "I think the only reason why Eric wanted me to be his girlfriend was because I lived in Wax Williams' old house."

Chapter Seven
Reductum Absurdum

TODD INSULIN: It was a wire story that ran in just about every newspaper in the country. The day after it ran, Wax became a hot topic on talk radio shows and late-night TV shows. A few columnists carried the discussion and analysis a little further, most of them trying to make it relevant to their favorite pet topics: taxes, big business, etc. Then a few reporters began to really follow the story. They interviewed performers in the adult industry, male and female. Got quotes from surgeons who said Dr. Banner was being irresponsible and that her patient was likely suffering through some kind of self-hating castration fantasy. A few reporters dug deeper and interviewed Mammon, Janna SayQua, and the Handles. They all seemed to be using the topic to increase awareness of *All Doll,* which Eva Handle described as the last full-length Wax Williams film.

DR. NORA BANNER: Wax called me about a month after I had given my deposition for Robby Rolland's case. He told me straight away what he had in mind. He wanted me to do a procedure to reduce the length of his penis. A most radical ablation. I really thought it was some type of joke. But he was completely serious.

***

It has been a muddy spring, slow to start but sweet once it did. He is living in a tent, camping along the Kancamagus River in New Hampshire. He has been there for almost five weeks and doesn't have plans to leave. He fishes each morning, hikes in circles throughout the day. In the evenings he reads from a field guide that was written about the area in the 1940s. An old passion of his has been reawakened: wildflowers. He always enjoyed wandering through the woods behind the Hacienda, happening upon small fields of untouched wildflowers. He especially likes daisies. He often hiked up to Lake Fortunate to skinny-dip late at night, usually alone but on occasion with one of the girls. He misses that now, but thinks he will never go back to Ampersand. A cold draft drifts up his pant leg. He feels his penis go icicle.

***

TED ROMLING: I learned from an article in the newspaper that Wax was going to have surgery to reduce the size of his penis. I got a call that day from Lyle Mammon. He wanted to know what I thought the fallout would be. I told him there wouldn't be any. It was a windfall. All plusses. The star performer in his stable had retired from the industry, but his retirement was making headlines all over the world. I predicted that *All Doll* and the entire back catalog of Wax's titles would sell like hell.

***

Day one he meets with Dr. Banner in her office after hours for a general physical. She takes a medical history, does some general blood work, gives him a stress test. "You're in excellent physical condition," she says. "Great score on your cardiac. Blood levels normal. You experienced no dizziness or pre-fainting symptoms."

She has dyed her hair a straw-colored blond since he first met her at the deposition when it had been a whiter blond. She has it cut shorter, too, but she still has the little twisted puffy points on the top. It looks like she's wearing a crown. She is a tiny woman, just a little over five feet tall. She's very slim. She is close to forty, he knows, but she looks much younger. A stethoscope rests around the back of her neck.

"I wish I had more medical background for you," she says. "But your files from childhood are what I would call scant."

"I didn't go to the doctor's much."

"You didn't go to the doctor's at all between the ages of three and sixteen. There's literally nothing in the way of well-child checkups, only a few dental records. Did your parents not care to know if you were healthy?"

Wax tells her that his parents didn't have insurance.

"Not true," she says. "The insurance coverage looks to be the same from when you were a baby right up through your treatment—and read the word treatment in big mocking air quotes—with Dr. Johnson."

Wax shrugs.

"Your most recent physical—three years ago—was just a horserace checkup. Your manager needed to get you cleared so he could use you to finance some real estate deal."

***

The thought of reduction first occurred to Wax when he worked with Suzie Glow on *Blond Lust.* She had a truly spectacular rack—42" double D—and her hips were slightly wider than her slim waist would have predicted. But she kept it all under control. She found a balance, moving carefully and knowing how to dress herself. She had a pretty face, but for some reason Mammon didn't consider her A-list.

"I got these implants too big," she said.

"Reduction," Wax suggested.

"No," she said. "You can't unring a bell."

***

Dr. Nora Banner: Medical professionals are deriding me for performing this reduction procedure on Wax. They say that I'm doing it to gain a reputation and to expand my practice. It's foolishness. How can gaining an international reputation as the doctor who made the world's largest human penis smaller bring me more patients? This is a procedure that no other man will ever need. And I'll probably never again have a male surgical patient. Men won't want me to operate on them. I should think they'll all be afraid to go under anesthetic with me in the operating room. They'll think I'm going to give them a Wax-trim after they've been knocked out.

***

"Wax, you have to give me a full accounting of your symptoms if I'm to be able to perform this reduction. I'll need to make the case for this procedure to the hospital if I'm to be granted permission to use their operating facilities. You may need to see a second physician to confirm my diagnosis and to agree, in kind, to the procedure we're planning."

"I don't understand why."

"Your fainting spells could be diagnosed as a psychological symptom, some conditioned response that you've developed to arousal. I don't think I can simply book a penile reduction surgery without someone from the hospital saying, 'Wait a minute. Did you say you want to give this man a smaller penis?' At the very least they'll want a psych consult. They may even want to give *me* a psych consult if we don't do this thing strictly by the book."

She explains that she could be seen as a physician prescribing an extreme and frivolous medical procedure to make a reputation for herself.

"You've got to realize that my colleagues are going to think I've gone round the bend. I mean, they know that I was summoned to give a deposition in the Rolland case. They're going to think I'm some kind of fetishist, or worse, a castrating witch."

Wax says, "What if I had more symptoms?"

"Like what?"

"Bedwetting."

"Enuresis," she says. "Is it true?"

"Not every night. But it's happened a few times lately."

***

LYLE MAMMON: He wants a sort of castration. A reduction, surgically. Crazy. The head is being reattached. I am hoping he keeps at least nine or ten inches. Doctors aren't sure if that's doable. Might have to go down to seven inches. Even better. Wax is still Wax. Even with half a cock. He could still work in features, if he wants.

***

Dr. Banner asks Wax to disrobe, tells him to climb up on the examining table and lie on his back. In this second physical examination, she tells him, she will observe his arousal cycle.

"I'm going to take some measurements—length, circumference at several points," she says.

She turns her back to Wax as he begins to take his pants off. Once he's on the padded table, he draws a white sheet up to his waist. "Okay," he says.

"I'm also going to use a magic marker to trace anastomotic vein networks from the base of your penis to its head. That might tickle. I'm going to take a few digital photos for reference."

She asks him to keep his eyes closed during the examination. "Can you do that?"

He tells her that he can.

"Will you be able to remain flaccid while I handle you?"

"Yes."

"A lot of men respond—become aroused—when I examine them."

"I won't."

"I should have known a man like you would have developed some techniques to control arousal," she says. "Would you like to wear a sleeping mask?" He likes her accent. She pronounces the word as "mauhsk." She is stylishly dressed beneath her starched, white hospital coat. At the deposition she wore a white sweater and a tan skirt, no stockings. Her shoes, Wax remembers, were also tan—open-toed with a low heel.

She asks him again if he can keep his eyes closed during the examination. Every time she asks this, the urge to open his eyes and look into her eyes grows stronger.

"I am going to be attaching temperature sensors to the middle finger of each hand and to the big toe of each foot. We'll look at the readings afterward to confirm rapid temperature drop in your extremities while your penis is erect. I'll be touching your nose and ears during the examination, as well, to get a feel for temperature drop in your face."

She draws down the sheet slowly, then he feels her touch his neck. Two of her fingers press lightly to get his pulse. She writes his heart rate down on her clipboard. He looks at her hands, which are dark on top with very pink palms. She wears no rings. Her fingernails are clipped short, unpainted.

"Hmm," she says. "You're starting without me."

He feels his heart begin to beat faster and the beeping of the monitor behind him echoes the feeling in his chest. He feels himself begin to get aroused.

He wonders if she is embarrassed. She described in her deposition how Robby Rolland became aroused when she examined him after his operation. She said that was normal and that she had been glad to see that recovery response from Robby.

He says he is sorry and tries to concentrate on losing his still-forming erection. Mind over matter. He feels his arousal lessen, can feel his penis losing its hardness one heartbeat at a time. He squints his eyes open and looks at her face as she watches his penis bounce lower and lower until it is finally resting again across his abs.

"Good," she says, taking him in her hands matter-of-factly. "What I'm going to do is manually arouse you and monitor your response. When you feel your feet and hands going colder or tingling, please let me know. I want to monitor you closely as you experience the fainting symptoms."

He sees her look at her watch and then at the clock on the wall. She writes down the time on her clipboard.

"I'm already seeing that the color is going out of your face. Are you feeling all right?"

"Yes."

"You've let the hair on your chest grow," she says.

As one hand combs through the hair on his chest and the other strokes him slowly, he understands that she has seen his movies. He wondered at the deposition if she'd been required to view the instructional tape that came with the pump. He hoped that she hadn't, and when she spoke to him in a most professional tone after her testimony and later when he called her to discuss the surgery, it fed his assumption that she had not seen his work. But now he knows otherwise.

"I've seen a few of your videos."

"Lots of people have," Wax says, aiming for a magnanimous tone.

"I remember a two-week vacation three summers ago watching *Lovers' Knot* two or three times a day. I've never masturbated more, not even as a teenager."

Mammon dialogue, Wax thinks. *Hidden cameras.*

"It was unhealthy, I know. Very compulsive, and I generally don't behave that way. That's likely why the memory of it is so strong."

"That doesn't make you a bad person." More magnanimity.

"What I want to do is determine the extent of capillary damage if, in fact, there is any. I'm afraid the only way I'll be able to do that is for me to conduct a close examination of your penis in an erect state."

He admires the smooth transition she makes from sexual chitchat to professional inquisitiveness. He feels her take three circumferential measurements of his penis and then another measurement for length.

"Of course I am aware that this all might sound like a phony pretext lifted from one of your videos, but it's true, nonetheless. I will be professional about this. I'm not requesting that you ejaculate. That isn't required."

"I'm with you so far," Wax says.

"However, based solely on my professional curiosity as a microsurgeon with a specialty in reattachment procedures and a secondary interest in urology, I would like to request that you allow me to continue to manipulate you. In this way, I'll be able to learn firsthand what's going on exactly. If you should happen to ejaculate during my examination, I will not be displeased and you should feel no shame. Your ejaculate will not go to waste. I could perform a number of tests on your semen, the results of which could be beneficial to our study."

She's still working her hands slowly in measured strokes. He tries to focus on his symptoms. He wants to be able to predict for her when he will pass out.

"Tell me when you begin to feel faint," is the last thing he hears her say as he opens his eyes and loses consciousness.

***

DR. NORA BANNER: I counted nineteen orgasmic contractions, and there was no volume diminution of seminal release from spasms one to nineteen.

BEN BETTIS: One of the tabloid TV news shows contacted me to buy the rights to the footage I shot of Wax fainting after his money shot with Janna in *All Doll.* I referred them to the Handles, who brokered a deal with Mammon to sell forty-five seconds of tape that showed Wax falling face flat on the floor as he reached down to help Janna up. It wasn't the best tape we had—they're saving that for inclusion in the reduction tape—but it brought a nice sum and got played and replayed day and night on cable news shows for almost a week.

LYLE MAMMON: I left a message with Dr. Banner's service telling her she should expand her unique services to women. Why stop at penis reductions? Why not do a few vagina enlargements? Or how about nipple inversion procedures?

***

Mammon walks across the empty restaurant like a toddler with a fresh load in his diaper. He stops about ten feet from Wax's table, makes a sour face, lifts his left leg, farts loudly, laughs, and continues on to Wax's table with his right hand outstretched for a shake.

It is odd to see Mammon without at least one female traveling companion. As if reading Wax's mind, Mammon says, "I'm a solo act today. Wax, I heard you're chopping off your schvantz. Is it true?"

"Yes, it is."

"Have you lost your fucking mind?"

"Lyle, I don't think you understand what I'm doing and why."

"Why then?"

"I have to do it."

"But why?"

"For my health."

Mammon says nothing. He has been calling Wax just about every day, leaving messages and call back numbers. Wax knows that Lyle has also been calling Dr. Banner's office.

"Circulation of my blood is being compromised," Wax says. "When my penis is hard, blood isn't flowing any place else."

"Is that why you passed out with Janna?"

"I'm cold all the time."

"How long have you been sick?"

"I don't know. At least this past year. It's just getting worse. I pass out now whenever I get an erection."

"Is this why you're retiring?"

Wax shakes his head. "No."

A waitress arrives at their table and Mammon opens his menu. Before selecting an entrée, he orders a beer and a ginger ale. Then he asks for an appetizer sampler that includes a selection of each appetizer on the menu. Wax orders a bottled water.

"I appreciate you meeting me like this, Wax. I needed to see you so I could know for myself that you're okay. You gotta admit, this operation you're doing is a bit cockamamie."

Nora is waiting in her car outside the restaurant. Wax wants to be with her now. *Lunch with Lyle was a bad idea,* he thinks. Wax opens his menu. He and Nora have plans for a dinner out later that evening. He will be checking in to the hospital the next morning, with the procedure set to begin at 10:00 p.m. The hospital thought it best that the operation take place after visiting hours.

Their drinks arrive. Mammon laughs.

"What?" Wax asks. "What's funny?"

"I'm thinking of the first time we had lunch together. You ordered a grilled cheese sandwich."

"It was the least expensive thing on the menu."

"We've had a lot of lunches," Mammon says, his tone aggressively wistful. "Lot of lunches. And this is our last lunch. Christ."

***

LYLE MAMMON: I know that deep down Wax was happy to see me again. We had a nice lunch. Like old times. I didn't say everything that I wanted to say. I didn't tell him that I have named him as the sole beneficiary in my will. I didn't tell him that everything that I own and all the money that I have in the bank will be his when I die. I didn't tell him. I don't think I need to. I know that he knows how I feel about him. Maybe he wasn't happy working for me all these years. Maybe I took advantage of the kid. If so, that's mea culpa. I'll admit it. I can't change that now. What we can do now is part right.

SEAN BOTHERS (GLOSS CORPORATION): There are a number of income opportunities presented here. I've shared a few with Lyle Mammon and others who have worked with Wax in the past. I'd like to get closer to Wax, but that's impossible now that they've relocated the operation to an undisclosed hospital. One of the most interesting inquiries that I heard about was from an online auctioneer who suggested that the removed section of Wax's penis could be sold in a competitive bidding process on the web. Another scenario: we slice wafer-thin cross sections of his penis and sell microscopic slides at a hundred bucks apiece. This flesh would otherwise be dispatched to a medical incineration service, to be burned with amputated feet and infected appendixes.

***

"If you're committed to this reduction procedure. We'll need to discuss exactly how much smaller you'd like to be," Dr. Banner says.

"I've been thinking about this."

"What are your thoughts?"

"I'm thinking I'd like to be a little less than average in size," Wax says.

"I'm sure you have noble reasons to want to be a little less than average, but that might not be possible."

"Why not?"

"We'll be removing a length of midsection from your penis and then reattaching the bits on either side of that midsection. We'll need to align like circumferences at proximal points of reattachment or else . . . or else I don't know. It wouldn't look right. It might not work.

"I want it to work," Wax says.

"I want it to work, too."

***

Wax hadn't thought about it before Lyle brought it up at lunch: videotaping the procedure. He brings up the topic with Nora, who tells him that she plans to film the procedure from start to finish.

"It's standard practice, Wax, for two very good reasons. Number one, the tape will provide incontrovertible evidence against a potential frivolous malpractice suit. And two, this is a historic procedure that must be documented."

Wax tells her that he understands and says he wouldn't think of preventing her from filming the operation.

"And I have a confession, Wax. I have also filmed all of our appointments so far."

The information surprises Wax.

"I've also obtained copies of the building surveillance tapes to document all of your comings and goings to my office."

More surprise. "Is that it?"

"And I've also been maintaining a video diary since you first contacted me about this procedure. I'm prepared to destroy it all once we've gotten through this. I'll let you burn every inch of tape, if that's what you want."

***

SEAN BOTHERS: I see a pay-per-view documentary of Wax's operation and recovery. Reality programming. There's definitely an audience. Not just a porn audience.

WAX WILLIAMS: Releasing the video of my examinations with Dr. Banner and the footage from the surgery will convince people that this was a procedure that I had to have.

***

Driving to the hospital, Nora asks Wax, "What's it like seeing yourself having sex on the TV screen?"

He thinks for a moment. "It's like putting on a mask and looking in the mirror."

"Wax," she says after a moment of quiet between them. "If you could be anything, anything at all, what would you be?"

Wax doesn't have to think about it for long. He knows what he wants to be. "I want to be a firefighter," he says. And he immediately feels embarrassed for saying it so enthusiastically. "It's probably too late for me to do that."

"I shouldn't think so," she says.

"Two summers ago I volunteered to put out wildfires on the Texas-Oklahoma border."

"You were a smokejumper?" she says. "That's what they call them, right? Smokejumpers?"

"I was one of the guys who supported the smokejumpers. I cleaned gear, packed food and blankets for them. I went up in the planes but only to drop supplies."

"You could definitely become a firefighter, but there is one thing that you should be aware of."

He can tell by the expression on her face that she is about to make a joke. "What's that?" he asks, trying to recall if Mammon has ever told him a firefighter joke. "What is the one thing about being a firefighter that I should be aware of?"

"I have noticed that young firefighters are almost always very handsome. Real beefcake types. Male models. Like yourself. But old firefighters are all so horrible looking."

She begins laughing so hard that she reaches out to tickle Wax. He laughs with her. "What are you talking about?"

"It's true," she says, howling. "It's true. Young firefighters are all studly calendar boys. And old firefighters are these grizzled, overweight men with mustaches too large for their faces."

***

DR. NORA BANNER: I bought something like fifteen Wax Williams Mega-Dildos to experiment with various points of incision and reattachment. Not the battery-operated ones. I got the solid ones that are made from some type of very sturdy, flesh-colored rubber. They're made from a cast of Wax's erect penis, so these dildos are full-scale surgical models—perfect for me to practice my cuts. The challenge for me is confirming reattachment points with corresponding girth. I have to remove a length of segment between the base and the head of the penis that has near identical circumferences.

***

Nora comes into his room with a white-haired man in a bulky sweater. "This is Dr. Barry Sing," she says. "Time for your psych consult."

Dr. Sing shakes Wax's hand. "Routine evaluation for every elective surgical patient."

"Right," says Wax, remembering that Nora had mentioned something about a questionnaire and some forms he'd have to sign. "I've got a growth," he says. "So I'd like to have it removed."

"Entirely?" Dr Sing asks.

"No, not all of it. I still want one. I'm a man. But I want some of it removed. A lot of it. Several inches. I'd like to have more removed than I'm leaving. I want to have a good scar."

"You're feeling sorry for yourself," says Nora, turning to leave the room. "Poor Wax. His penis is too big."

Dr. Sing takes a seat beside Wax's bed. "I've read Dr. Banner's notes. I'd like to understand why you're seeking this procedure."

"I came across a word that gave me pause—autopeotomy—cutting off one's own penis. That's not who I am. I don't want to cut off my penis."

"Chemical castration would prevent the fainting spells from arousal," Dr. Sing offers.

"Nora—Dr. Banner said the same thing. But it's not like I want to be a eunuch."

"But it is a treatment that would be reversible. A temporary solution."

"I want a permanent solution."

"Here's a theory for you to consider," Dr. Sing says in a singsong voice. "This permanent surgical solution that you seek is simply the fulfillment of your wish for career suicide. You don't want to make adult movies anymore, and you're using this procedure to terminate your career."

"You think it's psychological?"

"I think everything is psychological," says Dr. Sing.

***

NURSE JANE: I've done a few preoperative shaves, but I'd never had to shave a man down there before. The other girls had me all worked up about it. They wanted to show me one of his movies, but no way. The only advice they gave me beforehand was, "Try not to arouse him."

***

She maintains her professional demeanor throughout the task, working carefully around the base of his penis and scrotum. Wax is drowsy, half in a dream, but he can hear the razor cut as she drags it across his abdomen in measured strokes.

Wax recalls how he shaved himself when he was a teenager. He wishes he could just do this shaving himself.

Once she is done with the straight blade and has sponged away the excess shaving cream, she removes her rubber gloves to apply the medical aftershave lotion, which is more stinging than soothing. She notices his reaction to the cold alcohol, and it seems that her small hands rub his pubis a bit too long and a bit too vigorously. She then brings her face to within inches of his penis to closely examine the work she has done. "Looks good," she says before she begins toweling him off. "You're ready for surgery."

***

Make a true cut-point through the epidermis. Through integument. Through the *tunica albuginea*—the thick covering of the cylinders in the penis. Through erectile tissue—*corpus spongiosum* and *corpora cavernosa.* Through the *epididymis, vas deferens,* and urethra. Clamps. Examine work. Review the instructions she made for herself, having boned up on male reproductive anatomy. Trace the sperm route. Seminiferous Tubules. Straight Tubules. *Rete Testis.* Efferent ductules. *Epididymis. Vas deferens.* Urethra. Should have asked Wax if he wanted a vasectomy.

The lights and the cameras are not a distraction. The operating room is near silent. She hears electric current, breathing, feet in sterilized booties shuffling on the floor, climate control. Hears her cuts and her voice against the microphone beneath her mask.

Quizzing herself. *Epididymis* is part of the spermatic duct system that lies on the posterior aspect of each testicle, connecting it to the *vas deferens.* Instructing herself. Must maintain the patency of the *vas deferens* from the *epididymis* to the ejaculatory duct, the *ductus deferens.* Elementary knowledge. The testes perform two functions: produce testosterone to secrete into the blood stream and produce sperm. Smelling a surgically opened body through her mask always catches her off-guard.

Excision. Exsection. Talking to herself. Ectomy. Don't fuck it up. Thinking of Robby Rolland. This is easier. No wounds to deal with. No hematoma. No trauma. No need to deglove the penis. Two straight cuts. Six hours and forty minutes.

Microsurgery. Tubal physiology. Hemostasis—controlled bleeding. Extremely gentle handling of tissue. Precise dissection and exact alignment of tissue planes. Evaluate veins. Connections. *Anastomosis.* A branching system. A network. Like the veins of a leaf; like a river and its tributaries. Vascular structures carrying blood. No varicosity. Good dilation. Knew that already from the FMRI and the retrograde urethrogram. Examine the suspensory ligament. Thicker than she anticipated. It has supported an oversized structure for many years and shows signs of overdevelopment. She can't remember if that enlargement was visible across this pelvis. His abs are so well defined that she hasn't properly observed the physiology of the base of his penis.

She recalls the initial examination. Three hundred digital images of his growing member. Her own hands visible in many of the pictures. His face in the background, looking miles away from his large penis. Manual manipulation. Her heart in her throat. His face white as a sheet and then he's unconscious, his ejaculate reaching the ceiling.

His penis is now in three parts, its thick center placed gently into an ice chamber and carried out of the operating room. Testing to begin immediately. Not his anymore. Belongs to science and then to the top online bidder.

Meeting distal points. Her chief goal is to achieve bilateral symmetry, a balanced trunk and straight shaft from the glans and pubic bone. She works fast. Smaller needle. Smaller sutures. Lessen tissue damage. Decrease the formation of scar tissue.

***

BEN BETTIS: I had like a day and half to mount two swivel cameras in Wax's hospital room. I rented some lights from a local camera shop and a handheld digital camera to shoot impromptu stuff, nurses and doctors coming and going, reading charts and shit like that. The hospital had just wrapped taping for an eight-week reality series on first-year interns, so they were totally cool with what we were doing and very accommodating. They knew we weren't shooting a porno movie or anything. I did not shoot the procedure. Some company in New York that specializes in surgical video production was hired. I understand it was a six-man crew and it was a twelve-hour procedure.

***

Recovery. The ground floor hospital room is tiny. He hears traffic and construction work outside the low window beside his bed. The window is frosted so he can't see out, but he sees dark outlines of pedestrians passing by. His wrists and ankles are fastened to the bedrails with padded restraints. "You were thrashing around post-op and we didn't want you to tear your sutures," Nora says. His penis is wrapped loosely in a flexible cast. It stands straight up. There's a catheter tube—the heavyset nurse calls it a Foley—running up the outside of the cast, held in place by a few pieces of white adhesive tape. He can feel the catheter at its point of entry. He tries to pee but can't. He shifts his ass as little as possible, feeling every stitch of the incision. He closes his eyes and finds it all too easy to imagine that he was conscious throughout the procedure. He has a false memory, reinforced by the restraints, that the sedatives and painkillers didn't take effect until after all the cutting and sewing was done. Then the catheter lights up with bloody urine and this pain is new and almost more than he can bear.

He dozes off for perhaps an hour and wakes when two young nurses enter his room. "Here to clean and redress the wound." He can't tell which one spoke. They're both young and pretty. They seem unsure of their assignment, new to nursing. He hears one whisper something. Then they both shrug and turn simultaneously. They take positions on opposite sides of the bed and begin undressing his bandage. They work slowly, starting at the top, one handing the wrapping to the other as the bandage comes off to reveal a foam cast on the underside of his penis. One whispers again, an instruction to the other to hold his penis at the head and base while she removes the cast. He sees their every movement, but he feels nothing. He recognizes one of the nurses as the nurse who shaved him before the operation.

***

Ken Bettis: He had a few visitors—the Handles, Dee-Dee Sharp, some new girls of Mammon's that Wax had never met before. He got some flowers, fruit baskets. Mammon forwarded hundreds of cards and letters that had been sent to Wax care of the Hacienda. Mostly he played chess with me, watched TV, read. He also got lots of sleep.

***

"Look," Nora says holding a little round mirror under his penis. "I've managed to dorsally locate much of the scar tissue, so you won't see any scarring when you look down to pee."

***

LYLE MAMMON: I have seen the footage from Wax's surgery. I have also seen the footage that was shot during Dr. Banner's examinations of Wax—very hot—and I've seen a lot of the video they've been shooting during his rehabilitation. It is marketable. I'm sure we'll see it in stores someday. It's a hell of a story. Boy with a big cock gets it trimmed by a hot doctor and they fall in love. I'd partner with them to distribute... and I wouldn't take a nickel. It would sell like hotcakes, and I'd be able to preview a dozen coming attractions. We'd be in business again. But what I really want to pitch to Wax—and to Renee—is a *DormitOrgy* sequel called *DormitOrgy Reunion.* It's five years after graduation, and the kids from Pecker Hall have returned to Wadsworth University to relive old memories and to have themselves another little orgy.

***

Wax likes the heavyset day nurse who takes his vitals every two hours. She's a very pleasant woman. Her visits are quick. She's all business. She asks him to confirm his pain level on a scale of one to five. She checks the bag attached to his catheter and tells him that there is no blood in his urine. "That's a good sign." More than once she points to the bedpan on his side table and tells him he isn't checking out until he has filled it.

Wax's first few steps. He feels pain in his penis, then he feels like it isn't even there, so he lifts his hospital gown to see a shortened length of himself still gauze wrapped.

"How do you feel?" Nora asks.

"Like someone cut about eight inches off my dick and then sewed it back on."

***

LYLE MAMMON: I offered to let Wax come back to the Hacienda to recuperate after his operation, set him up in his old room. He could have helped edit the documentary. Brought along his doctor girlfriend. I'd even offered to vacate myself and all female residents if they wanted to be alone.

***

Dr. Banner begins what she calls her final post-op examination. Wax is prone on the high examination table. "What I'm going to do is establish your arousal cycle and confirm your fastest possible refraction. I will attempt to arouse you to climax, then I will run the clock to see how quickly you are able to become aroused again and then climax again."

"Can I ask why you're conducting this experiment?" Wax asks.

"Certainly. We'll document your arousal cycle now, and then once a week for the next six to eight weeks. I want to see if your performance has diminished due to the reduction procedure, to see if your performance has been enhanced due to the reduction procedure."

"Seems I could do this experiment on my own and give you the results."

Dr. Banner shakes her head. "I'm not interested in your refraction when masturbating. That's not a true measure of your arousal cycle. Besides, you could lie about it. As a scientist invested in this experiment, I need to gather the results myself, document the experiment firsthand."

"Do you have any predictions as to the results?"

"I believe that we will see an improvement in your refraction."

"That's good," Wax says. "Why do you think so?"

"Because the blood in your body will have fewer vacuous cells to fill. Those fewer cells will fill faster and you will be aroused faster."

"Will I climax faster?"

"I hope not," says Dr. Banner.

Printed in the United States
123218LV00003BA/149/A

9 781934 081013